A NECESSARY DISTRACTION

Maddie steeled her resolve as she had a thousand times previously and headed toward the door. Agitation built inside her, not all of it from the robbery they'd committed just moments ago. Soon she would be alone with Scott in his hotel room. And knowing she'd make any sacrifice necessary to distract the investigator while her friends got away with the money was enough to start her pulse racing.

"Take care," Constance cautioned. "Don't think you have to place yourself in…a compromising position to save us. We'll be all right."

Maddie nodded. "I'll be fine. Trust me."

"I do."

She cleared her throat, a rush of emotions at Constance's declaration of faith in her having clogged it. "Wait until I've been gone at least a quarter hour before you leave," she instructed them. "That should give me enough time."

"Time for what?" Dora asked.

"I'm not sure yet." And she had only the minute it took to walk across the hall to Scott's room to think of something.

The Gate to Eden

CATHY McDAVID

LEISURE BOOKS  NEW YORK CITY

To my father-in-law, Glen.
You were one of my first and biggest fans.
I miss you.

A LEISURE BOOK®

April 2006

Published by

Dorchester Publishing Co., Inc.
200 Madison Avenue
New York, NY 10016

ISBN 0-8439-5692-5

Printed in the United States of America.

Visit us on the web at www.dorchesterpub.com.

The Gate to Eden

So he drove out the man;
and he placed at the east of the garden of Eden
Cherubims, and a flaming sword which turned every
way, to keep the way of the tree of life.
—Genesis 3:24

Chapter One

Edenville, Arizona Territory, 1887

"Very nice." Thaddeus Newlin watched as the pretty little thing standing in front of him slipped the narrow sleeves of her camisole off her pale shoulders. Mr. Forrester had done well in choosing her, and Thaddeus considered giving his secretary a bonus.

"I ain't never been with a man like this before," the woman said shyly, lowering her eyes to the richly carpeted floor of the private railroad car. "You're my first . . . you know."

Thaddeus doubted her statement. She might not be a prostitute in the strictest sense of the word, but she'd certainly done this before. The faint stretch marks on her belly attested to previous childbirth. Not that Thaddeus cared. In fact, he preferred experienced women. Just not worldly.

"You don't have to be nervous, my dear." He played

along with her pretense. "I promise to be gentle." And he would be gentle. Until the end.

She placed one stockinged foot on the edge of the pinstriped settee, near his leg. Thaddeus felt himself stirring and smiled. He might have only half the hair atop his head he did at twenty, but he'd not yet lost his ability to perform.

Reaching out a large hand, he stroked her smooth, surprisingly muscular calf. "Why don't we see what we can do about removing this stocking?"

The woman—he couldn't quite remember her name—pressed a knuckle to her lips. "It were a long walk here from my place. Can I use the . . . the . . . chamber pot first?" It clearly pained her to have to ask for the convenience.

"Of course. It's in there." He pointed toward the door to his sleeping quarters.

She ducked into the room, quiet as a mouse. No sense wasting time, Thaddeus thought, and kicked off his boots. Next, he stood, removed his pants, and tossed them aside. They landed haphazardly on the elegant cherrywood rocker he'd had shipped all the way from Boston last year. By the time he completed undressing, he'd begun to wonder what detained his lovely guest.

Wearing only his long underwear, he walked to the door of his sleeping quarters and knocked. "Are you all right, my dear?"

His only answer was a soft scuffling sound.

"Hello." He knocked again, and the brass knob twisted. Thaddeus smiled and moved away from the opening door. "There you are."

"So, I am."

The door swung wide. The smile on Thaddeus's face died as the end of a Colt revolver was jammed into his protruding gut.

"Mr. Newlin. I can see by yer startled expression ye weren't expecting me." Behind the kerchief covering most of the man's features, the voice bubbled with false cheer.

Thaddeus instinctively moved backward, stumbling. The bandit kept the revolver trained on his every move. "What do you want?" Thaddeus demanded, sounding less in control than he would have liked.

"Ack, man. Are ye always in such a hurry?" The man continued to prod Thaddeus with the end of the revolver, forcing retreat. Eventually, the backs of Thaddeus's knees hit the settee, and he sat down rather unceremoniously.

A second man followed the first one into the room. He toted a burlap sack, the contents of which Thaddeus found impossible to determine. Just before the door closed, he thought he heard a muffled female cry. They must have overtaken and subdued the woman, he thought. Perhaps the stupid bitch could yet serve a purpose.

"The woman in there. You can have her if you leave this minute without harming me."

The first man turned to the second one. "Did ye hear that? Mr. Newlin has offered us the use o' his lady friend in exchange fer his life. What say ye to the deal?"

Lifting the edge of his mask, the second man spit on the floor.

"Sorry, Mr. Newlin." The first man leveled the revolver at Thaddeus's nose with a hand steady as an iron post. "Seems me pal isn't inclined to take yer offer, though 'tis generous. What else have ye to bring to the bargaining table?"

"Money," Thaddeus sputtered. He despised being strong-armed. Especially by a pair of thugs. Fury and frustration boiled inside him.

"Money is always good," the man said, a smile in his voice. "We accept. The only question now is how much."

He was of medium height and lanky. No more than a kid. Thaddeus took care to observe small details so he could give an accurate description of his robbers to the sheriff later. The man's cohort was shorter and stockier and appeared somewhat older. But not by much. They were both dirty and smelled like they hadn't so much as touched a drop of bathwater since the ringing in of the New Year two months earlier.

Their clothes were ragged and ill-fitting. Between their masks and hats, only their eyes showed. The first man's twinkled with amusement. The second man's burned with a hate so strong, Thaddeus's blood ran cold, and he wasn't a man to scare easily. Good God, what had he ever done to inspire such loathing?

"My wallet is in the pocket of my pants," he said, indicating his discarded garment with a slight tilt of his head. "There's a hundred dollars in it. Maybe more."

"Ooh! A hundred dollars. Did ye hear that?" Though he addressed his cohort, the slender man's gaze didn't veer from Thaddeus.

The second man made a sound of disgust and dropped the burlap sack on the floor.

"I'm afraid I share the same opinion as me pal over there." The first man cocked the revolver and pressed the tip of it into the side of Thaddeus's nose. "Most people would be tellin' ye I'm a poor excuse fer a shot. However, I'm thinkin' at this close range, even I won't miss."

Sweat dripped from Thaddeus's temples. He could feel it slide down his jaw and along the sides of his neck. Yet he couldn't bring himself to disclose the location of his store of cash.

In a move so quick Thaddeus barely had time to flinch, the man lifted his weapon and shot a gilded mirror mounted on the wall behind the settee. Then he promptly returned the revolver point to Thaddeus's nose.

"Shall we try this again?" The eyes drilling into him no longer twinkled and the voice had lost all joviality. "Where's yer money?"

The ringing in Thaddeus's ears was deafening. He was only vaguely aware of glass shards that rained on his head and shoulders. He made an attempt at speech, but the words coming from his mouth made no sense. Taking several short breaths, he tried again.

"The company payroll is being kept in the third car behind the engine. Hidden in an overhead compartment."

"And being guarded by a half-dozen men dressed as passengers. Ye think we don't know that?"

Thaddeus briefly wondered how two such disreputable low lifes learned of a payroll transfer he'd thought kept diligently under wraps. Obviously, there was a leak in his office of some magnitude.

"We're here fer yer personal money." The man shifted the point of the gun from Thaddeus's nose to his left eye. "Now, where is it?"

"My sleeping quarters. The wardrobe." He embarrassed himself by gulping. "There's a false bottom."

"Get it," the man barked and instantly, the second man disappeared through the door.

He emerged a minute later waving a fistful of bills that Thaddeus knew amounted to almost a thousand dollars.

"Get the money in his wallet, too," the first man said, still leveling the gun at Thaddeus's eye.

The second man did as he was told and when he had

all the bills together, stuffed them into a small leather bag tied to his waist.

"Stand up," the first man said, moving aside, but not lowering the revolver.

"What's going on?" Thaddeus demanded.

"Please don't waste any more o' me time, Mr. Newlin." The man sighed tiredly. "We're in a hurry."

Thaddeus stood slowly, fear twisting his belly. These men were planning something, and instinct told him it wouldn't bode well.

"Now strip," the man ordered.

"Just a damn min—" Thaddeus's protest died when the end of the revolver poked into his neck.

"Ye heard me, man. Strip. And be quick about it."

With effort, he, unfastened the buttons one by one of his long underwear. Shucking his arms out of the sleeves, he pushed the top half down around his middle.

"We're waiting, Mr. Newlin."

The second man pulled several lengths of coiled rope from the burlap sack.

"What are you going to do with those?"

"Don't worry yerself, Mr. Newlin. We're just havin' a bit o' fun. I promise, no permanent harm will come to ye." The man's voice hardened further, if that were possible. "Unlike yer plans fer the lass in there. Heard tell yer lovemakin' leans toward the rough side."

Damnation! Where had they learned so much about his business and his personal habits? First thing in the morning, Thaddeus would have every single employee questioned, including his secretary, Zachariah Forrester.

"Sit," the man said when Thaddeus had completely disrobed, and inclined his head toward the settee.

Thaddeus did as instructed.

"Feet apart."

"See here!"

"Feet apart, I said." The man stepped ruthlessly on the toes of Thaddeus's left foot with the heel of his boot.

Crying out, Thaddeus complied. The second man came forward and made quick work of tying both Thaddeus's ankles to the decorative wooden legs of the settee.

"Hands next," the first man said, and Thaddeus's wrists were bound in similar fashion to the fabric-covered armrests.

" 'Tis that not a pretty sight?" the first man asked, stepping back to view the whole of Thaddeus.

All four of his limbs were stretched to their limits, leaving him completely exposed. His face burned with a mixture of anger and shame.

"So help me, God, you will pay for this," he hollered.

"Undoubtedly, Mr. Newlin. But 'twill be God and not you who judges and punishes us."

"When I get my—"

"Gag him," the man interrupted and holstered his revolver.

The second man produced a kerchief from his pocket, which he attempted to cram in Thaddeus's mouth. Thaddeus refused to cooperate and bit down hard. The man grabbed his chin and wrenched his jaw open. The cloth was filthy, like the men, and tasted vile, causing Thaddeus to retch repeatedly. Then a rope was wound around his head. The rough hemp sawed into the sides of his mouth, and he was sure his lips bled.

Helpless, he watched in horror as the two men set the burlap sack in front of a window. While the first man opened the window, the second man struck a match on a framed painting hanging beside the window.

Thaddeus fought his restraints. He prided himself on his collection of original artwork, and the landscape had cost him a small fortune. When the second man touched the lit match to the burlap sack, however, Thaddeus went stone still. Were they intending to incinerate him alive? Dear God, no! This couldn't be happening. His eyes began to water uncontrollably.

"Did I not say ye won't be harmed?" The man walked over to Thaddeus. "Rest assured, Mr. Newlin, I am a man o' me word."

Their eyes connected, and Thaddeus experienced a momentary sense of confusion. Something about the man, both men, actually, wasn't right. But he couldn't quite place a finger on it.

The man glanced over at the burlap sack, which had started to smoulder. "The smoke will bring help long before those oil-soaked rags catch fire. Someone will find ye."

Thaddeus began struggling again in earnest.

" 'Tis been a pleasure, I must say, but we'll take our leave now."

The two men started toward the door to Thaddeus's sleeping quarters. The shorter one went through, but the taller one hesitated.

"On second thought, maybe we will take ye up on yer kind offer o' the lass. Seein' as yer goin' to be rather busy in the next few minutes." He picked up the woman's discarded dress and waved it over his head like a banner. "Top o' the evenin' to ye, Mr. Newlin."

With that, he disappeared through the door.

Thaddeus screamed his rage, but the muffled sound reached no farther than the four walls of his private railroad car.

* * *

On the other side of the door, the thieves immediately got down to business. By their calculations, they had no more than a minute or two before the smoke pouring from the window roused attention.

"Put this on," Maddie Campbell said in a loud whisper and threw the dress she held at her partner. "Newlin will surely give a description of Dora to the sheriff and I want her wearing different clothing. Dora, you wear Constance's dress."

Constance Starkweather removed her battered felt hat, setting free a thick black braid that came to rest in the center of her back. She tossed her hat onto the bed and started stripping out of her shirt and pants. Maddie followed suit, removing her hat and clothes as fast as she could. Her own dark blond hair had been pinned into a tight knot on top of her head. Dora finished dressing first. She grabbed the men's clothes, and began tossing them into a tattered carpetbag Maddie and Constance had brought along.

When all three finished changing, they donned cloaks. Maddie pushed open the heavy metal door leading outside. She winced at the loud screeching sound and prayed no one heard. One by one, the women jumped down from the railed ledge extending over the mechanism connecting Thaddeus's car to the one next to it. Before Maddie jumped, she tossed the carpetbag into Dora's outstretched arms.

Their dresses were cumbersome and when Constance landed, she caught the toe of her boot on her hem and hit the ground hard, landing on her hands and knees.

"Oomph!"

"Are you all right?" Maddie asked, all trace of the Irish accent vanished. Without waiting for an answer, she grabbed Constance's arm. Dora grabbed the other, and they hauled Constance to her feet.

"I'm fine," she answered in a voice so high and musical, it couldn't possibly be mistaken for a man's. "Sorry."

The three women linked arms and ran along the train on the side opposite the depot. The men's boots Maddie and Constance wore hindered their progress, as did the loose dirt heaped beside the railroad tracks. Already, the pounding of running feet on the depot platform echoed through the night. Someone in the distance shouted, "Fire!" By the time the women reached the caboose, they were out of breath and panting hard. The cold night air burned Maddie's lungs, and her side ached.

Dora held the carpetbag to her middle, her face contorted with pain. "Sweet Lord in heaven. That were close."

It could have been closer, thought Maddie. All in all, they'd been most lucky. Next time, they might not have the advantage of surprise. "Hurry. Let's get a move on."

She cut the other women no slack. When they'd signed on with her, they knew the risks and knew they'd be expected to keep up or be left behind. The mission would not be forfeited to spare one life. Not when the survival of hundreds depended on the money they'd stolen from Newlin.

While she would have much preferred to return straight home to Eden and her precious young daughter, Josephine, Maddie guided the other women in the direction of the depot. They'd made it this far. Now was not the time to lose everything by drawing unwanted attention to themselves.

Assuming a considerably more sedate pace, they picked their way to the crowd forming in front of

Thaddeus Newlin's private car. There, they blended in, adding to the growing number of curious spectators agog over the late evening spectacle. Through the open car window, the majority partner of the Edenville Consolidated Mining Company could be heard bellowing. Apparently, his rescuers weren't untying his bonds fast enough.

The burning rags had done their job. Someone inside opened another window and more smoke poured out. Maddie hadn't lied. Thaddeus Newlin came through the ordeal with only his pride injured. But the same couldn't be said for his private car. She suffered a twinge of guilt at damaging so many fine things. Especially when she and the others possessed next to nothing.

But it couldn't be helped. The task she'd taken upon herself allowed no room for regrets. She'd made a commitment, and she'd see it through until the end. As she'd told Thaddeus Newlin earlier, she was a man, or to be more precise, a woman, of her word.

"They say there were two of them." A wizened oldtimer turned to Maddie, eager to spread the news. "Younguns. Not from around here. And that the Irish feller were a crack shot." Something akin to glee lit the old man's face. "They found Mr. Newlin, buck naked, gagged, and staked out with ropes to one of them fancy pieces of furniture he's got in there."

"My gracious! Why I never . . ." Maddie pretended to be appalled.

Shielding a smile with her hand, she, Constance, and Dora exchanged knowing looks. From all appearances, no one at this gathering suspected the truth. Nor would they ever find out if Maddie could help it.

Chapter Two

Five months later

Air, hot and stale enough to suffocate the heartiest soul, blasted Scott McSween full in the face as he disembarked the train at Edenville.

"Welcome to hell," said another passenger getting off the train. "Folks 'round here call that breeze the devil's breath." He removed his bowler hat and wiped his damp brow with the back of his hand. "I'd like to meet the fellow responsible for naming Edenville and give him a piece of my mind, since it's obvious he's missing most of his. I swear, there ain't one blessed thing about this town that resembles paradise. Even in winter." He plunked his hat back on his head.

Scott stepped down onto the depot platform and pointed to the mountain in the near distance. "I take it that's the mine."

A collection of wooden buildings had been constructed into the side of the mountain, climbing the steep slope in a stair-step fashion. Zigzagging trestles extended from the uppermost building and reached clear to the mountaintop. Smoke poured from the mouths of three cylindrical stacks, the devil's breath carrying it off to mingle with a few wispy clouds drifting by.

"That's it." The man fell in beside Scott. The large leather valise he carried close to his side identified him as a traveling salesman. "Old Eden herself. Heart of the Edenville Consolidated Mining Company. The company actually owns three mines altogether. The Vista Linda and the Pinnacle are both northeast of here. But neither produces near what this grand lady does. Be interesting to know why old man Newlin keeps them open."

"Yes, it would." *Very interesting.*

"You think you're hot," the man went on. "Them godforsaken miners work in temperatures ten to twenty degrees hotter." He chuckled mirthlessly. "Don't know about you, but I'd drop like fly if put down in them tunnels."

Scott had feigned sleep for most of his two days on the train to avoid talkative passengers like this man. Now that he'd reached his destination, however, he was eager to learn all he could about the mine and the town that had seemingly sprung up overnight. Scott made it his practice to get the lay of the land before accepting any job. He liked to think he picked his clients, not the other way around.

"You a miner?" the man asked.

"Nope." Scott removed his jacket and hooked it over the arm not carrying his well-worn canvas travel bag.

"Didn't think so." The man stared openly at the Colt Peacemaker revolver strapped to Scott's leg. "A lawman?"

Not any more, thought Scott. But all he said was, "Nope."

"Where you from?"

"Texas." By way of Colorado, New Mexico, California, and Utah. But he didn't say that either.

They passed between two buildings, one of which housed the ticket office, and, after stepping off the platform, entered the street leading to Edenville. Already sweat plastered Scott's shirt to his back. How did people survive this heat? Next to him, the man tugged at his collar.

"Which hotel you staying in?" he asked.

"There's more than one?"

"Four, if you include the rooms over the three saloons. And a half-dozen boarding houses at last count, some reputable, some not so reputable." The man winked. "There's no shortage of sporting ladies here, if that's what you have in mind."

Scott had other things in mind. "I'm staying in the Edenville Hotel," he said, recalling the telegraphed instruction he'd received two weeks previous.

"So am I. Follow me, and I'll show you the way. Though you can't hardly miss it. The Edenville Hotel is the largest building in town."

They climbed onto the sheltered boardwalk at the first opportunity to escape the worst of the sun's burning rays. Taking in his new surroundings, Scott concluded that the oppressive heat didn't keep folks indoors. Edenville bustled with activity, even in midafternoon.

The buildings seemed crammed impossibly close. Every available space had been utilized, as if the residents resisted moving any farther away from the mining operation than absolutely necessary.

Most of the businesses were the same as any other

town, with the exception of an assayer's office and a greater number of banks. In place of a general store was the Edenville Mining Company Store.

"Where do all the miners live?" Scott asked.

"You can't see from here, but on the other side of town are rows and rows of houses." The man indicated the direction with an outstretched arm. "If you can call them houses. Wooden crates are more like it."

"Does the mining company provide them free to the employees?"

"Nothing in Edenville is free," he scoffed. "Rent comes right off the top of the worker's wages. After that, any amount owed to the company store, of which there is always something. You can bet your sweet hide old man Newlin and his partners get their dollar ahead of anyone else in town."

From what he'd been able to learn of Thaddeus Newlin, Scott suspected as much.

"Then, of course, there's all them women and children living in Eden."

"Eden?" Scott asked, his attention wavering. He'd spotted the hotel up ahead.

"It's what the men here dubbed the old tent and shack settlement about a mile outside town. Mexican miners abandoned it after building their own town of Rio Concho. The women moved in lock, stock, and barrel a month or so after the accident last year."

Scott's interest rose abruptly. "What accident?"

"You haven't heard?" The man beamed, obviously relishing the chance to recount the story. "A hundred and sixty-seven miners were killed when a tunnel collapsed. The worst accident in the history of the state. There weren't enough pine boxes available to bury the dead. Newlin had some shipped in special from Denver. I was here at the time and I tell you, if they'd lined up them boxes end to end, they'd have stretched all the way from the Edenville Hotel to the train depot."

"What caused the accident?" Once reminded, Scott vaguely remembered reading about it in a newspaper account.

"In my book, friend, it was the result of greed. Pure and simple. The miners had been blasting for weeks before the cave-in, opening a new tunnel. Newlin promised the crews a bonus if they finished before Easter, so they were pushing extra hard. Someone got careless and set off dynamite in the wrong place at the wrong time. The lucky ones died instantly. It took rescue workers six days to dig through the rubble."

"Any survivors?"

"A few. Most of them died from their injuries a few days later. And if that weren't bad enough, a scarlet fever epidemic broke out not two weeks later. I forget how many children died."

Scott had seen more than his share of death and horror through the years, but he still felt a touch of pity for the miners' families. "It must have been very difficult for the women."

"Terrible. And what Newlin did to them afterwards made it worse."

"What do you mean?"

They'd reached the hotel, but neither man made a move to enter. They stood out of the path of passing people, but many paused to give Scott and his Peacemaker revolver an inquiring, and often wary, look.

The salesman's laugh rang with disgust. "Newlin refused to pay them their husbands' back wages, for one. And he'd promised a bonus of fifty dollars to the family of any man killed in the line of work. Course, that was before the cave-in. Guess he never expected to lose so many men in one shot like that. Claimed the company suffered a grave financial loss and there wasn't any money left to pay the families. Hogwash, if you ask me."

Scott silently agreed. From what he'd learned, Thaddeus Newlin had risen from the depths of poverty to become one of the richest and most powerful men in the West. He hadn't done it by making friends or sharing his wealth.

"Miners earn good money, but so what?" The salesman shook his head. "It costs an arm and a leg to live in Edenville. Most of them women didn't have two nickels to rub together. What few could, left as soon as they managed to scrape up the money. The rest had nowhere to go. Not that Newlin cared. He had them evicted from their houses to make room for the families of the new miners he hired to replace the ones who died. The heartless bastard."

Scott had a curious mind. It was one of the reasons he was so good at his job. He thought about a bunch of women and children living in . . . what had the man called it? An abandoned tent and shack settlement. They must have been desperate. How, he wondered, did they manage with so many mouths to feed?

"Say, friend. I find myself in need of a refreshment." The man pulled a kerchief from his pocket and mopped his sweaty face. "Can I interest you in a whiskey?" He nodded toward a saloon across the street. "There's plenty more to tell about Newlin and this town, if you have a hankering."

"Thanks, but no." Scott did have a hankering, for both the whiskey and the information, but he had several more stops to make in town before dark. "Maybe later."

"I'll be in Edenville all week." The man smiled broadly. "How about yourself?"

"A few days. Maybe longer. I haven't decided yet."

"Perhaps I'll see you around, then. By the way," the man extended his hand, "name's Otis Tarrington. I'm a notions salesman, originally from Ohio."

"Scott McSween." Scott shook the man's hand, but he didn't offer his profession. "Nice to meet you. Are you any relation to the San Francisco Tarringtons?"

"Only a very poor relation, I'm afraid. You must get around, Mr. McSween."

More than he wanted. In truth, Scott hadn't stayed in one place long enough to hang his hat once during the last five years. Not since he'd left Texas and turned his back on everything he'd known and loved.

"I've been a few places," he said. "Thanks for the lowdown on Edenville and Newlin."

The two went their separate ways after that, Otis to the saloon across the street and Scott into the hotel. He walked to the front desk, his boots resounding on the wooden floor. For all its size, the hotel looked as if it had been slapped together in a hurry. The sparsely decorated lobby was dark, the shades drawn over the windows in a feeble attempt to keep the oppressive heat at bay.

"Can I help you, sir?" asked the clerk behind the desk. He didn't look old enough to have grown the outlandish mustache he sported.

"Yes. Scott McSween. I need a room."

The clerk became immediately flustered. "Mr. McSween. We weren't expecting you until tomorrow."

"I'm early," Scott said. "Have you a room available?"

"Certainly. That's not a problem." The clerk busied himself with registering Scott. "I'll send word to Mr. Newlin right away that you've arrived."

"Don't bother."

The clerk's head shot up. "But, sir. He would be most displeased with me if I didn't—"

Scott cut the clerk short by tossing him a gold dollar. The young fellow wasn't in such a tizzy that he couldn't snatch a tip in midair.

"You can advise Mr. Newlin of my arrival in the morning. If the question ever arises, I'll tell him I gave you a false name."

The clerk rolled the coin around in his fingers, his forehead creased with concentration. Newlin clearly wielded a significant influence over the citizens of Edenville as well as the employees of the mining company. But money generally talked, and it did so today.

"I would feel better about our agreement if you gave me the false name today," the clerk said. "Then tomorrow, I'll register you again under McSween."

"Fair enough."

Scott gave him the name of his mother's brother, a one-time favorite relative and the reason he became a U.S. Marshal. His uncle was also the driving force behind Scott leaving Texas. So much for the saying about blood being thicker than water.

The clerk led Scott to a small, sparse room.

Once the clerk left, Scott spent a few minutes washing up, using the china basin, pitcher of water, and towel left for him on the nightstand. That would have to do until he could get a bath later tonight. He'd meet Thaddeus Newlin tomorrow looking his best and not like he needed a job. Which he didn't. Private investigating paid well, and Scott could afford to be choosy. He had his uncle to thank for that much, at least. As a lawman, Scott had never come close to earning the kind of money he did now.

Marginally refreshed, he headed down the stairs and out onto the street. He took his time touring the town, strolling up one side of the main street and down the other. He stopped in the livery stable and inquired about renting a horse. The need for transportation would arise if he took the job Thaddeus offered. Like Otis Tarrington, the proprietor of the livery stable was a chatty fellow and a wealth of information. Everything he said agreed with what Otis had already told Scott.

A scantily clad and heavily rouged woman waving a brightly colored scarf called to him from a window above one of the saloons. With a smile and a tip of his cowboy hat, he declined her brazen invitation to come up and join her.

People looked him over as he passed, but no one talked except for the occasional "Howdy." He bought a newspaper from a scruffy-looking boy on the corner. He folded it in thirds and tucked it under his arm for later reading.

He approached the Edenville Mining Company Store and, on impulse, followed a finely dressed mother and her trio of children inside.

Business was brisk, a fact that astounded Scott as he perused the shelves and noted the exorbitant prices. The majority of customers were women. A man, however, stood at the counter, negotiating a purchase with the store manager who was easily identified by his shopkeeper's attire and the authority with which he spoke.

At a loud crash, Scott poked his head around a corner. Two of the three children he'd come in with stood beside a toppled tower of canned goods, expressions of alarm and guilt on their faces. The third child sat sprawled on the floor amid the fallen cans. He rubbed the top of his head as if it hurt.

"Why'd ya push me?" His mouth puckered into a surly pout.

Their mother flew into the aisle from another part of the store. "What in heaven's name is going on here?" She took in the scene, displeasure emanating from her every pore. "Get up right this minute, Norman."

The store manager appeared at her side. "Is something the matter, Mrs. Newlin?"

Scott had been prepared to move on until he heard the store manager call the woman by name. Hoping to learn something, he feigned interest in a nearby selection of porcelain ware.

"Yes, there is, Mr. Abernathy," Mrs. Newlin said, fixing an icy glare on the store manager. "This display of canned goods was set up right in the middle of the walkway where anyone could stumble into it. You're fortunate my son wasn't seriously injured. Believe you me, Mr. Newlin will hear about this."

She took her son by the arm and yanked him to his feet, then proceeded to brush him off with a heavy, almost brutal, hand. The other two children, a boy and a girl, tried to slink away. She shot them a menacing glare, and they stopped dead in their tracks.

"Perhaps the children would like a sarsaparilla?" Mr. Abernathy offered. He didn't point out that the cans had been stacked well out of the way and that Norman had been shoved into them by his siblings.

"Well, I suppose." Placated, she collected her unruly brood to her side. "Come along, children."

"If you'd be so kind to meet me at the counter, I'll be there right away to serve you." The store manager gave Mrs. Newlin a polite, and visibly forced, smile. "I'll need just a moment to attend to this . . . situation."

"Don't dally," Mrs. Newlin snapped. "I have several

more errands to run today." Gathering the folds of her skirt in her fingers, she moved away with the haughtiness of a queen.

Which, Scott supposed, she was in this town.

"Maddie," the shopkeeper called, looking around. "Where are you?"

"Here, Mr. Abernathy." At the other end of the aisle, a young woman straightened from a stooped position. She'd been so unobtrusive, Scott hadn't noticed her before.

She wore a simple handmade linen dress over which she'd donned a full-length white apron. Her blond hair was pulled into a neat bun at the back of her head. The severe style didn't detract from her hair's vibrant color or silky texture. Unpinned and falling loose around her shoulders, it would probably bring most men to their knees. She was of average height, but not average build. The layers of frumpy clothing did little to hide the outline of her figure, which, as far as Scott was concerned, possessed exactly the right combination of curves and long lines.

"Get over here, Maddie." The store manager indicated the toppled cans with a jerky nod and said in a tone harsher than circumstances necessitated, "Pick those up, lickety-split. I don't care if you have to move the whole blasted stack. Just make sure none of the cans extend into the walkway. Can't have people tripping into them at every turn."

"Yes, sir."

She angled past Mr. Abernathy, her head bowed. He didn't take his eyes off her until she had lowered herself to the floor and began arranging the cans. Then, with a grunt of satisfaction, he left to attend Mrs. Newlin and her children.

Perhaps sensing Scott's presence, she raised her

gaze. It met with his, and he was rendered momentarily still, something that seldom happened to him.

Her eyes were wide, luminous, and the most amazing shade of green Scott had ever seen. A spark of intelligence shone in their depths, belying her meek demeanor. She matched his blatant stare with one of her own. As they silently studied each other from across the distance, Scott felt his body respond.

He was no stranger to intimacy, but he could honestly say not once had merely looking into a woman's eyes caused him to stiffen like a randy juvenile on his first trip to a bordello.

Scott broke eye contact and turned away before his condition became apparent to everyone else in the store. Mildly disturbed by the intensity of his body's reaction, he sauntered down another aisle. He knew it would be wiser to leave, but instead he went to wait in line at the counter.

Finished with their sarsaparillas, the three sticky-faced Newlin children followed their mother out of the store. As they neared Maddie, Mrs. Newlin paused. In a voice intended to carry, she said, "Rest assured, Mr. Abernathy, I will still be speaking to my husband about the earlier incident. But I will let him know it was this . . . person's improper arrangement of the canned goods that caused the mishap and not you."

"Thank you, Mrs. Newlin. If there's anything I can do for you or Mr. Newlin, please let me know."

Scott considered himself a fair judge of character. It was practically a requirement in his job. And while he hadn't expected Mr. Abernathy to defend Maddie, it still rankled him when the man let her take the blame.

As the last boy passed Maddie, still on her knees stacking cans, he kicked out. A dozen cans went sailing. Scott saw a brief spark of anger cross Maddie's face before she schooled her features into a semblance of calm and began collecting the newly fallen cans. The boy accepted a congratulatory punch in the shoulder from his brother, the two of them snickering as they left the store. If Mrs. Newlin noticed, she didn't let on.

Scott resisted the urge to help Maddie. She would probably refuse anyway. Stubborn pride as well as intelligence shone in those amazing green eyes of hers.

"Can I help you with something, sir?" the store manager asked when the customer in front of Scott had completed her transaction.

Not having thought ahead, Scott studied the items on the counter and said, "Licorice. One rope."

The store manager's brows lifted. "Will that be all?"

"Yes."

As he wound the licorice rope into a coil and placed it in a paper sack, the man said, "I apologize for the disruption." He glared at Maddie. "God only knows why I continue to put up with her."

Scott wondered why Maddie put up with the store manager, but his question was answered in the man's next breath.

"I suppose I feel sorry for her and her little daughter. She's one of those women from Eden." The way he said "women from Eden" sounded more like he meant women of ill repute. "I have two of them working here in the store. Two too many, if you ask me."

Maddie must have lost her husband in the accident last year, Scott figured. She obviously needed a job. Badly, if she tolerated such poor treatment from her boss and customers like Mrs. Newlin. Unusual that she hadn't remarried, thought Scott. A pretty woman like her would have no problems finding a husband in a town populated with so many men, even with a small daughter. But then, there was that stubborn pride of hers to take into consideration.

"That'll be ten cents," the store manager said, handing Scott the paper sack containing the licorice.

He was disappointed not to see Maddie by the canned goods on his way out. When had she left? But then he spotted her standing by the door, dusting a display.

Once again, their gazes connected. Scott's reaction was more sudden than before and every bit as intense. Surprising himself, he paused and held out the paper sack. "Here. Take this home to your daughter."

Her chin lifted ever so slightly. "Thank you kindly, but I can't." She spoke with a hint of Southern accent.

"Please. It's only a rope of licorice."

"I know what it is."

So she'd been watching him, too. "Then why won't you take it?"

She didn't hesitate to answer, and her voice contained no apology. "There are almost two hundred children living in Eden. It wouldn't be fair to bring home a treat for one and not the rest."

"I understand." He didn't really. But then, he could tell even after such a short acquaintance that Maddie was a complicated woman. Complicated and far too interesting. He reminded himself he didn't need any distractions. Not if he accepted the job Thaddeus Newlin offered. "Good day to you, then." Scott tipped his hat and took his leave.

Once outside, he decided he had enough time before dusk to make one or two more stops. The saloon and Otis's promise of whiskey beckoned, but Scott decided against it. He preferred to be clearheaded when he met with Newlin in the morning and not nursing the lingering effects of strong drink.

He gave one last glance back at the company store. He came to a jarring halt at the sight of Maddie standing in the open doorway, her green eyes fastened on him. Neither of them moved for a very long moment. This time, however, it was she who walked away first.

Chapter Three

The springs on the old surrey creaked as the four women boarded. Once they were all in and seated, their driver, Granny Fay Hartford, snapped the reins and clucked to the bedraggled and mismatched pair of horses pulling the rig. They started out slowly and, as Maddie knew from experience, would gain no speed during the mile-long drive home.

"Gonna rain tonight," Granny Fay said, searching the overcast sky with eyes that didn't see as well as they once did. It was her job to deliver and pick up whichever women from Eden were working or had shopping to do in town.

The arrangement made sense. One of the horses belonged to Granny Fay. The other, the younger one, had been a gift from Delilah Montgomery, the madam at the Strike it Rich Saloon and Gambling Hall. A payment for services rendered, so to speak. The women of Eden had agreed to help Delilah with a particularly delicate problem. In return, Delilah helped them, providing a horse, money—a generous monthly allotment—and most importantly, information.

The old surrey and its set of harness hadn't been a gift from Delilah, but she'd negotiated with the seller on behalf of the women and convinced him to lower the price to one the women could afford. Mechanically sound, the surrey was nonetheless a sight, with its peeling paint, bent canopy frame, and crooked wheels.

Maddie would have liked to have the surrey repaired, but it was an extravagance she couldn't justify. Food, clothing, shoes, medical supplies, school supplies, seed for the garden, equipment, building materials, and feed for the livestock came first.

"How was work?" Dora asked. She sat next to Maddie in the rear seat. "Anything new?"

"The private investigator Newlin hired arrived in town today."

"Land sakes!" Constance blurted. "Why didn't you say something? He wasn't due until tomorrow."

The surrey bumped and shook as they traveled the dirt road leading out of town toward Eden, knocking the women into each other. Between Granny Fay's poor eyesight and the weary horses, they hit every pothole in their path.

"I'm saying it now," Maddie replied with a shrug. "He showed up at the company store." She recalled the look of him, as she frequently had during the last few hours. Tall, wide-shouldered, and cool as the waters of the Gila River on a January morning. His eyes were gray, not unlike the sky above them, his skin sun-darkened, and his features undeniably masculine. He was an imposing man and not altogether unattractive, if a female went for that sort, which Maddie most definitely did not.

"Where was I when all this took place?" Constance fumed.

"At the hotel. Fetching Abernathy's lunch."

"Are you sure it was him?" Gertrude Michaelson asked. She worked as maid in the Edenville Hotel. "I've been checking the guest register every day like you told me and his name wasn't on it."

"I'm sure," Maddie said. She couldn't explain why, but some instinct told her the man she met in the company store was Scott McSween.

"I think Maddie's right," Dora chimed in. "I made a towel and bedding delivery to the Strike it Rich Saloon just before quittin' time. Lulu told me there were a salesman in the bar this afternoon, talking about a man he done met on the train. She didn't catch the man's name, but the salesman said he were real interested in Edenville and Newlin. And that he wore his Colt like a lawman does."

They took a moment to digest this latest piece of news. Not much happened in town the women of Eden didn't learn about sooner or later. It had taken many months to set up and implement their information system. But once in place, it ran like clockwork.

Besides Maddie, Constance, Dora, and Gertrude, eight other women from Eden held town jobs, each in an establishment where people gathered and conversations could be easily overheard. Places like the company store, the laundry, the hotel, restaurants, and the homes of important citizens, such as Thaddeus Newlin. In addition, the women had contacts—Delilah and Lulu to name just two—who passed along any noteworthy tidbits they came across.

Lulu, unlike Delilah, hadn't always been a prostitute. She'd been a miner's wife, widowed after the accident like the rest of them. But her baby had been born dead during the scarlet fever epidemic that followed, and she'd been unable to cope with the loss of both husband and child. She tried living in Eden. After a time, unhappiness drove her into the bed of a despicable man. When he finished with her, he cast her out as if she warranted no more importance than yesterday's garbage. Physically and emotionally beaten, Lulu chose to work for Delilah rather than return to Eden, even though she would have been welcomed back with open arms.

"What about Clint Damschroeder?" Constance voiced the same question on Maddie's mind. "We still gonna go through with the robbery next week?"

Clint Damschroeder was one of three minority partners in the Edenville Consolidated Mining Company. They, along with Thaddeus Newlin, the majority partner, ran the Edenville Consolidated Mining Company. But Newlin was the one in charge, and everyone knew it.

"I think we'd best wait for a while," Maddie said. "Until we know more about Mr. McSween and his plans."

In the four robberies they'd pulled off, Maddie and her recruits had stolen more than three thousand dollars. With hundreds of mouths to feed, it went neither far nor long. And the arrival of Scott McSween in Edenville meant the prospect of future robberies dimmed. Maddie didn't like it, but she wasn't sure what to do about it. Yet.

"I agree with Maddie." Granny Fay leaned forward, her elbows resting on her knees, the reins loose in her hands. "We've worked too hard to risk it all now."

"We're going to need flour soon," Gertrude added. "Mice ate through the sacks, and we lost half our supply in the last rainstorm. And the younguns will need warm clothes before long."

"I know," said Maddie.

She thought again of Scott McSween. Until today, fear of being caught hadn't bothered her much. They'd been clever and careful in pulling off the robberies and taken no chances that weren't calculated. But something about McSween put her on edge. He was different from a lot of men, including the sheriff of Edenville. Not just bigger and stronger, but smarter. She still hadn't figured out why a man like he was would offer to give her his licorice rope.

"Lookie there." Constance nudged Maddie in the ribs with her elbow. "Don't that beat all? I swear, your little Josephine is just the cutest thing."

As they approached the rickety wooden gate marking the entrance to Eden, a group of children ran out to meet the surrey, laughing and hollering in their excitement to be reunited with mothers who'd had a long day away from home. Constance's son, Archie, led a small gray donkey, which Josephine rode bareback. The women had found the donkey roaming the desert shortly after moving into Eden—he was probably left behind by the former residents—and made a pet of him. The giggling girl clutched the donkey's stubby mane as he trotted, her long black hair coming loose from its ribbons.

Maddie was instantly reminded of her late husband, William. The resemblance between him and their daughter was so strong, Josephine might have sprung from William alone like the Greek goddess Athena had from her father, Zeus.

Maddie's heart swelled at the sight of Josephine—and Eden. What had once been a collection of dilapidated structures occupied by a bunch of desperate and poverty-stricken women had been transformed into a real community. The women had pooled their talents, skills, resources, and intelligence and, together, they'd survived. Not well, necessarily, but at least they had roofs over their heads and were no longer starving.

And it wouldn't have happened without the joint effort of a great many individuals, including Maddie and her band of thieves.

As Granny Fay reined the horses to a stop, Constance's son lifted a squirming Josephine to the ground. With arms outstretched, she ran toward them, calling, "Maw, maw," in a slurred voice, the result of her bout last year with scarlet fever.

Maddie climbed down from the surrey and gathered her three-year-old daughter into her arms. Josephine gave Maddie a sound kiss on each cheek. The girl's slight build and ragged clothes pained Maddie so greatly, it hurt her to breathe.

Damn Newlin, she thought to herself. Damn him and the other partners for taking their husbands from them, then leaving them utterly destitute and homeless.

Nothing could bring the dead miners back. But the money was another matter. As she did daily, Maddie vowed to reclaim every red cent the Edenville Consolidated Mining Company owed the women. And she'd take it from Newlin's and the partners' pockets one coin at a time if need be.

Scott didn't make use of the buggy Thaddeus Newlin sent for him the following morning. Instead, he accompanied a crew of second-shift miners as far as the base of the mountain.

He figured the buggy driver wouldn't freely converse with him, while the miners did. Scott had learned early on to keep his mouth shut, listening rather than talking.

Conversation that morning confirmed what he already knew. Mining was an inherently dangerous occupation. Conditions were appalling, safety was taken lightly, and accidents happened on a regular basis. Edenville, however, had a reputation exceeding other operations. The tragic explosion last year hadn't been the first such disaster. Merely the worst.

Before entering the mining company headquarters, he kicked the toes of his boots into the threshold, dislodging the dirt and dust he'd picked up on his walk over there. He straightened his hat and shirt collar, but he didn't remove his Colt revolver.

Inside the office, he was greeted by an impeccably dressed young man who was obviously expecting him.

"Mr. McSween. Welcome to Edenville. I'm Zachariah Forrester, Mr. Newlin's secretary. He's in a meeting at the moment with the mine superintendent. Please have a seat, and he'll be right with you."

"If you don't mind," Scott said, noting a thin white scar marring the man's otherwise handsome face, "I'll have a look around while I wait."

"Of course."

The secretary returned to his desk and picked up a sheet of paper. He appeared to be reading, but Scott could tell the man watched him with keen interest from the corner of his eye.

Muffled voices came from behind a closed door near the secretary's desk. Scott couldn't hear what was being said, but the tone was angry. Evidently, Mr. Newlin's meeting with the mine superintendent wasn't progressing well.

Framed photographs of the mining operation lined the entire length of one wall. Scott pretended to study these while he bided his time. In truth, his thoughts wandered, which they had been doing with increasing frequency since yesterday afternoon. Distractions were a dangerous liability in his profession. But for some inexplicable reason, he couldn't get Maddie off his mind.

She intrigued him, and it had nothing to do with her pleasing looks, though she was pretty enough to distract any man. She'd acted meek in front of her boss, but Scott would bet his last bullet in a showdown the woman was anything but. There'd been strength in her green eyes when she'd stared at him yesterday. More so, there'd been defiance and, if he weren't mistaken, a challenge.

He had the odd impression she knew him, which didn't seem feasible. If he'd met her before, he would remember. Maybe the unsettling familiarity he'd sensed had been one of kindred spirits recognizing each other. Even at a glance, he could tell he and Maddie were more alike than different, right down to the anger and resentment simmering deep inside them.

The idea of seeing her again, of becoming better acquainted, appealed to Scott. But, he reminded himself, that alone wasn't good enough reason to accept Newlin's job offer. Scott would base his decision to accept or decline entirely on the outcome of their meeting. Still, Maddie provided an added incentive for remaining in Edenville.

Moving along to the next picture, he allowed a slight smile to pull at his lips. No matter what transpired during the meeting, he'd make a point of dropping by the company store on his way back to the hotel. Maddie was definitely a woman worth taking a few extra minutes out of his day to visit.

At a sudden loud noise, he spun around. The door to Thaddeus Newlin's office swung open. An older man wearing soiled work clothes and carrying a battered hat stepped out. Though he bore no noticeable bruises, he looked as if he'd lost a long, grueling fist fight. Shoulders slumped, he brushed past the secretary's desk without either an acknowledgment or a good-bye and left without looking back.

The secretary stuck his head in Thaddeus Newlin's open doorway. "Sir. Mr. McSween is here."

"Send him in," a voice boomed.

"Mr. Newlin will see you now." The secretary gestured Scott into the room.

The office reflected its owner's personality. Combining heavy pine furniture with elegant appointments, the decor conveyed a feeling of both power and wealth.

"Good morning, Mr. McSween." Newlin, already standing, came around from behind his desk to shake Scott's hand. "Welcome to Edenville. I trust you're comfortable in the hotel. It's not much, but it's the best we have."

"Very comfortable. Thank you."

Newlin indicated an oversized, elaborately carved pine chair situated in front of his desk. "Would you care for some coffee? Or I have something stronger available if you wish."

"Nothing," Scott said. "I had coffee with breakfast at the hotel."

Newlin dismissed his secretary with a nod, and the man slipped out of the room. He pulled the door closed behind him, but left it open a crack, something Scott found interesting.

Guessing his thoughts, Newlin said, "You can trust Zachariah. After the first robbery, I had all my employees checked and double-checked. The leak in my office didn't come from him."

"Actually, I was thinking maybe you didn't trust me."

That earned a laugh from Newlin. "I was surprised to hear you refused the services of my buggy and driver."

"When a horse isn't available, I prefer to walk."

"A few days in this heat, and you'll change your mind."

"If I stay."

"Speaking of which . . ." Newlin leaned back in his chair, and openly assessed Scott. Propriety mattered little to men used to calling the shots.

If he intended to intimidate Scott with his frank stare, his ploy failed. Scott didn't so much as blink during the interplay, which lasted several seconds. To Scott's satisfaction, Newlin spoke first. It was a small reminder that Newlin needed Scott and not the other way around.

"As I told you in my correspondence, three of the four partners in the Edenville Consolidated Mining Company have been robbed in the past six months. Myself twice. The robberies have clearly been personal attacks. In each case, not only was money taken, the victims were tortured."

Tortured was a strong word, though Scott could see why Newlin might use it. None of the men had been physically hurt in the robberies. But they had all been publicly embarrassed in some fashion. To a man in Newlin's position, that would be torture.

On the first occasion, he'd been tied naked to the settee in his private railroad car. On the second, he'd been kidnapped and taken down into a remote tunnel in the farthest depths of the Edenville mine. There, he was left alone, handcuffed to an ore cart and blindfolded. When he was finally discovered the following day, he'd been on the verge of hysterics. The other two partners had suffered similar fates.

Whoever these robbers were, they possessed intimate knowledge of Newlin and his partners. The punishments they inflicted were specifically chosen to play on the victim's darkest fears or reveal his most carefully guarded secrets.

For that, they'd earned Scott's respect, which certainly made the job offer more attractive. He didn't chase down criminals who weren't worthy opponents.

"I've been getting almost no help from the sheriff," Newlin continued, his mouth twisting in disgust. "The man is worthless and incompetent."

"Tom Lunsford has a good reputation. He's honest and hardworking." Scott had once been similarly described. No more. He'd learned firsthand that when a man went against the tide of public opinion, a good reputation counted for little. Even with his family. "I can't help believing he's doing his best."

"His best isn't good enough," Newlin roared, then made a noticeable effort to contain his escalating rage. "It's obvious Lunsford doesn't possess the skill or experience to bring these robbers to justice. You do, if your reputation is to be believed."

"Believe it," Scott said flatly.

Newlin smiled. "I do." He shifted in his chair, his smile altering to a look of condescension. "I thought your actions at the Galveston lynching were stupid."

Scott didn't react. He'd been expecting Newlin to bring up the lynching. Everyone who heard of it did. "You're not the only one."

"Are you including yourself in that group?"

"No."

"Really?" Newlin's bushy brows shot up. "You still abide by your position even after losing your job and . . ."

"Everything that mattered to me?"

"Yes. Since you put it that way."

"For the record, I wasn't fired. I quit."

"And what of it?" Newlin's laugh had a brittle edge to it. "The end results were the same."

"Not entirely." And not to Scott.

He had turned in his badge by choice, not force. If he clung to that difference out of misguided self-respect, so be it. He'd ridden away from Galveston with little else except the conviction he'd done the right thing.

"You killed two innocent men who'd attempted a lynching." Newlin's accusation sliced through the momentary silence.

"I killed two men in self-defense. Innocent is an arguable point."

"The prisoner you were protecting had raped and murdered a young girl of sixteen, then had the gumption to brag about it. Can you blame her family and friends for wanting him dead?"

"No."

"Then why protect him, for God's sake?"

"According to the law, he was entitled to a fair trial."

Newlin stared at him incredulously. "That's it? That's your reason?"

Scott drew in a long breath. He hadn't yet made a habit of defending himself, and he didn't intend to start today. Especially with Newlin, a man whose own morals and ethics were highly questionable.

The State of Texas had cleared Scott of any wrongdoing and determined he'd been carrying out the duties of his office. Few people, however, agreed with the State's ruling. They regularly condemned Scott, labeling him a murderer and a traitor. No better than the scum he'd been protecting. He never went to prison. But he was a prisoner just the same—of prejudice, hatred, and his past.

It was doubtful he'd escape any time soon.

"I was a U.S. Marshal for four years. During that time, I served my government. No questions asked. I give the exact same service to my clients. If that's not good enough for you . . ." Scott stood, careful to mask his emotions with casual indifference. He refused to lose the upper hand by showing weakness.

"Wait just a minute!" Newlin surged to his feet. "I don't give a tinker's damn about you killing those two men. Hell, it's the reason I brought you here in the first place. I admire a man who doesn't back down in a fight. Come on," he said when Scott didn't move. "Sit back down and let's quit this nonsense.

"I don't need your job, Mr. Newlin."

"So I hear. My sources tell me you're an individual of some means."

"Your sources are right."

"I can make you rich."

Scott turned to leave.

"Listen to my terms before you refuse, McSween. I'm quite certain you'll agree they're very generous."

Scott thought of Maddie, with her glorious blond hair and snapping green eyes, and felt his refusal begin to waver. He knew better than to let a woman figure into his decision regarding a job. But his instincts told him Maddie wasn't just any woman. And Scott had excellent instincts.

He sat and named an exorbitant weekly fee. "And all expenses paid. *All* expenses," he reiterated. If the majority partner of the Edenville Consolidated Mining Company wanted him, he'd have to pay through the nose.

Newlin's only reaction was to ball one hand into a fist. "You drive a hard bargain."

"But I also deliver the goods."

"I expect daily reports. If I'm not here, you can speak to my secretary, Mr. Forrester."

"I'll report when I have something to tell you."

The two men stared at each other. After several seconds, Newlin growled, "Agreed," and slammed the fist he'd made onto his desk.

"I'll need a horse."

"See Mr. Forrester on your way out. He'll arrange for whatever you require." Newlin snatched an envelope from a pile of papers and ripped it open.

Scott rose, not caring that he was being dismissed. The spoils of battle had gone to him. Newlin could keep his last shred of dignity.

Tipping his hat to his newest client, Scott left the office, then stopped to speak to the secretary. He assumed Mr. Forrester had listened to the entire conversation, for he showed no surprise at Scott's request for a horse.

"Your hotel room has been taken care of through next week," Mr. Forrester said crisply when they finished conducting their business.

Outside, Scott let the sweltering heat seep through his clothes and into his skin as he contemplated his first move. Paying a visit to Tom Lunsford made the most sense. He'd spotted the sheriff's office on his earlier walk through town with the miners. And as luck would have it, the sheriff's office wasn't far from the company store.

All last night and all morning Scott had fought a powerful hunger for another rope of licorice—and the pretty lady he hoped to entice into waiting on him. He saw no reason not to indulge his hunger after interviewing the sheriff.

Then again, why wait?

Chapter Four

"May I help you?" Maddie asked.

She faced Scott across the counter. Though she'd likely been on her feet a good portion of the day, she still looked neat and tidy. And not especially happy to see him. She wore the same apron as yesterday and maybe even the same homespun dress. Both garments, however, had been cleaned and pressed. She must have risen before dawn, or gone to bed at midnight.

He'd failed to notice the dark smudges beneath her eyes on his first visit to the company store. But he had noticed the smattering of freckles sprinkled across the bridge of her nose and the curve of her delicately shaped mouth. The freckles charmed him. Her mouth, and thoughts of how it might feel parting against his as his tongue sought entry, had kept him tossing and turning half the night.

Scott stepped closer to the counter. "I'd like two hundred licorice ropes."

Her face registered shock at his request. "I beg your pardon."

"Two hundred licorice ropes. Isn't that how many children you said lived in Eden?"

Her spine snapped ramrod straight and in a clipped voice that reminded Scott of Newlin's secretary, she said, "I don't appreciate having pranks played on me, Mr. McSween."

"You know my name?"

"Edenville is a small town."

A reasonable explanation. Towns like Edenville were notorious havens of gossip, something that often worked in his favor. But it pleased him nonetheless that she'd taken note of his name and remembered it.

Not to be outdone, he countered, "So it is, Maddie." If he weren't mistaken, something akin to alarm flickered in her sea-green eyes. "I heard the store manager holler for you yesterday. He used your name."

She noticeably relaxed. "Yes, of course."

"He doesn't impress me as a very pleasant person. Neither do some of your customers," Scott said, remembering Mrs. Newlin and her brood of unruly children.

The gaze Maddie fixed on him was unfaltering and void of emotion. "I need the job."

Scott simply nodded, having guessed as much already. His admiration for Maddie rose a notch, as did his disrespect for Newlin. The majority partner of the Edenville Consolidated Mining Company might be his newest client, but that arrangement didn't require Scott to like the man.

"How about those licorice ropes?"

Maddie peered around the store as if concerned their conversation might be overhead. Her glance briefly rested on a second woman clerk stocking shelves, then cut back to Scott. "You aren't serious," she whispered.

"I'm very serious," he replied softly and leaned closer to her. It may have been his overactive libido, but he swore a current of heat passed between them. Thick and heavy and charged with electricity, like the wind that raged just before a summer thunderstorm.

"If you're considering giving the licorice ropes to the children of Eden, I can't allow it."

"Did I say that?"

"We don't accept charity from strangers," she answered primly.

He couldn't resist smiling. "Two hundred licorice ropes, if you don't mind. And what I do with them is my concern."

Her lips thinned in perfect imitation of a disapproving schoolmarm, and she made a show of examining the candy on display at the counter. "I'm sorry, sir," she said with mock formality. "There aren't more than twenty pieces here."

"Have you any in the stockroom?"

"I'll have to check."

"Much obliged."

She stepped out from behind the counter and came around. "I'm afraid the task will require several minutes."

"I'm in no hurry." Scott didn't mind waiting. Not when there was such a variety of interesting things to occupy his attention. Like Maddie's curvaceous backside as she stooped to retrieve a piece of trash on her way to the stockroom.

He passed the time by leisurely strolling up and down the aisles. The other clerk finished stocking a box of dry goods and cast Scott a wary glance. More than wary, her eyes were decidedly cold and unfriendly. He wondered why. Did he look particularly threatening, or was she just distrusting by nature? He nodded politely, and she scurried away as if he'd growled at her. Strange, he thought.

Shouts from the stockroom made him forget all about the clerk. He hurried back to investigate. From behind a curtain separating the stockroom from the store, he heard the manager berating Maddie.

"That's enough out of you. I'm sick to death of your insubordination. You'll do as I say, or I promise, Maddie Campbell, you'll rue the day you walked in here asking for a job."

"Release me this instant." Maddie's voice resonated with fury.

Scott ripped the curtain aside and stepped into the stockroom. His blood ran hot at the sight of the store manager with his meaty hand on Maddie's arm, his face twisted into an ugly grimace. Scott reached for his revolver, ready to shoot if necessary.

"Get out," the store manager hollered at Scott. "This doesn't concern you."

"I'll get out when you release the lady."

"It's all right, Mr. McSween." Maddie shook her arm, freeing it from the store manager's grasp. "The situation is under control."

"The hell it is!"

"You heard her." The store manager appeared to have lost some of his bluster, but he stood his ground. "Now leave."

"Maddie," Scott said. "You don't deserve this kind of treatment. Not from the likes of him."

"I'll thank you to mind your own business, Mr. McSween." She hugged her waist and turned away from both men.

Scott stared at her, dumbstruck. Could she really be that desperate for a job? When she continued to face the wall, he shook his head in disgust and exited the stockroom. Somebody, probably the store manager, whisked the curtain closed after him.

Despite Maddie's insistence that he leave, Scott stuck around. She might not welcome his interference, but, by God, if the man so much as laid a pinkie on her again, she'd get Scott's interference and get it good. Shifting his weight to one leg, he leaned against the doorjamb and stuffed his hands in his pockets. He noticed the other clerk observing him from a distance, her look now one of curiosity as opposed to distrust.

"You sass me again like that again in front of a customer and you're fired." The store manager's voice carried over the curtain.

"You won't fire me."

He laughed scornfully. "You think just because—"

"If you fire me, I'll go straight to Newlin and tell him you've been skimming profits for the last year. *And* that you're taking bribes from suppliers on the side."

For the second time in ten minutes, Scott smiled. Maybe he'd been too hasty in assuming Maddie needed defending. The lady could take care of herself. Very well, apparently.

"You have no proof," the store manager sputtered.

"But I do, Mr. Abernathy. If you don't believe me, go to your desk and remove the journal you keep in a locked box in the bottom drawer. You'll find two of the pages are missing. I don't need to tell you what records that journal contains."

"I—I refused to be blackmailed."

"The way I see it, you have no choice. Now, if you don't mind, I have customers to wait on. And the store closes in ten minutes."

"Bitch!"

Scott could hear the shuffle of feet and then Maddie speaking, her tone lethal enough to cause the hairs on his arms to stand upright.

"Don't you ever touch me or Constance again. Is that clear?"

The curtain shot into the air. The store manager stormed out of the stockroom and past Scott.

"A word of caution, my friend," Scott called out.

Abernathy stopped dead in his tracks, spun around, and glowered. His cheeks burned a deep red.

Scott responded by scratching his jaw contemplatively. "It's never a smart idea to land on a lady's bad side."

"She'll be gone by morning."

"Sorry, mister, but I won't take that bet." Chuckling, he pushed off the doorjamb.

The store manager tore down the aisle, shoving past the other clerk who had resumed stocking shelves the instant her boss appeared. She stared after him, then at Scott. Her eyebrows lifted in surprise and confusion.

Maddie emerged from the stockroom, calm and composed. She started at the sight of Scott.

"I thought I told you to leave."

"I'm not very good at following orders. One of my few faults."

"Somehow I doubt that." Maddie drew herself up, gathered her skirt, and squeezed by him. She smelled like cinnamon and nutmeg, reminding Scott of his mother's kitchen.

Pushing the unwanted memory to the back of his mind where it belonged, he followed Maddie and caught up to her in three strides. "What? That I'm not good at following orders or have few faults?"

She whirled on him. "Go. Before I lose my job."

"You won't lose your job. You said so yourself."

Her eyes narrowed. "How much did you hear?"

"Everything."

She sighed tiredly. "Mr. McSween—"

"Maddie." He cut her off, stepping near enough to hear the quiet swish of her petticoat. The sound triggered an image of his hands buried deep in the folds of that petticoat, lifting it over her head as he undressed her. "Let me take you home."

"Absolutely not!"

"It's not wise for you to be out on the streets alone so late in the day." He thought she might retreat from him, but she didn't. Part of him wished she would. The part reacting to her proximity.

What was it about her that affected him so profoundly? Granted, she was pretty, though not uncommonly pretty. Then again, she *was* uncommonly feisty. Not many women had the gumption to confront their boss. Or him, for that matter. She had done both.

"I won't be alone," she insisted and took her leave without further ado.

He watched her skirt around the display of canned goods she'd restacked the previous day, and disappear down another aisle.

"No, you won't, Maddie Campbell," he said under his breath. "In fact, I can pretty much guarantee it."

Checking the wall clock on his way to the door, he went outside. He spotted a bench beside the entrance and sat down. Then, slouching against the side of the building, he stretched out his long legs and adjusted his hat so that the brim covered his eyes. Maddie had said the store closed in ten minutes. Scott would cool his heels until then. He knew he should probably drop by to see the sheriff, but decided to postpone his visit until morning.

Several minutes later, he remembered the licorice ropes.

Maddie wasn't surprised to see Scott waiting for her and Constance outside the store a half hour later. He'd been nothing if not persistent from the moment they'd met.

From beside Maddie, Constance hissed, "What's he doing here?"

Both women gazed out the window at Scott. They'd been on their way to the door when Constance stopped to refasten her high-top boots. Lucky for them she did, or Maddie wouldn't have caught sight of Scott through the window.

"I think he wants to take me home," Maddie said through tight lips.

"You are not serious!"

"Afraid so."

"You can't let him, of course."

"I'm not sure I can stop him."

"Maddie!"

"Calm yourself. He isn't coming with us." Maddie closed her eyes and pinched the bridge of her nose. "But I may have to let him walk us to the surrey."

Constance puffed up like a riled hen. "Have you completely lost your mind?"

"If I refuse, with no good reason, I could rouse his suspicions." Maddie didn't think Scott had connected her and Constance to the robberies, even with him witnessing the scene between her and Mr. Abernathy. Still, the possibility remained. He was rumored to be a very clever man and from what she'd witnessed of him so far, the rumors appeared true.

"It's too dangerous," Constance insisted.

"Yes and no."

"Quit speaking in riddles."

"I can continue to . . . discourage him, but what will that accomplish?"

"For pity's sake, Maddie." Constance didn't hide her irritation. "We could lose everything."

"Yes, you're right. But on the other hand, with him underfoot, so to speak, we can easily keep watch on him and his activities."

"I don't know." Constance drew the words out. "It's awfully risky."

"Agreed. However, there's also opportunity. Opportunity we wouldn't otherwise have."

"Are you interested in him?"

Maddie squirmed under Constance's critical apprisal. "Naturally I'm interested in him. Newlin hired him to track us down and have us arrested."

"That's not what I meant."

"I have no idea what you're talking about."

Worried Constance might be right, Maddie feigned indignance. What if she did have a personal interest in Scott McSween? He'd taken a fancy to her, that much was obvious. And, heaven help her, she was flattered.

Of all people in Edenville, why him?

The charcoal gray suit he wore emphasized his tall, lean build; the revolver at his side accentuated his rugged good looks. He had yet to remove his hat entirely in her presence, but she suspected the thick brown locks curling beneath the rim covered his entire head. She had tried to convince herself all last night she didn't find his appearance appealing. Her bout of insomnia proved differently.

"Come on." Maddie pulled Constance along with her toward the door. "Might as well get this over with."

Constance spun Maddie around and clasped her hands. She peered up at Maddie, her expression filled with concern. "Please, be careful. I couldn't bear it if something happened to you."

"He's only walking us to the surrey. I'm not facing him in a shoot-out."

"Not yet you aren't."

There was an air of foreboding in Constance's voice, and despite the insufferable heat, a chill slid up Maddie's spine.

"Evening, ladies." Upon seeing them approach, Scott came to his feet in a long fluid motion that caused Maddie's breath to hitch.

Making a point to be polite yet cool, she said, "Mr. McSween, fancy meeting you here."

Instead of being put off, he merely smiled, and Maddie did her best to resist responding with an answering smile. She shouldn't—*couldn't*—give him the slightest encouragement, not without disastrous results.

He gestured for them to proceed with him down the boardwalk and onto the street. "After you." Once on the street, Scott fell in step beside them. Taking Maddie's elbow as they crossed, he guided her out of the path of an oncoming rider.

The touch of his hand was nothing like that of Mr. Abernathy's. She thrilled to the sensation of his distinctly proprietary fingers pressing into her flesh.

On the far side of the street, they paused under the shade of an overhang. Thankfully, he released her.

Maddie made introductions. "Mr. McSween. This is my dear friend, Constance Starkweather. Constance, this is Mr. McSween."

"Ma'am." Scott inclined his head.

"How do you do?" Constance answered primly.

"It would be my pleasure to escort you ladies home."

"We don't need you to take us home, thank you." Constance raised her chin a good three inches. "We have a ride waitin' for us."

Scott turned to Maddie.

She confirmed Constance's claim by motioning to the end of the street where Granny Fay waited in the dilapidated surrey with its mismatched team of horses. Two other women were with Granny Fay, having already finished their jobs for the day.

"Then I'll see you to your ride."

He didn't insist exactly, but Maddie doubted he'd take no for an answer. Scott McSween got what he wanted. And for whatever reason, at the moment, he wanted her.

"Thank you," she said, and started down the street. "That would be nice."

Constance opened her mouth to object, but Maddie hushed her with an imperceptible shake of her head.

"Does the surrey pick you up every day?" Scott slowed his stride to match Maddie's.

"And drops us off."

"Do many women from Eden work in town?"

"A few." She refrained from giving specifics. The less he knew about them, the better.

"I don't suppose there are a lot of jobs available in Edenville for reputable women."

"No." Turning the tables on him, she asked, "How's the investigation into the robberies progressing?"

Constance swallowed a gasp. Maddie ignored her.

For his part, Scott didn't so much as blink. "Besides my name, you also know the reason for my visit."

"News travels quickly."

"I only accepted Newlin's job offer an hour ago."

So he *had* taken the job. Until this moment, they weren't certain. Maddie shot Constance a sidelong glance as if to say, *See, my plan has paid off.*

"Any leads yet?" She surprised herself with the forwardness of her question.

"I work fast. But not that fast."

"How long does it usually take for you to capture a criminal?"

"That depends on the criminal. A week or two. Maybe a month."

A week or two! He had to be exaggerating. "And are you always successful?"

"Always."

No, he wasn't exaggerating. Scott McSween exemplified confidence.

"Anything you can tell me about the robberies?"

"Me?" Maddie's heart gave a little jump. "No, why would you ask?"

He looked at her, and she swore his gray eyes saw clear through her to the many secrets she harbored within herself.

"The women of Eden have suffered a great deal," he said, "starting with the accident. If you were to hold Newlin responsible for your suffering, and I'm not saying you do, you might be of a different opinion regarding the robberies than most people."

Maddie couldn't stop her emotional outpour. A year of grief and anger gave voice to her true feelings.

"Are you implying that if I knew the identity of these robbers, I might help them or hide them because I hate Newlin with every breath I take and hope to God he rots in hell for all eternity?"

Without her realizing it, they had come to a stop about twenty feet from the surrey.

"Something like that." Scott's eyes continued to study her.

She didn't wilt beneath his intimate scrutiny. "Yes, Mr. McSween. If I had the chance to help these robbers, I would do it gladly and without the least hesitation." She tilted her head, challenging him to dispute her. "Can you blame me?"

He didn't speak for several seconds, then said slowly, "Not at all."

Constance, who had been watching in horrified silence, made a strangled noise and fled to the surrey.

"Your friend appears upset."

"It's been a difficult time for all of us. Constance lost her husband of fourteen years in the cave-in and her six-year-old son to scarlet fever four weeks later. If it weren't for her older son, I don't think she would have gone on living."

"I'm sorry."

A lump formed in the back of Maddie's throat. "They're waiting for me. I have to go." She walked away without saying good-bye.

When they were out of hearing distance, her fellow passengers bombarded her with questions. She tried her best to answer them, but her head spun wildly. A quick peek backward confirmed McSween remained where she'd left him.

"Maddie!" Constance wailed, her palms pressed to her cheeks. "Whatever has gotten into you? He'll find out now for sure we're the robbers and have us arrested. Then what will happen?"

"No." Maddie already regretted her impetuous outburst, but she nonetheless defended herself. "Hating Newlin after what he's done to us is to be expected. Mr. McSween won't see anything strange in that."

Constance sniffed and wrung her hands. "I pray you're right."

So did Maddie. If she'd made a mistake, said too much, they would all pay the price and pay dearly.

Chapter Five

"Come here, you little imp." Maddie chased after her daughter, catching her in the middle of their small, tumbledown shack and swinging her high in the air. "I've got you."

Josephine made squealing noises and what passed for a laugh. She flung her arms around Maddie's neck and held on with all her might, a grin big as life on her sweet cherub face.

"I love you, too, sweet pea," Maddie said in Josephine's small ear. "More than anything on this earth.

"Wuv maw maw."

Maddie snatched one of her daughter's flailing fists and pressed it to her cheek. Her heart ached with an almost unbearable combination of joy and pain. "Yes. That's it, sweet pea. Love Mama. You said it." She kissed her daughter's hand and fought to control her emotions. "Are you sleepy yet? Somehow, I don't think so."

A knock sounded at the door. Maddie swung around and called, "Who's there?"

"It's me," came a familiar voice. "Dora."

"Come in." Maddie set Josephine on her feet and went to the door. It squeaked as she flung it open, the hinges rusted through in some places.

Dora entered, balancing her fifteen-month-old daughter on her hip. Josephine made happy gurgling noises at the sight of their guests.

Behind them, the sun was setting. The last lingering rays slanted across the horizon, bathing the desert in a reddish-gold glow. For Maddie, dusk was the most beautiful time of the day. It never failed to fill her with hope for the future, even during her bleakest moments.

"I come by to tell you Lavinia has called a council meetin' fer tonight."

At Josephine's insistence, Dora put her daughter down to play. Though almost two years older, Josephine went right to the younger girl, scooped her up, and squeezed her like a rag doll. They both giggled.

Maddie tapped Josephine's shoulder to get her attention and wagged a finger at her. "Be careful." To Dora, she said, "When's the meeting?"

"Soon as everyone can git themselves there."

Maddie sighed. She shouldn't be surprised. Not after what happened that afternoon with Scott McSween. No doubt the instant Lavinia heard about him accompanying Maddie and Constance to the surrey, she'd called the meeting. It was her prerogative as head of the council. In fact, any of Eden's elected council members—which included Maddie—could call a meeting if they so chose.

"I still got a few more folks to tell. You don't have to rush."

"We'll be along shortly." Maddie resigned herself to her fate. She would surely be called upon to explain her actions regarding Mr. McSween. Not that she had an explanation. Leastwise, not a reasonable one.

Dora didn't immediately leave.

"Is there something else?" Maddie asked.

The other woman stared at the floor. The cracks between the planks were wide enough in some places to see ground below. Not to mention snakes, rats, lizards, and insects.

"What is it, Dora?"

"I . . . I know I ain't the smartest person. Never did have much schooling. Pa said third grade was more'n any girl ever needed." She gave an uncomfortable laugh, and her plump cheeks grew pink.

"You're much smarter than you give yourself credit for," Maddie said sincerely and meant it. "And very brave. We wouldn't have been able to pull off any of the robberies without you."

Dora shuffled her feet, still staring at the floor. Finally, she blurted, "I just want you to know, no matter what happens tonight, I still think you're the nicest, kindest person in the whole wide world. What you've done fer me, what you've done fer all of us, well, we wouldn't be here today without you."

She clasped Maddie to her in an impulsive hug. At their feet, the two little girls imitated them.

"Thank you, Dora. I appreciate it."

"Guess I'll see you at the meetin', then."

"I'll be there."

They separated, and Dora left with her daughter. Maddie no sooner closed the door than Josephone threw herself at it and yanked on the handle.

"No, sweet pea." Maddie removed her daughter's

hand and tilting her chin, forced Josephine to meet her eyes. "We'll see Dora and Sue Ann in a few minutes at the meeting." She spoke slowly and clearly while pretending to brush her hair. "But we need to fix your hair first and wash your face."

The little girl wailed loudly, the sound unnatural and gut-wrenching. Tonight, it grated on Maddie's nerves and she grasped Josephine firmly by the shoulders.

"That's enough now. Be quiet!"

The little girl stopped wailing, her expression a mixture of surprise and trepidation.

Maddie instantly regretted losing her temper. It wasn't Josephine's fault she didn't understand. It was Newlin's and the blasted scarlet fever epidemic. One had stolen Josephine's father from her, the other her hearing.

"I'm sorry, I'm sorry." Kneeling, Maddie pulled her daughter into a fierce embrace. "Don't cry. Mama loves you very much."

Typical of young children, Josephine's mood changed instantaneously. She was suddenly all smiles, laughing and wiggling in an attempt to escape Maddie's embrace.

"Come on. Let Mama fix your hair."

Maddie went over to the pine chest on the floor in the corner beside the bedroll where she and Josephine slept. On top of the chest lay a comb and brush, along with a tiny array of various personal items. Josephine snatched a bright red ribbon and pushed it into Maddie's hand.

"You want me to put this in your hair? All right."

There were very few furnishings in their shack, only the scant belongings Maddie and her late husband had brought with them when they traveled to Arizona from West Virginia.

The home provided to them by the Edenville Consolidated Mining Company had come with basic furnishings, so they weren't required to purchase a bed, or dresser, or table and chairs. Maddie could live without a bed and dresser. But she so longed to sit in a real chair when she and Josephine took the simple meals she prepared in a cook pit outside their shack.

That, and a stove to warm the shack. Last winter, she and Josephine woke up shivering every morning. It was a wonder they hadn't both caught pneumonia and died.

Every day during that dreadful winter, Maddie promised herself she would survive. For her daughter, for the robberies, and for the chance to get revenge on Thaddeus Newlin.

She didn't remember who first hatched the plan to go after Newlin and the partners. Not that it mattered. Once voiced, the idea grew and came together with astounding speed. It was unarguably daring, but they were desperate and starving and, in some cases, dying. They had little to lose and everything to gain.

For some, like Maddie, the prospect of reclaiming even a small portion of what Newlin took from them gave her reason to anticipate each new day rather than dread it. When the newly formed council learned she could handle a gun better than most men, she'd been immediately recruited and put in charge of the robberies.

Disguising themselves as men had been Constance's idea. Speaking with an Irish brogue had been Maddie's. Her late husband, William, was Irish, coming to America two years before he and Maddie met. She had loved listening to him talk. When they were courting, they'd sit for hours on the front porch of her home. While she sewed or tatted, he'd tell her stories about his home in Ireland. And though not the handsomest man in town, he'd been funny and charming and good to her despite his faults. She hadn't loved him in the strictest sense, but she had come to care for him immensely.

How could she not when he'd rescued her from a life she despised? Maddie might now be a poor widow living in a hovel in the middle of nowhere; still, she would choose this life any day over the one she'd left behind in West Virginia.

Using William's manner of speech not only aided with her disguise, in Maddie's mind and heart, it honored him and his unnecessary death.

Finishing with Josephine's hair, she turned her daughter toward her. "There!" She handed Josephine a small mirror and said directly into her ear, "Don't you look pretty."

The little girl stared at herself. *"Piddy."*

"Yes. Josephine is pretty."

Maddie returned the brush, comb, and mirror to the top of the chest after repinning her bun. They left their shack just as the sky was going from blue to violet, and walked the short distance to the center of Eden where the council meetings were customarily held. Last winter, bonfires were lit to warm the women as they talked. Tonight, only a small campfire burned. A half dozen pots and pans of tea were steeping for those who wanted it.

Not that they had real tea. Instead, they used dried parts of different plants they found nearby, such as sage and mesquite. Some of the women had experimented and come up with a variety of blends that were tolerable if not tasty.

Most everyone was already there by the time Maddie

and Josephine arrived. They headed first to a group of children playing outside the circle of gathering women. It was the job of the adolescents to watch the younger ones during council meetings, which, while not held in secret, were attended only by members and usually at night.

The residents of Eden were aware of the council's doings, particularly in regards to management of the community, but not privy to the details. Especially when it came to the robberies. Gossip couldn't be controlled, much less stopped, so the council made every effort to minimize it in order to protect those not directly involved.

Josephine ran directly to Archie, Constance's son. The twelve-year-old professed not to like her, but Maddie knew differently. Ever since his younger brother died, Archie had taken a shine to Josephine and could always be counted on to watch over her closely, if not play with her.

Tonight, he obviously wanted to socialize with his friends. Maddie sympathized and tried to dissuade Josephine. The little girl would have none of it.

"It's all right, Miz Campbell. I'll keep an eye on her."

"Are you sure, Archie?" She hated to burden him. He usually got stuck with Josephine during the day when Maddie worked. "It doesn't seem fair."

"Naw. If I ignore her, she'll just leave after a while and go play with the other girls.

They both knew he was lying. He wouldn't ignore Josephine, and she wouldn't leave him to go play with the other girls.

"I suppose." Maddie reluctantly agreed. "If she gets irritable or difficult, come get me. You promise?"

"Yes, ma'am."

Another lie. He wouldn't come for her no matter how irritable or difficult Josephine became.

Maddie showered Archie with a grateful smile. For all her misfortune and sorrow, Constance was infinitely blessed in that she had a wonderful son.

"This meeting will now come to order." Lavinia Claybourne took her place at the head of the group, ringing an old school bell. Nearly fifty years old and whipcord thin, her keen intelligence, sense of fairness, and ability to create order from chaos made her a natural choice for leader. By the same token, she could be a formidable opponent when challenged, and not many crossed her. "Everyone, please be quiet."

The eleven council members obediently settled down. Some found seats on logs, overturned buckets, or whatever else was handy. The rest stood, among them Maddie. She hung toward the back of the group, anxiety twisting her stomach into a tight knot.

How would she answer the questions regarding Scott McSween that would surely be put to her?

She didn't have long to wait. After a brief account from Patience Carmichael regarding the state of their food supply—mice were eating through their sacks of flour and cornmeal and coyotes were killing their chickens—Lavinia turned her attention to Maddie.

"It's come to my attention Maddie Campbell has some news to report regarding the private investigator Newlin hired."

Maddie felt every gaze fasten on her.

"Come forward, Maddie, and tell us what you've learned." Lavinia waved her to the front.

Was that a trace of annoyance Maddie heard in Lavinia's voice? Probably. While they usually got along well enough, the head councilwoman didn't like hearing news through the grapevine. In hindsight, Maddie should have reported to her the minute she returned to Eden.

She wove her way through the parting crowd, her stomach clenching tighter with each step. In some ways, facing Newlin and the partners during the robberies had been easier than speaking in front of these women.

Looking into their faces, her courage began to falter. She peered above the tops of heads to where the children were playing tag. The sight of Josephine, running and laughing, helped calm Maddie.

"Mr. McSween visited the store today," she began haltingly. "He insisted on escorting Constance and me to the surrey." Little by little, her confidence returned. "During our conversation, I was able to learn that, as of this afternoon, he formally accepted Newlin's offer."

There were gasps throughout the council members. In all honesty, they'd been expecting news of this nature for the last two months—ever since one of their secret informants advised them of Newlin's plan to hire a private investigator for the purpose of tracking down and capturing the robbers. Still, the realization came as a shock to many. Several voices rose above the rest.

"What do we do now?"

"There ain't enough food to last more'n a few weeks. Not with them mice and coyote gettin' into everything."

"Lord have mercy on us."

"Order, order." Lavinia rang the bell and kept ringing it until the voices quieted. "There's no need to panic yet, ladies. We have come through worse than this and survived. We'll survive again." Her heartfelt assurance brought the momentary disruption to an end. When all was quiet, she said, "Maddie, you've met him, this private investigator. Give us your impression of him."

Maddie swallowed. She could hardly share what she thought of him with the council members. Then again, did she really know? Where Scott McSween was concerned, her feelings were tangled worse than the branches of any tumbleweed.

She searched for something to say that would shift attention away from her. "He appears to be most competent. He stated it generally takes him a few weeks to a month to capture a criminal and that he's always successful."

Shock rippled through the group.

"Are we gonna be arrested?" someone shouted.

"From our conversation today, I don't believe he knows we're responsible for the robberies," Maddie said. *Not yet, anyway.*

"Are you sure?" someone else asked.

"No, I'm not absolutely sure. I suppose he could have been tricking me."

"What were ya doing talking to him anyway?" Patience Carmichael asked. A disapproving scowl made her already sharp features more pronounced. "Seems kind of foolhardy to me and downright risky."

Several shouted their agreement. To the casual observer, Lavinia's face probably bore concerned interest. Maddie was less certain. From her nearer vantage point, she swore the other woman's eyes gleamed with inquisitiveness. Did Lavinia somehow suspect Maddie of holding back information?

No. She had to be mistaken. It was merely a trick of her overactive imagination coupled with a guilty conscience. She shouldn't have been so forward this afternoon with Scott McSween, and she absolutely must stop having . . . inappropriate thoughts about him.

"Ain't you all been listening?" Dora stepped forward, her voice overflowed with righteous indignation. "Maddie done found out that Newlin hired the private investigator. That's pretty darn important information if you ask me."

"We would have found out," Constance countered.

"Sooner or later." Dora said, gesturing expansively. "But not today. McSween has no idea about us. Thanks to Maddie, we know an awful lot about him."

"Dora has a good argument," someone else said.

"We can't take the chance." Constance sat on a milking stool, winding a tattered handkerchief between her fingers. "The man has it in for us, and Maddie practically tells him right then and there we're the robbers. At the rate she's going, we'll all be in jail before the end of next week."

The barb hurt. Maddie guessed her friend to be the one who squealed on her to Lavinia. And while disappointed, she couldn't fault Constance. Not entirely.

"Constance Starkweather!" Dora planted her hands on her hips and gaped at her cohort in crime. "Where are your loyalties?" She shook her head in disgust. "You should be ashamed of yourself, picking on Maddie like that after all she's done for us. We'd've starved to death without her."

Dora had probably gone too far, but Maddie resisted interfering. With most everyone seemingly against her, it felt good having someone on her side.

Just as Lavinia began speaking, she was cut off by a shrill whistling coming from the vicinity of the gate. Heads turned in unison and all talking ceased.

Two guards patrolled Eden at all times, trained in the use of firearms by Maddie. In addition to leading the robberies, she supervised Eden's security. The guards used whistles to sound an alarm in the case of a visitor. In the case of an intruder, shots were fired.

A buggy and lone driver made its way through Eden,

stopping just short of where the council had gathered. The members watched in silent fascination. Unlike their old surrey, the buggy's black leather top and sides gleamed in the light of the rising moon. Each spoke on the shiny wheels was in perfect alignment with its neighbors. The fine horse pulling the vehicle tossed his head and pawed the ground impatiently.

Several of the older boys stumbled over themselves as they hurried forward. The woman driver handed the reins to the tallest of them, then allowed the boy to assist her from the buggy.

"Aren't you the gentleman," she said in a low, husky voice and gave him a smile that could only be described as stunning.

He turned beet red.

Taking in her surroundings with a definite air of bemusement, the woman collected the skirt of her satin dress in gloved fingers and sashayed to the front of the group.

Dora scurried to her seat, while Maddie faded into the background. Only Lavinia stayed her place.

"What brings you here tonight, Delilah?"

"I heard about what happened in town today. I guessed you might call a meeting and decided to attend." The town madam arched brows plucked to delicate perfection. "You know how much I enjoy giving my opinion."

"You have no vote in what goes on here."

"Not officially." Delilah pouted prettily. "But there are plenty who would listen to what I have to say."

There were, Maddie silently agreed.

Without Delilah Montgomery's help, the women wouldn't have lasted those first months after the accident. It was she who suggested they occupy the abandoned Mexican tent and shack town. She arranged for their move and provided them with enough food to last until some of the women could find jobs—jobs she arranged for through her many connections.

But even with her generous assistance, survival for the residents of Eden was a never-ending struggle. Three hundred people were a lot to feed, clothe, and house, requiring drastic measures. By October, the council had been formed and the first three members elected. Their sole purpose was to carefully manage the community and its limited resources for the good of all. By Christmas, more members were added, Maddie being one of them. And plans for the first robbery were put in motion.

Delilah and Lulu were the only citizens in Edenville who knew the true identity of the robbers. They were both trustworthy. Lulu, because she shared a history with the women of Eden. Delilah, because the women provided a loving home for her illegitimate son.

"By all means. Speak your mind," Lavinia said.

"Thank you." Delilah addressed the group. "Ladies, I'm sure you're very concerned about the private investigator Newlin has retained and what effect his presence in Edenville will have on you and your safety. Rest assured, I will do everything in my power to protect you and . . ." She drew a breath before continuing. "And the children."

"There ain't much you can do if Maddie don't quit jibber-jabbering with the man," someone shouted.

"Well. I don't know as I can blame her." Delilah batted an imaginary fan and rolled her eyes. "Have you seen him? Quite delicious, if I do say."

Her antics resulted in a few scattered titters.

"And from all accounts, right handy with a gun," someone near the front interjected, obviously not amused.

"Among other things, I'm sure." Delilah sighed. "But back to business. There has not been so much as a hint that you all have anything to do with the robberies. And no reason whatsoever for Newlin or this McSween gentleman to draw that conclusion. Has it occurred to you that Maddie's conversations with McSween could be an excellent opportunity to collect information?"

"At what cost?" Constance demanded.

Delilah turned to her, mild irritation flashing in her eyes. This wasn't the first time the two had sparred. "Very little, from what I can tell."

"I disagree." Constance slowly rose and folded her arms over her well-endowed bosom.

"You're making a mountain out of a molehill."

"Easy for you to say. You don't live here and have nothing to lose if we're arrested."

Delilah's head jerked as if she'd been struck. She took several seconds to compose herself before responding. "I have everything to lose. My son means the world to me."

Constance had the grace to look guilty. "I'm sorry. I spoke out of turn."

Maddie guessed Constance was recalling her youngest son and felt a pang of sympathy for her friend. For both her friends. In a way, Delilah had also lost her son when she'd been forced to give him up for adoption.

"This bickering is getting us nowhere and not the reason I called the meeting." When Lavinia had everyone's attention, she continued. "The fact is we have a serious problem. Our funds are low, along with our food supply. If we don't find a way to rid ourselves of the mice and coyote, we'll soon be out of food altogether."

"What about a cat?" Delilah's usual cheery mood had returned. "There are at least dozen running lose behind the Strike It Rich."

"Patience suggested the same thing. We agreed Dora will bring one or two home with her tomorrow. And we have that old trap. We can use it on the coyote if someone can get it to work right. But that still leaves us with the problem of Newlin's private investigator. We'd been planning another robbery for next week." Lavinia's gaze encompassed the entire council. "I assume we're all in agreement that, under the circumstance, we must postpone it."

There were nods and murmurs of consent throughout.

"How long until your food runs out?" Delilah asked.

"If we don't lose any more flour, two weeks," Patience answered. "Three, if we ration."

No one spoke for several moments. They were already rationing. Most days, the adults skipped one meal, if not two, so the children could eat.

Maddie thought of the licorice ropes Scott McSween had wanted to buy for the children. Had she been wrong to refuse him?

"I might be able to help." Delilah rubbed her chin thoughtfully.

"You've already helped so much," Lavinia said. "We can't expect you to support us."

More murmurs of agreement followed. The women were desolate, but also proud. They'd accepted Delilah's assistance in return for taking in her son and when there was no other choice. But their goal was to be self-sufficient.

"I wasn't referring to money." Delilah's smile, the one that had men emptying their pockets in order to spend an hour in her company, broadened. "I have an idea."

"Do tell."

Delilah didn't let Lavinia's sarcasm dim her enthusiasm. "Hear me out. You need food. To buy food, you need money. To obtain money, you have to steal from Newlin and the partners. But you can't steal from them as long as the private investigator is in Edenville, looking for you. Seems to me, the solution is simple. Get rid of the private investigator."

"Get rid of McSween?"

"Yes. Send him on a wild goose chase. While he's off gallivanting to God knows where, you can rob one of the partners. You'll have the money you need to tide you over, and McSween will be miles away from here."

Lavinia chuckled dryly. "And how exactly might we accomplish this small feat?"

"Feed him false information." Delilah shrugged one slim shoulder, implying the answer was simple. "You already have the means."

"Which is . . . ?"

Delilah turned her head. So did everyone else.

"Why, Maddie, of course."

Chapter Six

"Come walk with me," Delilah said, and without waiting for a response, linked arms with Maddie.

"Just for a few minutes. It's late, and Josephine needs her sleep."

"You, too, I imagine."

"Yes. Fortunately, I don't have to work tomorrow."

"I wish I could say the same thing." Delilah chuckled. The sound was rich and full. "No rest for the wicked, as they say."

Maddie smiled. She liked the town madam. In her opinion, Delilah was honest, generous, and forthright. And while there were those in Eden who snubbed their nose at Delilah despite the help she'd given them, Maddie didn't feel she herself was in any position to cast stones. Stealing was stealing, regardless of the reasons, and she would no doubt have to atone for her sins someday.

The two friends strolled toward the playing children, most of whom resisted being called away by their mothers.

"I apologize for putting you on the spot with Lavinia and the council. And I'm sorry I let Constance irritate me so much." Delilah sighed. "I know she's been a big help to you with the robberies. But, dear Lord, she can be so damn sanctimonious."

"Constance means well. She's concerned about her son. He's all she has left."

"At least she *has* her son." Delilah's voice fractured. She didn't hide her emotions well where her child was concerned. "And now I must apologize again. That was uncalled for. I can't imagine what's gotten into me tonight."

"The private investigator has us all on edge."

"Doesn't he." Delilah arched her brows. "You most especially."

Maddie ignored the thinly veiled implication. "I admit that I'm surprised the council voted to let me feed false information to Mr. McSween."

"It's a good idea, if I do say so myself."

"I suppose. If I can pull it off."

"The man is positively smitten with you. Why else would he have returned to the store today and insisted on escorting you and Constance to the surrey? And when a man is smitten, he'll believe anything you say." Delilah leaned in close to Maddie. "Trust me, I know. It's why I've done so well over the years."

Maddie should have been taken aback at Delilah's outrageousness, but she found herself laughing instead. Some of the tension of the long day left her.

"I'm not very experienced or knowledgeable where men are concerned. I may have to seek your advice concerning Mr. McSween."

"And wouldn't I simply *love* to give it."

Maddie had never been serious with a man other than her late husband. And while their lovemaking might have lacked the sweeping grand passion she'd once dreamed of, it was never a duty for Maddie. The truth was, she had enjoyed the intimate aspects of marriage.

"There he is." Delilah stopped abruptly and drew in a sharp breath, her face alight with unabashed joy. "Isn't he darling? Oh, my. He's getting so big."

Her son, Henry, hopped over the crouched form of another boy, the two of them engrossed in a game of leapfrog. He misjudged and tumbled onto the ground in front of his playmate, the two of them giggling.

"I don't want him to see me." Delilah stepped behind Maddie. "It's been over six months, but he might still recognize me. I couldn't stand another awful parting. Not tonight."

Across the way, Henry's adoptive mother dipped her head in acknowledgment at Delilah. Delilah returned the nod but, otherwise, didn't move. They'd agreed not to speak to each other in front of Henry lest they confuse him. He'd only recently stopped talking about Delilah. At almost four years old, it was hard to tell how much he remembered of his former life.

"He looks just like his father," Delilah said after several moments of quiet observation. "God help him."

The town madam had made this remark to Maddie on several occasions. So often, in fact, Maddie sometimes found herself examining the faces of different men in Edenville and searching for resemblances to Henry.

Some speculated that Newlin was Henry's father. Maddie doubted it. Newlin didn't take up with prostitutes. This, she had learned from their primary informant, a man whose real identity was so carefully guarded, she didn't dare think of him by name for fear of accidentally speaking it. His rare visits to Eden were always under the guise of another purpose.

"Henry's a good boy," Maddie said. "Never any trouble."

She and Delilah watched Henry's adoptive mother lead him away by the hand. They'd traveled no more than a few feet when the boy charged ahead, pulling his adoptive mother with him and shouting, "Come on. Hurry."

"He was always a good boy. The girls at the Strike It Rich absolutely doted on him." Delilah dabbed at her teary eyes as Henry disappeared around the corner of a large canvas lean-to that served as a laundry. "Constance doesn't know what she's missing."

Maddie tended to agree, but hated taking sides in the ongoing dispute. When Delilah first brought Henry to Eden, the council had suggested Constance take in the boy. Still devastated over the death of her youngest son, she'd refused. Delilah had taken insult at the refusal. To this day, the two women remained at odds.

"I think, given time, she might have come around. We all handle grief differently."

"I should hate Fat Mike for making me give up my only child," Delilah said, referring to the owner of the Strike It Rich. "The man is a ruthless tyrant." She flashed Maddie a sad smile. "But Henry really is better off here than he would be growing up in a saloon."

"If things change, you can always take him back."

"Things aren't going to change. Can you see me as a miner's wife?" Delilah bit back a sharp laugh, then sobered. She stared at the lean-to behind which Henry and his adoptive mother had disappeared. "But someday, when he's a man fully grown, I hope to tell him I'm his mother."

Maddie started to say something, but held her

tongue when Archie approached with Josephine in tow. From the dirty streaks lining her daughter's cheeks and the grim set of her mouth, she'd evidently been crying. Maddie bent down, and Josephine ran the last few feet to her.

"What's wrong, sweet pea?"

The girl made tiny whimpering sounds, and her slender body shook.

"I'm sorry, Miz Campbell," Archie said glumly as he approached them. "She got too close to one of them cholla cactus. I yelled for her to stay back, but . . . she didn't . . ."

"How bad is she hurt?" Maddie squatted beside Josephine.

"A big cluster got stuck to the front of her dress. She went and touched it before I had a chance to knock it off with a stick."

Maddie tried to take her daughter's right hand. Josephine resisted, uttering garbled sounds of protest and pulling away. After much coaxing, she finally relented, and Maddie winced at the sight of a dozen or more inch-long stickers protruding from her daughter's small fingers.

Delilah bent her head to look. "It's not so bad."

Maddie concurred. Cholla cactus were everywhere in and around Eden. Any number of women and children had suffered worse than Josephine. But they, at least, had understood what happened to them and why. Josephine didn't, and Maddie had yet to find a way to communicate the dangers of the desert to her small daughter.

Maddie picked up Josephine, careful not to press on the stickers. "Don't blame yourself, Archie. She'll be fine in a day or two and forget this ever happened."

"Iffin' you don't want me to watch her anymore—"

"Don't be ridiculous," Maddie cut him off. "She adores you. Now, go on home before your mother worries herself sick."

"Yes, ma'am." Shoulders hunched, he shuffled off, kicking up dirt with the toes of his boots.

Delilah stroked Josephine's tangled hair. "I should be leaving, too. I'm sure by now Fat Mike is wondering where I am and when I'll be back. He's probably worn a hole in the office carpet with all his pacing back and forth. Not that a little pacing wouldn't do him good, mind you."

"You're incorrigible," Maddie chided.

"I'm honest."

The two of them started walking. Josephine, having cried herself out at last, laid her head on Maddie's shoulder. When they reached the buggy, Delilah climbed in. Once she was seated, the young boy tending her horse handed over the reins.

"Thank you, handsome." She winked broadly.

He broke into a huge grin and darted off, no doubt to brag to his pals.

"Men. They're the same at any age. You remember that, Maddie, when you're dealing with Mr. McSween."

"I'll try."

"If you need help removing the stickers from Josephine's hand, I'll gladly stay."

"No. You go on. We'll manage." Maddie kissed a dozing Josephine's forehead. "Granny Fay showed us a trick she learned a long time ago from a freed slave woman. You cut the stickers off at the skin, then after a day or two, they soften enough so you can pull them out without too much pain."

"If you're sure."

"I'm sure. You take care driving home."

The horse flung his head high and shook it impatiently. "Easy there, big fellow." Delilah tugged on the reins to quiet the animal. She then turned to Maddie, her expression solicitous. "It's none of my business, and if you tell me to go jump in a lake, I won't be the least bit offended."

"When has the possibility of being offended ever stopped you from speaking your mind?"

"You know me too well." Delilah laughed, but there was an edginess to it which caused Maddie's stomach to knot again.

"What is it?" she asked.

"I can't help it," Delilah blurted. "I worry about you and Josephine. With you working most days at the company store and going off on those robberies, you can't always be available to take care of her. The child needs help. She needs to see a doctor. Maybe something can be done about her . . . condition. The older she gets, the harder it will be for both of you."

"Doctors charge fees. I don't have any money. I can't even afford to buy her a new pair of shoes for winter."

"Take a larger cut from the robberies. As leader, as the one putting your life on the line, you're entitled. That was the agreement."

"No! I won't allow others to go hungry because of me."

"What about the company payroll? I don't know why you stick to such small pickings."

"We voted before the first robbery. We won't steal from the miners. None of what happened with Newlin is their fault."

"I just hate seeing you and Josephine suffer if something can be done for her."

So did Maddie. With every beat of her heart. She instinctively held her daughter tighter.

"I've upset you, and I'm sorry," Delilah said softly.

"You haven't upset me, and I appreciate your concern. But this is how it has to be."

"Your decision, of course." Delilah waved and clucked to the horse. "Good night, love."

Maddie watched the buggy bump along until it faded into the darkness and thought if anyone understood the agony she went through, it was the town madam. Not a day went by they both didn't confront and grieve over their respective failures as mothers.

Guilt flared inside Maddie. Guilt and anger. Thaddeus Newlin was responsible for every terrible thing that had happened to her in the last year. To all the women.

But no amount of resentment toward him changed the fact that Delilah was right. Something had to be done about Josephine. And not only about her condition, but her immediate safety and well-being, too.

If Scott McSween were successful, and Maddie arrested for the robberies, Josephine would be left alone in the world. Maddie silently vowed not to let that happen and to protect her daughter at all costs.

But to accomplish that, she would have to involve herself with the very man who could quite possible destroy everything of importance to her.

Scott walked through the door to the sheriff's office without knocking. He'd stopped by twice before and both times, the same aging and disinterested deputy had informed him the sheriff was on a call and unavailable. On this visit, a younger man sat behind the desk, looking considerably more alert and actually capable of protecting the citizens of Edenville from danger.

"Tom Lunsford?" Scott asked.

"In the flesh." The sheriff stood and extended his hand. "You must be McSween."

Scott accepted the handshake. "Also in the flesh."

"Have a seat."

"Thank you." Scott sat in a badly scarred straight-back chair with weak and squeaky joints. It swayed under his weight. He'd possessed a similar chair in his office back in Galveston. The memory didn't warm him. Nothing about his former occupation did.

"I figured you'd show your face here eventually. How can I help you?" The polite inquiry didn't come with a smile.

"I need information. What can you tell me about the robberies that I don't already know?"

The sheriff studied him briefly, and Scott sensed the other man's unwillingness to cooperate. Understandable, considering the circumstances. According to Newlin, Scott had been brought in because Sheriff Lunsford couldn't get the job done. If their places were reversed, Scott would resist cooperating, too.

Then again, there'd be no need to bring in a private investigator as the robbers would be caught and behind bars by now.

In Lunsford's defense, however, Newlin was a pain in the neck and went out of his way to make an already difficult job even more so. Despite the discernable friction between them, Scott believed Lunsford to be a decent man and, from what he'd heard, a passably good sheriff.

"What do you have so far?" he asked.

Scott outlined what Newlin had told him, adding what he'd gotten from talking with the miners and asking around town.

"Not much more I can tell you."

Not much he *would* tell, Scott thought, but didn't press. He'd run up against lawmen like Lunsford in the past, both as a U.S. Marshal and a private investigator, and had learned the hard way that a show of force would be met with a brick wall. Better to coax the information out of Lunsford than demand it.

"Well, if you think of anything, I'm staying at the Edenville Hotel." Scott rose.

"If I do," Lunsford remained seated, "I'll be in touch."

Scott started to leave, then paused, feigning indecision. "I was told the leader speaks with a thick Irish accent."

"So they say."

"You've been sheriff here a while. Ever run across anyone with an Irish accent?" Scott had asked this question around town all morning with minimal results. Even Otis Tarrington, the notions salesman and a wellspring of information, had drawn a blank. Not surprising. People came and went in mining towns like ants in an anthill.

Lunsford was slow to respond. "Only one."

"Was he any help when you talked with him?"

"No. Because I haven't." Lunsford's mouth curved with the beginnings of a smile. He evidently found Scott's question amusing.

"Why not?"

Lunsford pushed back in his chair and lowered his head. His big body shook with laughter. "Because the man's dead."

And so was Scott's lead. Still, he didn't give up. People, especially foreigners, tended to stick with their own. "Are there any more Irish around these parts?"

"None I'm aware of."

"Would you mind telling me this fellow's name?"

"What good would it do you?"

"Maybe there's folks in town who knew him."

"Some, I reckon. He had a wife and kid."

Scott tried not to show his excitement. "Do they still live in Edenville?"

"Nope." Lunsford lifted a leg and propped his boot on his desk with a loud thud. Irritation and boredom played across his relatively handsome features. "They live in Eden."

"He was one of the miners killed in the accident?"

"Yep." Ignoring Scott, he leaned back in his chair, picked up a stack of Wanted posters, and leafed through them.

"Interesting." *Very interesting.* Scott had thought all along the robberies were connected in some way to the accident. But how? Finding out could be the key to locating the gang of robbers. "Well, thanks again, Sheriff." He headed toward the door, his intention to visit the mining offices and speak to the clerk in charge of personnel records. He suddenly remembered Lunsford hadn't given him the miner's name and turned around. "I'm sorry. What did you say this Irish fellow's name was?"

The sheriff tossed the Wanted posters onto his desk. "Campbell. William Campbell. His widow, Maddie, works in the company store."

Scott went still. He couldn't hear the rest of what Lunsford said over the ringing in his ears.

Scott nudged the big bay gelding along. After leaving Lunsford's office, he'd made straight for the company store, only to be told Maddie wasn't working today. He then hightailed it down Main Street to the livery stable. Throwing a saddle and bridle on the horse Newlin's secretary had arranged for, he mounted and rode out of town. His destination, Eden.

Maddie's late husband was Irish.

Admittedly, this bit of news rattled Scott. He cautioned himself not to jump to conclusions. Likely, William Campbell and one of the robbers both being Irish was simply a coincidence. But he had to start somewhere. Maddie might know someone or something without realizing it.

The question most pressing on Scott's mind was whether she would agree to talk to him once he arrived.

He ignored the rush of anticipation building inside him, assuring himself it had everything to do with the case and nothing to do with the prospect of seeing her again.

There'd been no need to ask for directions. Enough people had told him about Eden that he could find the place blindfolded. The deep ruts carved in the road by wagon and buggy wheels were also a giveaway. He figured on following them right up to the gate.

He figured right.

Less than a quarter hour into the trip, the gate to Eden appeared in the distance. The squared arch above the gate rose at least eight feet high, twice the height of the surrounding fence, and looked ready to collapse at the first strong breeze. Various structures stood behind the fence. Scott wasn't close enough to discern more than a few tin roofs and the lazy drift of smoke from a large fire.

As he rode nearer, he saw figures of varying sizes moving around within the confines of the community. Dim voices carried across the desert. A dog barked, a donkey brayed, and a rooster crowed.

His horse began to trot, encouraged by either the excitement of reaching their journey's end or the nervous energy coursing through his rider.

Scott heard the rifle shot a split second before the bullet struck the ground two feet in front of his horse's front hooves. The frightened animal reared and whinnied, almost knocking him off.

"Easy, partner." Scott fought for control, putting his weight in the saddle and jerking back on the reins.

Just as the horse's hooves came down, another shot whistled through the air. Scott felt the bullet pierce the crown of his cowboy hat and experienced a rare moment of fear. The shooter meant business. And had excellent aim.

His horse snorted and danced in a circle.

"Hold it right there," a female voice hollered.

Scott had every intention of obeying. "I will, damn it," he hollered back. "But quit your firing."

"Come any closer, and I'll take your head off."

He fully believed her.

The horse began to settle as Scott forced both of them to relax. He'd been warned of Eden's strict policy regarding men, but hadn't expected to be shot at by an armed sentry. His mistake. And not one he would make again.

Activity behind the fence became more concentrated in the center of the small community. Three women materialized at the gate, each brandishing a rifle. Two of those rifles were leveled directly at Scott. The third woman held hers at her side, as if it were a natural extension of her arm. She walked ahead of the others, her posture erect and her demeanor calm. Gut instinct told him she'd been the one firing at him.

Scott recognized her immediately. How could he not? He'd know that blond hair and lush figure anywhere.

Maddie Campbell.

The same woman he'd been dreaming about for the past two nights, thinking about his every spare waking moment, had very nearly killed him.

"Well," he said to himself as he dismounted, his earlier sense of anticipation returning tenfold. "This should prove to be an interesting conversation."

Chapter Seven

“That’s some welcoming committee you have,” Scott said, a grin forming at the edges of his mouth.

Maddie stopped and stared at him, her heart racing and her temples pounding. Had he been anyone else, she might have put a bullet clean through him and hoped he made it back to Edenville before he bled to death. Too many women in Eden had been brutalized by men sneaking past their meager defenses. As a result, the guards took no chances. Shoot first, ask questions later.

It required no more than a few close calls for the men to heed the message. Stay clear of Eden.

Scott had told her he wasn’t good at following orders. Well, it had nearly cost him his life. And she’d been the one pulling the trigger. Thank God she had recognized him.

“What are you doing here?” To her dismay, her voice shook. A person might think she didn’t make a regular habit of firing on trespassers.

"I came to see you."

Her breath caught. Striving to remain calm, she slowly let it out. If Constance and the other guard, Hannah Wallace, were to witness the extent of her turmoil, they would surely report it to Lavinia. The head councilwoman had spoken out against Maddie's continued involvement with Scott and yet the vote had gone in favor of Delilah's plan to feed him false information. Maddie would have to watch her every step from now on, lest someone get the wrong impression.

"No men are allowed in Eden."

He squinted at her, the setting sun striking him in the face. "Like I said, I came to see *you.*" He had a way of making the innocent comment sound intimate.

A small jolt went through her, and she involuntarily pressed her fingertips to her middle. "Why?"

His gray eyes tracked her movement, unconcealed longing glimmering in their depths. In the next instant the longing vanished, but not before the echo of it reverberated through her. Heaven help her, she desired him. Her knees wobbled at the realization.

"I have some questions I'd like to ask you," he said.

"Questions?" Speaking coherently proved difficult for Maddie.

"About the robberies."

Constance uttered a soft hiss.

"I already told you," Maddie said. "I don't know anything." If only that were true, maybe her insides wouldn't be a bundle of nerves.

Despite having two rifles aimed directly at him, Scott appeared at ease. His confidence irritated Maddie. And intrigued her on an entirely different level.

"You also told me if you had the chance, you'd help the robbers."

"Meaning if I knew something, I'd keep it to myself." She sighed, feigning boredom. "This conversation is over, Mr. McSween."

"I learned something today about the robbers. It may or may not have a connection to you."

She laughed sharply in an attempt to mask her shock and surprise. One day on the job and he'd already connected her to the robbers. At this rate, she'd be in jail by tomorrow.

"And what did you learn?"

"One of them is Irish. So, I'm told, was your late husband."

Maddie almost laughed again, this time with relief. "Unless you believe he's come back from the dead, I can assure you William had no part in the robberies."

"But maybe someone he knew did."

Someone he knew very well.

"Mr. McSween—"

"Please. Hear me out."

"No." Maddie wanted nothing more than to end this charade. Sweat dripped in rivulets down the back of her neck, and her muscles ached from constant tension. "I can't help you. I won't help you."

He went for the pistol at his side. Constance and Hannah reacted instantly, cocking their rifles and stepping closer.

"Wait!" His hand went up. "I'm not going to shoot." Moving an inch at a time, he removed the pistol from its holster and handed it, stock first, to Maddie. "Here."

She looked at the gun, but didn't move.

"I just want to talk. We don't have to go inside Eden." He indicated Constance and Hannah with a tilt of his head. "They can stay with us. Hell, they can even keep those damned rifles pointed at me the whole entire time if it makes you happy."

From the corner of her eye, Maddie caught sight of Constance. The woman gave a tiny nod. Maddie understood the silent signal and reconciled herself to the inevitable. Here was her chance to feed Scott false information, and Constance expected her to take it.

Where was Delilah and her well-intentioned advice when Maddie needed her?

"All right." She could see by his raised eyebrows he'd expected her to put up more of a fight.

"Shall we walk?" he offered.

"Fine." She tucked his pistol in the waistband of her skirt.

Constance and Hannah followed them. They lowered their rifles but kept their thumbs on the triggers. Scott remained oblivious to the threat. Once again, Maddie marveled at his easy confidence. What, she wondered, caused a man to develop such a high disregard for danger?

Maddie herself had acquired a healthy respect for it at an early age. She still carried a scar on her torso from where a confederate soldier sliced her with a knife when she was no more than a few months old. Her brother was similarly marked on his face. The soldiers committed these atrocities in front of their mother, whom they then repeatedly raped. As soon as the Weatherspoon children could hold a gun, their father, a Union Army veteran, had taught them to shoot.

Danger lurked around every corner, her father had said. Maddie didn't run from it, but neither did she embrace it. Until the robberies.

"What can you tell me about your husband? Did he have any friends?"

Scott's questions jarred Maddie back to the present. "Yes. Many."

Everyone had liked William. He charmed them much the same he had Maddie.

"Who were they?"

"I can tell you their names if you'd like. And where to find them."

"You'd do that?"

"Of course." Maddie met his stare straight on. "They're dead. Buried beside William in the cemetery outside town."

The hope in his eyes dimmed. "None of his friends are left alive?"

"I suppose there are a few who knew him still living in Edenville. Not every miner was killed in the accident. But I haven't kept in touch with them or their wives. I'm sure you understand why."

For a moment or two, they strolled in silence, Scott leading his horse alongside him. Maddie listened to the crunch of sand beneath their feet, and to the drone of flying insects. The distant sound of children's voices carried on the breeze. She uttered a silent prayer of thanks that Josephine was safe and away from Eden. Constance's son, Archie, had taken her and a group of children into the nearby desert to hunt rabbits with handmade slingshots. God willing, they would be successful. It had been a more than a week since anyone in Eden enjoyed fresh meat. Even just a little went a long way.

"Are there any other Irish miners in Edenville?"

Maddie drew in a long breath. "No. None that I know of." The rush of fresh air must have restored her thinking, for an idea of how to sidetrack Scott suddenly popped into her head. "Wait. There was a man." She compressed her lips, pretending to concentrate. "I can't remember his name exactly. O'Sullivan. . . . O'Shannon. . . . O'Shea! Yes. That's it. Rory O'Shea.

He visited us once when William brought him home for Sunday dinner."

"Where is he now, do you know?"

"He arrived with a crew from the Vista Linda Mine, on temporary loan to Edenville. He may still be at Vista Linda."

"When was this?"

"Some months before the accident."

Scott's expression remained stoic, yet Maddie sensed his rising excitement. Her plan was working, and she nearly went limp with gratitude. Maybe he would even go so far as to travel to the Vista Linda Mine and check out this fictitious Rory O'Shea. That would buy the council several days in which to plan their next move.

But then, assuming he did visit the Vista Linda Mine, what would he do when the wild goose chase she'd sent him on didn't pan out? Would he return and confront her for lying to him? She could always claim a faulty memory, she supposed. Miners did come and go with regular frequency.

"Do you remember what this O'Shea fellow looked like?"

"Hmm. Not terribly tall. Brown hair, I think. It was only one afternoon and a long time ago."

"Was he young or old?"

"Young. That much I do remember. And very nice. He had a courteous manner about him." Maddie smiled to herself as she recited some of the gossip she'd heard concerning herself in the guise of the robber. Behind her, Hannah coughed.

"Thank you, Mrs. Campbell," he said. "You've been very helpful."

She hoped she had. But not to him.

He moved closer to her. Not enough to alert Constance or Hannah, but enough to start Maddie's heart beating double-time. Unable to resist, she peered up at him. Their eyes met, much as they had a few days ago on his first visit to the company store. And like before, she felt a connection to him that simultaneously thrilled and terrified her.

And then he touched her.

A small touch, really. Hardly more than a brush of his fingertips across the back of her hand. But it was enough to send ribbons of warmth curling along the length of her arm.

Flustered by her reaction to him, she parted her lips and gasped softly. Watching her, Scott smiled.

Maddie immediately averted her head and moved aside. When, after several moments, Constance and Hannah said nothing, she dared to relax.

Her reprieve didn't last. From around the east end of the fence came the sound of shouts and laughter. The children were returning, just in time for supper. Though she couldn't imagine Scott harming them, she preferred not to test the theory.

"If your business here is complete, Mr. McSween, I suggest you leave."

He grinned at her. "Promise you won't shoot me in the back as I ride away?"

The man had a lot of gall, she'd give him that. If Maddie were so inclined, she could nail him between his shoulder blades at a hundred yards.

"Not today. But don't assume I'll be so accommodating in the future."

"I wouldn't think of it." He swung his horse around, grabbed the saddle horn, and mounted. "Good-bye, Maddie. It's been a pleasure." Lifting his hand in a mock salute, he dug his heels into his horse's flanks and took off at a lope.

Damn his conceited hide!

"You did good," Constance said. She and Hannah came to stand alongside Maddie. "Real good." They all three watched Scott ride away.

Maddie turned toward the approaching children. "I'm not so s—"

The words died in her throat when she saw Josephine. The three-year-old was astride their pet donkey and guiding him into a dense patch of cholla cacti. All thoughts save those of her daughter's safety fled Maddie's mind. She started out at a brisk walk, which quickly accelerated into a run as Josephine and the donkey wound their way deeper into the patch of cacti . . . and deeper into danger.

Someone threw a ball. The children chased after it with sticks, yelling instructions to one another. Scott slowed his horse to a walk and shifted sideways in his saddle in order to watch them. He'd only loped the horse for Maddie's benefit. Given his choice, he'd prefer a leisurely ride back to Edenville during which he could mull over the information she'd given him about this supposed Irish miner.

It did occur to him that she might be lying. She had plenty of reason—she'd made that much clear yesterday when he escorted her to the surrey from the company store. But if she had lied, the question was, why? What did she have to gain? And who was she protecting?

Either way, Maddie knew something about the robberies. He'd be wise to stick close to her.

Then again, maybe not. The sparks he'd felt when

their hands brushed could have ignited a large brush fire.

It would be in his best interest to visit the Vista Linda Mine over the next few days. Not only to check out Maddie's story, but to put some much-needed distance between them. First, however, he'd speak with the superintendent of the Edenville Mine. The man, if he were employed at the time, might remember the temporary crew.

Suddenly, one of the older boys in the group of children stopped playing. He waved an arm over his head and hollered at the top of his lungs. Though Scott couldn't hear everything the boy said, there was an unmistakable urgency in his voice. The other children also stopped playing, and they, too, began waving their arms and hollering. Dropping his stick, the boy broke into a dead run.

Scott looked in the direction the boy ran. He spotted a young girl riding a small donkey bareback. She appeared unaware of the other children and their frantic efforts to get her attention. Scott reined in his horse, not sure if he should do something or not. The girl didn't appear in any immediate trouble, though she was surrounded on all sides by cholla cacti.

Being somewhat closer to her than the boy, Scott shouted, "Hey, you."

She didn't hear him. With a big smile on her face, she leaned down, wrapped her arms around the donkey's neck and hugged him, a picture of charm and innocence.

In the next second, all hell broke loose.

The donkey spun in a half circle, evidently unsure how to navigate the prickly obstacle course. He backed into a large cactus and with an ear-piercing squeal, hopped forward. Imbedded in his tail and rump were several large clusters of stickers. Long ears laid flat, he swished his tail from side to side, succeeding only in implanting more stickers into his hide.

Scott had never seen a donkey move so fast. The agitated animal bolted from the cacti patch, his hind end high in the air as he bucked and bucked. The little girl struggled to stay seated, though it was obvious she couldn't hold on for long. Her small body slipped from side to side as the donkey bounced along, heading not toward Eden, but the open desert.

Without pausing to think, Scott nudged his horse into a gallop and took chase. As if happening in slow motion, he saw the little girl, so slight to begin with, come off the donkey's back and fly through the air. She landed hard on a pile of rocks. Finally free of his passenger, the donkey trotted in a wide circle before coming to a standstill. Sides heaving and legs quivering, he waited for someone to retrieve him.

No one did. Everyone converged on the little girl.

Scott reached her first. Jumping down from his horse, he dropped the reins and went on his knees beside her. She lay on her side in a tiny crumpled heap.

A curtain of black hair covered her face. He carefully pushed it back. "Are you all right?"

She lay deathly still, not responding.

"Josephine! Josephine!" The boy stumbled to a halt in front of them. Bracing his hands on his knees, he tried to catch his breath. "How is she?"

"Unconscious. I don't know yet if she hit her head or just had the wind knocked out of her." Scott observed the rise and fall of the little girl's chest. It was steady, but shallow. "Is she your sister?"

"No, sir." The boy had difficulty talking. "Son of a

bitch. This is all my fault. I was supposed to be watching her."

He might have been young, but he swore like a man full grown.

"Don't go blaming yourself. It looked like an accident to me." Scott very carefully tilted the little girl's chin. He was aware of the small crowd gathering around them and their collective gasp at the bleeding wound revealed on the back of her head.

"Oh, my God!" Maddie sagged to the ground next to Scott. She reached out a trembling hand and stroked the little girl's cheek.

"Your daughter?" he asked.

Maddie nodded, her eyes moist with tears. "Her name is Josephine."

"She took a pretty nasty bang to the head. I don't see any broken bones, but she may be bleeding inside. Is there a doctor in town? I could ride out and bring him back with me."

"He won't see us," Constance said. "We've tried."

Scott stared up at her. "What do you mean he won't see you?"

"He's the company doctor, on Newlin's payroll. Since we're no longer wives and children of mining employees, we aren't entitled to medical services."

"That's horseshit!"

Constance blanched.

"Excuse my language. But I've never heard anything so ridiculous in my life."

"Ridiculous or not, it's true." Maddie gazed worriedly at her daughter. "She's so little. I shouldn't have let her go riding."

"Is there another doctor in town?"

"Yes. But he's a worthless quack and I won't let him near Josephine." She climbed to her feet. "We have to get her to the infirmary inside Eden. Granny Fay will know what to do."

"Granny Fay?"

"She was a nurse with the Union Army and is as smart as any doctor." Maddie bent down for Josephine with shaky arms that refused to cooperate. "I can't lift her," she sobbed. "Oh, God."

"Here. I'll carry her," Scott said.

"No!" Constance stepped in front of him.

"Maddie can't do it. See for yourself."

"No men are allowed in Eden," Constance stated firmly.

"Make an exception."

"The rules are in place for a reason."

Scott glared at her and snapped, "Are you willing to risk this girl's life on a silly rule?"

Constance gasped and retreated a step.

Scott gently lifted Josephine into his arms and stood.

"Please, Constance." Maddie rushed to assist him, supporting Josephine's lolling head. A small moan escaped the little girl's lips and her eyelids fluttered, but she didn't rouse. "There, there, my darling," she crooned and kissed the child's forehead. "You're going to be fine."

"Bring my horse," Scott told the boy and started walking toward Eden. The boy immediately went after the animal, who'd wandered in search of edible vegetation. Someone else had already collected the donkey.

After handing her rifle off to Hannah, Maddie walked beside Scott. She produced a handkerchief from her skirt pocket and pressed it to the wound on Josephine's head. Constance walked directly behind Scott, her rifle raised and ready to fire should he decide to drop Josephine and go for the gun tucked in the waistband of Maddie's skirt.

As if reading his mind, Maddie glared at the rifle and asked, "Is that really necessary?"

Constance didn't deign to answer. "Stay back, children," she ordered.

They didn't take her seriously and pressed close around Scott and Maddie.

The procession crossed the open desert to Eden, the sun beating down on them. At the gate, Scott noticed two hand-painted signs nailed to the railing. One read NO TRESPASSING, the other KEEP OUT. Disregarding both warnings, he passed through the gate. Inside, another crowd waited. Judging by the size, every resident of Eden had come out to greet them.

Scott turned to Maddie. "Which way is the infirmary?"

"Left," she said. "Follow me."

He could hardly believe the severe poverty in which the women lived. Though clean and tidy, the place was nothing but an assortment of broken-down tents and shacks—hardly fit to house a dog, much less respectable women and their children. He wanted to choke Newlin with his bare hands. How could the man treat innocent people with such callousness and still sleep at night?

"There. Up ahead." Maddie indicated a large tent that had been patched and repatched so often, none of the original canvas remained. "Is Granny Fay back from Edenville yet?"

"She just drove up," someone reported. "Archie's done gone for her."

Maddie left Scott's side, went to the tent, and lifted the flap so he and Josephine could enter. Once inside, he paused a moment to orient himself while Maddie fumbled to light a lantern. She succeeded at last, and Scott looked around. Like the rest of Eden, the tent's interior was neat and organized, though sparsely furnished. It was also high enough in the center for him to stand upright. He laid Josephine on one of two old cots, hoping its spindly frame was capable of supporting her.

He no sooner stepped back than Maddie clambered to her daughter's side. Constance had also come into the tent, giving Scott the distinct impression he wasn't going anywhere in Eden without an armed escort.

The tent flap whipped open and an older woman entered, her crinkled face alight with curiosity. "You that private investigator Newlin hired?"

"You must be Granny Fay."

"Mrs. Hartford to you." Her gruffness didn't quite mask the hint of amusement in her tone.

Scott smiled, deciding he liked Granny Fay. "How do you do, ma'am?"

"Been better, been worse." She pushed past him and went to Josephine. "What happened?"

Maddie replied, and the two women engaged in conversation.

Scott suffered a moment of awkwardness, which Constance ended by waving her rifle at the tent opening. "Come with me, Mr. McSween."

He would have liked to remain, but realized he had no choice except to accompany her. "Sure."

"No!" Maddie whirled to face them. "I want him to stay."

"What?" Constance's mouth fell open.

Scott felt a bit loose in the jaw himself. "Maddie—"

"I said I want him to stay." Her snapping green eyes slitted and fixed on her friend. "And I'm the one in charge here."

"We—we'll just see what Lavinia has to say about th—this."

"Fine."

Constance inched backwards, then stooped and disappeared through the tent opening.

She no sooner left than Maddie returned her attention to Josephine's care.

Granny Fay gave Scott a thorough once-over. Hands on hips, she made a tsk'ing sound. "Look at you. Hardly here five minutes and already you're stirring up trouble."

Chapter Eight

Lavinia would be hopping mad, but Maddie was determined Scott should stay.

Just once, she wanted someone to be strong for her and not the other way around. Protect her. Stand up for her. Slay dragons if necessary.

Scott had shown himself to be that person, unwelcome as he might be in Eden.

Unfortunately, he was also her sworn adversary.

As a child, Maddie had cared for her ailing parents more than they'd cared for her. The same held true for her husband, William. He had been a hard worker and supported their family, but left all the big decisions to Maddie. Because of Josephine's condition, the child required more attention than most children, though Maddie didn't regret giving birth to her daughter for one instant. And since the mining accident, the women of Eden had looked to Maddie to as one of their leaders, expecting her to take dangerous risks on their behalf.

Maddie was tired of the endless demands. Bone-weary tired. Especially now, with her daughter injured and lying unconscious.

When, despite Constance's objections, Scott had carried Josephine inside Eden, Maddie could have kissed him, so great was her gratitude. His gentle manner, his obvious compassion and concern, affected her deeply.

He gave the impression of being rough and hard and devoid of tender feelings. But Maddie had glimpsed his benevolent side, and it attracted her more than his good looks, confidence, and masculine appeal. He genuinely cared about her. And if anything bad happened to Josephine, Maddie would need a caring someone to watch over her while she fell to pieces.

"Are you sure about this?" Scott asked, and squeezed her shoulder. "You could be asking for trouble."

Trouble would be arriving momentarily in the form of an incensed councilwoman. "Very sure."

Maddie peered up at him from where she sat on the stool. Compassion and concern were again evident in his face, this time for her. She automatically reached up and covered his hand with her own, allowing his strength to flow into her. For several seconds, they communicated without the benefit of speech.

All at once, Josephine made an awful sound, and her small body began to convulse.

"Oh, my God," Maddie cried, bolting to her feet. "What's wrong with her?"

Ignoring her question, Granny Faye snapped, "You, lawman. Fetch that wooden bowl off the table." Scott jumped to do her bidding. "Maddie, give me a hand." She went around to the other side of the cot.

The two women lifted Josephine to a sitting position. Granny Fay snatched the bowl from Scott and positioned it beneath Josephine's mouth. For the next minute, the little girl vomited.

It was the longest minute Maddie had ever endured.

When Josephine at last finished, they lowered her onto the cot, tilting her head to avoid pressure on her wound. She called for her mother, more of a moan than any real words, then fell back into an unconscious state. Granny Fay set the bowl on the ground beneath the cot and used a washrag to wipe Josephine's mouth and face. All the while, Maddie stroked her daughter's glossy black hair, the pounding in her temples finally receding. She was vaguely aware of Scott standing at the foot of the other cot.

"Don't fret yourself," Granny Fay said. "It's natural for someone with a head injury to get sick."

As Maddie watched, Granny Fay gave Josephine a thorough examination.

The older woman pried open the little girl's eyelids and peered into her eyes. "Pupils are the same size, which is a good sign. No leaking from her ears or nose. Breathing is steady." She carefully probed the wound on the back of Josephine's head. "Bleeding's stopped, but she has a lump the size of my fist. I reckon she'll wake up with a whopper of a headache."

"But she *will* wake up?" Worry tore at Maddie, its icy tentacles strangling her heart.

"Can't say for sure. Head injuries are hard to predict." Granny Fay studied Josephine's small, still body. "A person can look fine one minute, then drop dead the next."

"I couldn't bear it if I lost her." Maddie's legs buckled, and she automatically reached out for a handhold. How many more trials were in store for her? Hadn't she suffered enough? Surely God wouldn't take Josephine from her, too?

"Easy now." Suddenly Scott was there beside her, grasping her upper arm and steadying her.

Temptation beckoned, and Maddie succumbed. As she leaned against him, a soothing calmness stole over her. For the first time in a very long time, she felt safe and at peace. Everything would be fine. Josephine would recover, and they would survive another winter.

The tent flap flew open, and Lavinia entered with Constance bringing up the rear.

"What in the Sam Hill is going on here!" the head councilwoman demanded. Her hawklike eyes went straight to Maddie and Scott.

Maddie instantly stiffened and tried to pull away from Scott. He gradually released her, his fingers lingering in the same proprietary manner as the other day when he took her arm while crossing the street. She should have been annoyed at this bold display, but she wasn't.

"Thank goodness you're here," Granny Fay said, standing upright. "She went plumb white all of a sudden and prit near fainted. Lucky that lawman feller caught her or both these cots would have patients lying in them."

A grave exaggeration or Granny Fay's version of the truth? Either way, Maddie didn't begrudge a gift horse.

"Do tell." Lavinia didn't appear convinced, but neither did she dispute Granny Fay's accounting. "Mr. McSween. I'm Lavinia Claybourne, head of the council. I understand Mrs. Starkweather asked you to leave Eden and that you refused. We have a rule here. No men are allowed."

Was that really how Constance had explained the situation? And if so, why did she lie? Maddie glanced over and noted the stubborn set of Constance's jaw, and realization struck. She knew then Constance had twisted the story so Scott would take the blame, not Maddie. Her reasons might have been to protect Maddie. More likely, she wanted Lavinia's wrath to be directed at Scott, a place she felt it rightfully belonged.

"I did refuse Mrs. Starkweather's request," Scott said.

"No, he didn't," Maddie said. "Mr. McSween was more than willing to leave. I'm the one who insisted he stay."

"You!" Lavinia gaped at Maddie. "Why would you invite trouble into our home by doing such a thing?"

"He was kind to Josephine. He offered to ride to town and return with the doctor. When I didn't have the strength to lift her, he carried her across the desert to the infirmary. Who knows what might have happened without his help?" Maddie's throat closed, and she swallowed in an effort to ease the pain. "Forcing him to leave so soon after he arrived seemed inhospitable in light of all he'd done."

Lavinia considered briefly. "Perhaps you're right."

From behind her, Constance sputtered a loud objection. Lavinia silenced her with a raised finger. Granny Fay chose to stay out of the discussion and took a seat on the three-legged stool Maddie had previously occupied.

"Mr. McSween," Lavinia said, her demeanor less abrasive, though far from cordial. "We appreciate everything you've done for Mrs. Campbell and her daughter. While we don't have much in the way of food, we could offer you some buttermilk biscuits and tea and a chance to wash up before you return to Eden."

"Thank you, ma'am, but I'm not hungry. And I'm not leaving until Maddie tells me to." His tone invited no argument.

"Maddie," Lavinia began sternly. "Rules are rules. Mr. McSween can't stay. You must ask him to leave."

"No."

"I'm afraid—"

"I won't. You and I both know I'm owed this consideration."

"Are you now?" There was considerable challenge in Lavinia's retort.

Maddie met the challenge head on. "Yes, I am. I've always taken less than my share. According to our agreement, I'm entitled to more."

Constance inhaled sharply, while Lavinia's eyes narrowed with warning. "Watch what you're saying."

"You need me. And I'm happy to serve the community. But in return, I ask this one favor." She pulled Scott's revolver from her waistband and presented it to Lavinia. "Take this. Post guards around the tent and another one inside. Just let him stay." As an afterthought, she added, "Please."

An overwhelming silence filled the tent as everyone waited for Lavinia's answer.

She didn't keep them waiting long. One of the qualities that made her a competent leader was her ability to make quick decisions.

"All right." She reached for Scott's gun. "Two guards outside, one on each end of the tent. Granny Fay remains inside with you at all times, or someone else should she have to leave for any reason. If Mr. McSween is spotted in Eden unescorted, he'll be shot on sight. Do you understand?"

Maddie nodded.

"And you?" Lavinia asked Scott.

"I give you my solemn word, I won't harm any of the women."

Lavinia scrutinized him, her gaze like ice. "I wish I could believe you."

A shuffling noise drew their attention. They all turned in time to see Constance disappear through the tent flap. Maddie suffered a pang of guilt—she had some bridges to mend where Constance was concerned. The other woman had been a good friend since before the accident, not to mention a trustworthy and invaluable partner in crime.

But not tonight. Tomorrow, after Josephine was recovered from her fall, Maddie would talk to Constance.

That was, if Josephine did recover.

The little girl continued to lay unnervingly still. Maddie went to her daughter's side.

"Send one of the guards if you need anything." Lavinia moved to stand next to Maddie. She looked down at Josephine and for the first time since entering the tent, smiled. "She's such a dear child. I'll pray for you both."

"Thank you." Maddie took Lavinia's hand in hers. "For *everything.*"

Lavinia squeezed Maddie's fingers before releasing them. Her eyes cut briefly to Scott. "Be careful," she whispered.

"I will. I know you don't understand why I asked for him to st—"

"I understand more than you think I do. I wasn't always this old and ugly."

"Oh!" Feeling herself flush, Maddie quickly said, "It's not like that between us."

Lavinia pinched Maddie's chin between her thumb and forefinger, back in full force as head councilwoman. "Regardless of what happens with Josephine, I want him gone by sunrise."

A fair demand. "I promise."

"Good night, then." Before stepping outside, Lavinia paused with her hand on the tent flap. "Mr. McSween. As I trust you'll have no use for your revolver while you're here, I'll leave it with the guard at the gate. You can pick it up on your way out."

Scott nodded solemnly. "I appreciate that."

With Lavinia gone, the tension inside the tent lessened considerably. Granny Fay popped off the stool, remarkably spry for a person of her advanced years.

"Sit," she instructed Maddie. "You'll wear yourself out with all that standing." She picked up the wooden bowl from the floor. "Keep an eye on Josephine while I wash this out." On her way past Scott, she said, "Make yourself useful and hand that bucket over there to the guard out front. Tell her we need fresh water."

Scott didn't appear to take offense at Granny Fay's bossiness. Grinning, he dutifully carried out the task.

Maddie sat on the stool and straightened the collar of Josephine's shirt, more for something to do than anything else. Next, she removed the little girl's shoes. Josephine's only response to her mother's ministrations was a thin moan.

"Should we try waking her?" Maddie asked. "I've heard it isn't good for a person with a head injury to sleep." *If* Josephine was sleeping. She might be unconscious. Maddie couldn't tell.

"Naw. Sleep is the best thing for her." Granny Fay dried the wooden bowl with a ragged towel, then put both items away on a small wobbly table in the corner of the tent. Underneath the table sat a crate covered with a sheet of canvas. It contained the community's paltry selection of medical supplies. "Trust me, the good Lord knows what's best for her. When she's ready to wake up, she will."

When she's ready to wake up, she will.

Maddie clung to the phrase like a drowning sailor would to a lifeline, repeating it over and over.

Doubts, nonetheless, crept in, unbidden and unwanted.

Would Josephine be the same when she did wake up? People with head injuries sometimes weren't right afterward. Maddie remembered a man from her hometown who fell two stories through the floor of a hayloft. Afterward, he walked with a limp and talked funny. Some of the children were cruel and made fun of him.

No! Maddie refused to consider a similar bleak outcome for her daughter. She'd survived scarlet fever, she'd survive this. Maddie gripped the side of the cot with such force, her fingers cramped.

"Are you all right?" Scott sat on the empty cot across from them. "You look ready to do battle."

"If that's what it takes to save Josephine, then yes."

Scott watched Maddie hover over her daughter. She'd dozed from time to time during the long night, waking the instant Josephine so much as twitched.

It pained him to witness such devotion. His own mother had refused to even acknowledge him after the shootings at Galveston, so great was her shame. She hadn't cared that he almost died in the lynching attempt—probably would have preferred it to having a murderer for a son.

He didn't believe he was a murderer. He'd been carrying out his job and nothing more. Sadly, few people agreed with him, including his family.

Five years had passed since he'd last spoken to or heard from his parents. The saddest part of all was that he'd stopped caring a long time ago.

"I'm sorry she's hurt." He rested his forearms on his knees. "I wish I could have gotten to her sooner."

"You tried." Maddie folded Josephine's small limp hand inside hers. "That's more than anyone could ask."

On the tent wall, shadows danced in the light of the lantern. Scott couldn't remember seeing the sun set. He estimated it was well after midnight. Her chores finished hours earlier, Granny Fay sat in a corner on the only other available seat and appeared to be dozing.

Scott removed his hat, set it at the foot of the cot, then inched closer to Maddie. "I hollered, but she didn't hear me."

Tears filled her eyes. She pressed her fingertips to her mouth and held back a sob. Seeing her in such distress shook Scott, and he had to refrain from reaching out to comfort her.

"She's deaf," Maddie said dully.

"What?"

"She can't hear. Not much, anyway. If I speak directly into her left ear, she can understand some of what I say."

Scott was dumbstruck. He could do no more than stare at Josephine for several seconds.

She was pretty, but not in the same way as her mother, except for the smattering of freckles across the bridge of her nose and the shape of her delicate ears. Ears that didn't hear. Which explained why she'd ignored all the attempts to get her attention.

Not that he had any experience when it came to offspring, but he figured raising a deaf child couldn't be easy.

"How old was she when you learned she was deaf?" he asked, finally finding his voice.

"She lost her hearing last year during the scarlet fever epidemic."

Maddie's revelation stunned Scott, and he sat up, causing the old cot to creak.

She truly had been to hell and back. In the span of a day, she'd lost her husband, her home, and her sole source of income. And shortly after, her only child became deaf after a bout with scarlet fever. The fact that Maddie had come through the ordeals with her sanity intact was a testament to her determination and strength of character. His admiration for her grew yet again.

"You must want to kill Newlin with your bare hands."

She didn't so much as bat an eyelash. "The thought has occurred to me on more than one occasion."

"How do you do it?"

"Refrain from killing Newlin?"

He chuckled, then stopped when he realized she hadn't been joking. "No. How do you manage to work and raise a child? A deaf child at that?"

"We take turns. The women who don't have jobs in town care for the children of those of us who do."

"Is that hard for you?"

She stared at him dumbly. "No one's ever asked me that before." Maddie returned to absently toying with Josephine's hand. "I hate leaving her. Every time I do, I feel like a piece of my heart is being ripped away."

"But you still go."

"I have no choice. My wages put food on the table for a lot of people."

"You support more families than your own?" He now understood her earlier remark about serving the community.

"Everyone's wages go into a community treasury. The money is spent for the good of all. Those who don't hold jobs in town work in other capacities. They wash laundry, tend the garden and livestock, gather firewood, clean, cook, teach school, mend fences, stand guard, whatever is needed. The children all have jobs, too. They were out hunting rabbits this afternoon."

Scott wasn't sure what to make of this arrangement. He'd never heard of anything like it. Except, he thought, for Indians. From what he'd learned of their culture, however, it was the men who went off to hunt for food or wage war while the women stayed behind. In the case of Eden, Maddie and those like her filled the roles of providers and defenders.

Unusual, he supposed, yet it evidently worked. The women were apparently making do, though not prospering.

But how did they support themselves?

Even with a garden and livestock, it would require a significant amount of money to feed and clothe a population of almost three hundred. Whatever Maddie and her fellow laborers earned, it couldn't be enough. Newlin and the mining company certainly weren't helping them. Perhaps the local churches or the Ladies' Aid Society, if there was one in Edenville, lent assistance.

He thought of asking Maddie but decided it was neither the time nor place, not with her so distraught over her daughter's condition. And besides, Eden's finances had no bearing on his case. It was just his natural curiosity getting the best of him, as it frequently did.

Instead, he asked, "Where'd you learn to shoot?"

Maddie let go of Josephine's hand and straightened, putting her closer to Scott. If she were to turn slightly, her thigh would touch his knee. If she were to lean back, he could drape an arm around her shoulders. Or plant a kiss on her temple after brushing aside the loose wisps of blond hair falling from their pins.

Scott imagined drawing Maddie to him, her tantalizing curves yielding beneath his palm, supple, yet firm. Desire, strong and more demanding than any he had ever known, gripped him in that moment and refused to set him free.

His aroused state intensified when, arching her back, she reached up and massaged the spot where her neck joined her shoulder. Mesmerized, he watched and wished with every fiber of his being that it was his fingers manipulating her taut flesh. Inspired by the flickering lantern light, his mind journeyed down an imaginary path filled with images of him and Maddie.

"My father served in the Union Army for three years," she said.

Scott blinked, his vision of her half-naked form fading. "I'm sorry. What did you say?"

"My father was a corporal in the Union Army and an excellent marksman. He taught my brother and me to shoot."

"Unusual skill to pass on to a daughter."

"He wanted me to be able to protect myself. I practiced every day until I got good."

"You're better than good."

"He swore not to let same thing happen to me that happened to my mother."

"She was attacked?"

"She . . . suffered . . . at the hands of some Confederate soldiers."

"Badly?"

Maddie spoke as if in a trance. "There'd been a series of battles in the northeastern part of the state. Skirmishes, mostly. Not close enough to home to concern my mother. One day, a group of stragglers came passing through. They were starving and wounded, which didn't excuse the terrible abuses they inflicted upon her."

Anger raged through Scott as he pictured Maddie's mother alone and defenseless, unable to protect herself, much less her two small children. War wasn't all glory and honor. And it wasn't always fought on the battlefield. Unspeakable atrocities had been inflicted upon countless innocent people—on both sides of the conflict.

"She was never the same afterward and took to drinking," Maddie continued in the same monotone. "Or, so I'm told. I was only a few months old at the time. My brother was the same age as Josephine is now. We don't remember ever seeing our mother sober."

He gently squeezed her arm. "Maddie, you don't have to talk about this."

"No. I want to." She didn't shy from him. If anything, she appeared to take comfort from his touch. "It helps keep my mind off . . . other things."

Like whether Josephine will ever wake up. Scott squeezed her arm harder. He didn't have to hear her say the words to know what she was thinking.

From the corner where Granny Fay sat came the sound of soft snoring. The guards, Scott assumed, remained on watch outside the tent, though all was quiet. He had no idea how much time had passed when Maddie finally broke the silence.

"The war changed my father, too. I forget how many wounds he sustained, but he was hospitalized three separate times for weeks on end. And each time he was released, he returned to the front, not home. That, more than anything else, bled the life right out of him. My first memory of him is standing by his bedside, holding my brother's hand and watching my father cough and cough until he passed out from exhaustion. He never got well. To this day, he spends the better part of every winter confined to bed."

"How did he support your family?"

"He worked in the coal mines when he could. It's what he did before the war, it's what most able-bodied men in Boone County, West Virginia, do. My mother died eight years ago, though I suspect she died inside long before then."

"I'm sorry."

Maddie shrugged, failing in her attempt to mask her hurt and sadness with indifference.

"My brother and I pretty much raised ourselves. We kept goats and chickens, selling the milk and eggs to neighbors or the company store. When I was eleven, we discovered a more lucrative means of earning income." She turned a sorrowful smile on Scott. "You may find this hard to believe, but people will pay a lot to see a girl shoot a half-dozen tin cans off a fence railing. We'd pass the hat, and my brother got very good at handling the money."

"That was no life for the two of you."

"There were days it was that, or starve."

Scott harbored little respect for parents would allow their young children to support them by target shooting for handouts. But it did, however, explain Maddie's ability to fend for herself so well.

What had it been like to be so poor? He thought of the fat bank account in Galveston with his name on it. His family, while not exactly wealthy, hadn't lacked money, and Scott grew up wanting for nothing. As a private investigator, he lived comfortably. His leanest years were those he'd been a U.S. Marshal. Except when he'd been hunting down or transporting criminals, he'd rarely gone without a meal or a roof over his head.

"Is your brother a coal miner like your father?"

Maddie hesitated before answering. "No. He left Boone County right after our mother died. He . . . travels a lot. I'm not sure where he is now."

"What about your father? Is he still in Boone County?"

"Yes. Leastwise, the last I heard," she said with a tinge of bitterness. "My mother wasn't gone three months when he remarried. Guess he couldn't tolerate living alone. I didn't set much store by his new wife, so when William came courting, I encouraged him."

"He was from Ireland."

She nodded. "A lot of foreigners worked in the coal mines. We married soon after we met. When Josephine was six months old, we came to Arizona. William loved the West. He read every dime novel and newspaper article he could get his hands on. He was convinced mining for gold and silver would be less difficult and less dangerous than mining coal and that we'd be rich in a matter of weeks. He was wrong on all accounts."

Scott realized he and Maddie were more alike than he first thought. Both their lives constituted a series of disappointments. Both had been abandoned by their families in some fashion or another. Both had left home to escape unhappiness, only to find there was no escaping.

"I suppose you're wondering why I wanted you to stay." Maddie swivelled sideways on the stool, her green eyes—luminous in the lantern light—sought and held his.

Her thigh brushed his knee. Scott became acutely aware of the physical intimacy, slight though it was and limited by several layers of clothes. With her body at an angle, he was afforded a perfect view of her breasts. Full, lush breasts, the shape of which were enticing, the feel of which he could only imagine.

"Whatever your reasons," he said, clearing his throat, "I'm glad you asked."

"Aren't you the least bit curious?"

"It doesn't matter."

She smiled then, somewhat crookedly. "Are you always so accommodating?"

"No. Only for you."

Her smile receded. She'd been joking, of course.

Not Scott. "You're special, Maddie Campbell."

They stared at each other, not moving and not speaking. Seconds ticked by.

"I'm glad you stayed," she said at long last and tilted her head. Her hand came to rest delicately on his knee.

He needed no further invitation and cupped her cheek in his palm. Her skin was like porcelain, flawless and incredibly smooth—and moist from her tears.

"Don't cry, Maddie." Slipping his fingers beneath her jaw, he drew her toward him. And damned if she didn't come willingly. "Everything will be all right."

His lips brushed hers in a featherlight caress. Then again. He didn't want to scare her off. Maddie surprised him by pressing her mouth fully to his, and a groan escaped from deep within his chest. He had barely savored her incredible sweetness when she placed a restraining hand on his chest and abruptly pushed away. Eyes wide and filled with shock, she twisted sideways.

Scott's body was slow to respond to the sudden change. Hell, he might never return to normal. He started to ask her what was wrong and then he heard it. A tiny noise, like a kitten's mew. He craned his neck to see around Maddie.

Josephine's dark brown eyes stared up at them from the cot. She took one look at Scott and screamed.

Chapter Nine

Josephine's scream sounded odd, not quite normal. Without meaning to, Scott winced. Too late, he saw the hurt shimmering in Maddie's eyes and wanted to kick himself.

"I'm sorry."

"It's—"

"Maw, maw," the little girl squawked and reached her slender arms out to Maddie, distracting her from Scott.

"Granny Fay," Maddie hollered over her shoulder. "Josephine's awake."

"I heard." Granny Fay stood and stretched, blinking the sleep from her eyes. "And so, I reckon, did everyone else in Eden."

Maddie put her face next to Josephine's. "Mama's here, darling."

The little girl hugged her mother fiercely, her small body shaking as Maddie kissed her. The utterances she made became choppy and more distorted, but they were still speech, of a sort.

"She can talk," Scott said. Amazement had him sitting up straight. He'd taken for granted deaf people were also mute.

"She can say a few simple words." Granny Fay walked around to the other side of the cot and smiled down at mother and child. "Well, what have we here?"

A guard poked her head inside the tent. Scott recognized her as having been with Maddie that afternoon when he'd first arrived at Eden.

"Was that Josephine I heard? Is she awake? How is she?" Holding her rifle at an awkward angle, the guard stepped fully inside the tent.

Scott immediately pegged her as young, inexperienced, and sorely lacking in confidence.

"How would I know?" Granny Fay made a motion with her hands, shooing the guard away. "If everyone would give some elbow room here, I might be able to tell you."

The guard obediently retreated a few steps. Eyes glued to Granny Fay, Maddie scooted backward on her stool. She continued squeezing Josephine's hand, nearly crushing it in the process. Scott didn't think a well-placed stick of dynamite could blast the two of them apart.

"She called me Mama, and she knows me. Does that mean she's all right?"

"It's a good sign." Granny Fay smiled, and the wrinkles on her weathered cheeks deepened in response. "A very good sign. Josephine, girl," she bent down and, pinching the little girl's chin between her forefinger and thumb, peered closely at her, "you had us pretty worried there for a while. How are you feeling?"

Josephine didn't answer, but recognition registered on her face.

"You're looking no worse for the wear, if I do say." Granny Fay conducted a quick examination of Josephine. "Eyes clear and bright. You can move your arms and legs. Does your head hurt?"

Maddie patted Josephine's hand to get her attention. She pointed to her own head, made a face like she was in pain, and said, "Ow!" She then pointed to Josephine. "You?"

Josephine nodded, gingerly touching the top of her head.

"What about your stomach?" Granny Fay asked.

Maddie translated Granny Fay's question using a similar combination of gestures, facial expressions, and speech. Josephine responded by rubbing her stomach and frowning, indicating it was indeed queasy.

Scott watched them, admittedly fascinated. He'd known any number of elderly people who were hard of hearing. To talk to them, he'd simply shouted.

But Maddie didn't shout, though she'd told him Josephine had some hearing in one ear. Instead, she'd developed a method of communicating with her daughter that was unlike anything he'd ever seen.

Would she never cease to amaze him?

Josephine put a hand to her throat.

"She's thirsty," Maddie said and leapt from the stool. Locating a tin cup on the small table, she filled it from the bucket of fresh water Scott had retrieved earlier.

As she brushed by him with the cup of water, her skirt caught on his knees. She tugged at the fabric. It clung to him briefly before releasing. The sensation wasn't very different from what her hand had felt like on his knee minutes before when they'd been kissing.

Scott caught a fold, allowing the material to slide through his fingers.

For an instant, their gazes connected and, like Josephine, they didn't need to talk to communicate. He knew she was remembering their kiss.

So was he.

If he lived to be a hundred, he wouldn't forget it, so strongly was the memory seared into his mind. And for the rest of his life he'd ponder what would have happened if Josephine had not awakened at the exact moment she did.

He could still taste Maddie, still feel the heat of her mouth on his, soft and giving. So very giving. And not shy by any means. She'd eagerly met his advances with an ardor equaling, if not exceeding, his own.

Would she be as bold in bed as she'd been in his arms?

Scott gritted his teeth and shifted in his seat. It did nothing to alleviate the physical discomfort brought on by imagining the answer to that question.

Maddie returned to Josephine. She and Granny Fay eased the little girl to a half-sitting position so she could drink from the cup. The effort exhausted her, and she sank back down onto the cot after only a few sips.

"Josephine, sweetheart," Maddie crooned. "You hardly drank anything."

"She will when she's able. Best not to force her." Granny Fay made Josephine more comfortable by freeing the hem of her blouse from the waistband of her skirt. "She's awake and in pain, but acting normal enough. I'm thinking she'll be up to her old tricks in a day or two."

"I'm sure glad to hear it," the guard said and stepped closer. She cast a fearful glance at Scott. "Mr. McSween. If you'll please come with me. My orders were to escort you to the gate the moment Mrs. Campbell's daughter woke up."

He was leaving. Just like that. Now that Josephine had recovered, Maddie no longer needed him, and his continued presence in Eden wouldn't be tolerated. Even if she were to ask him to stay—which he highly doubted, given the way she was fussing over Josephine—the guard would never agree. Orders were orders. He should know, he'd followed enough of them in his career as a U.S. Marshal. And broken almost as many in the years since.

The problem was he didn't want to go, didn't want to leave Maddie. And he couldn't explain why. It had nothing to do with their kiss or the fact he desired her, desired her with a longing so deep he felt raw inside.

No, he wanted to stay for another reason, one too confusing and too complicated to put into words.

The guard hefted her rifle, perhaps to bolster her courage. "Mr. McSween."

"Yes, ma'am." He rose from his seat on the cot and placed his hat on his head. He reached for Maddie's shoulder, hoping to give her a reassuring pat, but she abruptly twisted away from him.

"What's wrong with her!" she cried out and went on her knees beside Josephine's cot.

Scott froze in place, staring at the little girl, as did everyone else.

She lay there, eyes closed, her complexion pale, and as unmoving as when Scott had found her in a crumpled heap after she'd been thrown from the donkey. His heart jerked inside his chest. Had she fallen unconscious again? Or worse?

Granny Fay bent over Josephine, then broke into a sunny grin. "Why, there ain't nothing wrong with her. She's asleep is all."

"Asleep?" Maddie's voice trembled. "Are you sure?"

"'Course I'm sure."

"Should we wake her just to . . ."

"See for yourself."

Maddie did. She checked Josephine all over, delicately touching her face, head, and arms. The little girl quietly stirred, her small mouth moving soundlessly. Then, turning her head, she issued a soft sigh and settled into a deep slumber.

"You worry too much," Granny Fay scolded. "She's hurt and needs her rest. Simple as that. And so do you, Maddie. If you don't mind me saying, you look like something the cat drug home."

"I'm fine."

Granny Fay huffed as if her experience as a nurse were in question. "Go on. Get some sleep."

"I can't. What if something happens to her during the night?"

"I'll stay with her. Sleep right beside her on that there cot."

"But what if she wakes up, and I'm not here? She'll be afraid."

"If she does, I'll send for you. Your place ain't far."

"I don't know." Maddie wavered.

"You're gonna have your hands full the next few days taking care of her. You'll need your strength. You being dead on your feet won't do either of you any good."

"She's right, Maddie," the guard said, sympathy tinging her voice.

"Darn tootin' I'm right. Been nursing sick folks for prit near twenty-five years."

"I suppose." Maddie fidgeted, not yet ready to acquiesce. "Do you *promise* to send for me if she wakes up?"

"I swear on my Elwood's grave, God rest his worthless, two-timing, sorry-excuse-for-a-husband soul."

Evidently, Granny Fay had not enjoyed the happiest of marriages.

"Mr. McSween." The guard beckoned Scott. "If you please."

She was clearly eager to see the hind end of his horse riding away from Eden. She looked ready to bolt if he so much as sneezed wrong. Bolt . . . or shoot.

He reluctantly moved to follow her, hating to leave Maddie but having no choice.

"Wait." Maddie placed a loving kiss on her daughter's forehead, then rose, a picture of grace and strength. "I'm coming with you."

The guard squared her shoulders. "Lavinia said you were to stay here."

"I insist." Maddie resolutely walked around the cot to join them.

"Maddie," Scott said, "it's not necessary for you to come with us."

"I believe it is," she told him. "You're my guest in Eden, here at my invitation." She stared pointedly at the guard. "Not a prisoner. And I won't have you treated like one."

The guard's scowl said otherwise.

Scott had trouble believing Maddie would openly defy the councilwoman's order. She'd demonstrated her mettle before, and he knew her to be more capable than most. But this was sheer stupidity. If he didn't know differently, he'd think it was she and not her daughter who had taken a hard knock to the head.

Maddie had clearly lost her mind. Totally, completely, and indisputably gone over the edge. She didn't always see eye to eye with Lavinia, and after tonight they might never get along again. And with good reason.

Why hadn't she stayed with Josephine and let Scott leave without her? Had saying good-bye, thanking him for all he'd done for her and her daughter, been important enough to put her position on the council at risk?

It had seemed so back in the tent. There, Scott had been her protector and defender, sticking up for her and Josephine. But now that they were walking along through the center of Eden—with Hannah Wallace's hard stare burning into their backs, her rifle raised and ready to fire—Maddie began to question the wisdom of her actions.

She wasn't usually an impetuous person. Her escapades, though daring, were well thought out and planned long in advance. But for some reason, Scott brought out her reckless side. Even now, walking beside him, she was acutely aware of the heat generated by his body, the appealing male scent of him, and her entirely feminine reaction to both those things.

Yes, she had lost her mind. And she didn't need Hannah Wallace to remind her how much trouble she'd gotten herself into.

"If you need anything," Scott murmured from the corner of his mouth, "you can reach me at the hotel."

Rousing from her daze, Maddie whispered, "Thank you. I appreciate the offer." She did, more than he realized. She couldn't remember the last time someone had made her an unconditional pledge of assistance. Without warning, tears pricked her eyes. She blamed the long, emotional night and not any affection she might harbor for Scott. "But I doubt it'll be necessary."

"Still, the offer stands. And if it turns out Josephine does need medical help, rest assured, I'll bring the company doctor here, hog-tie him if I have to."

She had to smile. "Somehow, I don't see Newlin allowing it."

"He won't have to know."

"Sooner or later, he'll find out. Nothing that happens in Edenville escapes him."

"Money can buy silence."

Maddie didn't know how to respond. Scott standing up to Lavinia and Constance was one thing. Deceiving Newlin, quite another. Especially when he worked for the man. Could he really care for her enough to put his job on the line?

Oh, dear Lord. It was too much to think about when her emotions were already as frayed as the end of an old rope.

"I can't ask you to pay for a doctor," she stammered.

"You didn't ask me," he said in a tone that managed to be both frank and intimate.

She almost stumbled, so weak had her knees gone. Scott McSween was danger incarnate. To her, to her daughter, and to everyone in Eden. Yet she was utterly unable to resist her attraction to him. How else could she explain that kiss back in the tent? And she would have kissed him more fully if Josephine hadn't awakened. No matter that her injured daughter and a dozing Granny Fay were but a few feet away. She'd have enjoyed it, too.

It had taken only one brief caress of their lips to send a shower of sensation from the top of her head to the tip of her toes. If she closed her eyes and concentrated, she could feel him kissing her even now—would probably always feel it long after Scott left Edenville. Which he would, as soon as he caught his quarry. Her.

Maddie let the sensation slide over her again, knowing this was all she'd ever have of him. The prospect should have gladdened her. It didn't. With a passion so strong it shook her to the core, she yearned for another of his kisses.

Yes, she had without question truly lost her mind when it came to this man.

"You two," Hannah snapped. "Be quiet up there."

For once, Maddie did as her subordinate commanded and not the other way around. She needed a clear head, and talking to Scott had a tendency to cloud her thinking.

The gate loomed ahead in the predawn darkness, looking larger and more imposing than it did in broad daylight. Much farther away, where night sky met earth, a thin strip of purple along the horizon heralded the soon-rising sun.

If Maddie were smart, she'd bid her two companions farewell and head straight to her shack for a much-needed nap. Oh, but she'd proven over and over again she wasn't smart when it came to Scott McSween and instead, continued walking alongside him.

They'd crossed paths with no one on their way to the gate. From all around, nocturnal noises reached Maddie's ears. A dog barking. The hoot of an owl. The sudden swish of brush as some small creature scurried into hiding. Moist air settled on her skin, a sure sign of impending rain given the late summer season. A glowing three-quarter moon provided enough light for the party of three to navigate without difficulty.

"Where's my horse?" Scott asked, cranking his head around to address Hannah.

"Tied on the other side of the gate. Lavinia left instructions for him to be watered."

"I'm oblig—"

A rifle shot rang out, shattering the otherwise peaceful night.

Scott grabbed Maddie before she could react and pushed her behind him, shielding her from . . . what? Reaching for his gun, he came up empty-handed and uttered a ripe curse.

"That came from the south end of camp," Hannah said, staring in the direction of the shot. She clearly wanted to investigate.

So did Maddie. She darted out from behind Scott. "I'll go find out what's happening. You stay here with Mr. McSween."

"Absolutely not!" Scott took her by the arm, his grip firm.

Her boss, Mr. Abernathy, had held her in such a fashion. Scott's touch, however, didn't anger her. She found his protectiveness endearing.

"It's my job as head of security," she said. Many the night she'd been called out to investigate a disturbance.

The shot had roused a good many people from bed. Everywhere heads were poking out of doorways and tent openings. The sound of someone coming toward them at a dead run had them all whirling around.

"Hannah! Hannah! You there?" It was Archie Starkweather, Constance's son.

"What is it?" Hannah rushed forward to meet Archie, who had slowed to a stop.

"They told me at the infirmary you'd left with that private investigator." The boy's breath came in huge gulps, and his shirt had come untucked. "We got him!" he gasped, a happy grin splitting his face.

"Got who?"

"The coyote. He's caught in the trap we set." He wiped sweat from his forehead with the back of his arm. "Miz Stolworthy tried shooting him. But he lunged at her. She got scared and missed. Miz Lavinia sent me to find you."

"Why didn't she fire again?" Maddie asked. "He can't hurt anyone while he's stuck in that trap."

Archie looked chagrined. "She's out of bullets."

Maddie knew what that meant. Bullets were ruthlessly rationed, two per guard. They were stored in a locked box in the supply tent. Only Lavinia had the key. Her choices would have been to leave the scene for more bullets or send for Hannah Wallace, the other guard on duty. Not knowing that Scott wasn't still in the infirmary with Maddie, Lavinia had obviously chosen the latter.

Hannah frowned, her uncertainty plain. If she went with Archie, that would leave Scott alone with Maddie. But if she didn't go, Lavinia would be upset with her.

"Come on, Miz Wallace," Archie pleaded. "They said to hurry."

"Go," Maddie told Hannah, her tone the one she used when giving orders. "You're a decent shot. And the coyote needs to be killed. I'll see Mr. McSween to the gate."

Hannah appeared to be relieved to have the decision taken from her. "All right." She left with Archie after first assuring the awakened residents that all was well. A few went with her and Archie; the rest returned to their beds.

For the first time in their short acquaintance, Maddie and Scott were alone.

"Shall we?" He gestured, and they started out slowly.

Conversation didn't come easily. Maddie didn't trust her voice or the myriad emotions it might reveal.

Soon—too soon, almost—they left the last row of tents and shacks behind and came upon the gate. Scott's horse, tethered on the other side as Hannah promised, flung his head and whinnied at the sight of them.

"I think someone's eager to go home," she said, stopping on the Eden side of the gate.

Scott turned to face her. "It's certainly not me."

Was he teasing her?

She looked up and found herself utterly lost in his smile. Neither of them moved for several long moments. There was something about the sensual curve of his mouth that fascinated her. She felt as if she stood before an open doorway with no clue as to what lay on the opposite side. Treasure or peril? Should she stay in her place or step over the threshold? Her head and heart couldn't seem to agree on the answer.

She began to say something, what exactly she didn't know, when another shot rang out. She started, more in response to Scott's sudden tensing to the shot, but quickly relaxed.

"I suppose," he said, "your poor coyote has gone to meet his maker."

"Not so poor." She made a face. "The rascal's been killing our chickens for weeks now."

"Guess he hadn't heard the rule about no males allowed in Eden."

They both smiled, and the charged atmosphere between them lessened. Until Scott stepped closer. "When can I see you again?"

"I don't think that's possible."

"Why not?" Another step, closer still.

Maddie swallowed. "It's complicated."

"If you're still mourning your husband . . ."

"I'm not."

She wasn't sure she'd ever mourned William. Not properly, leastwise. The magnitude of the accident had left them all numb from grief at first. They'd hardly had time to recover when the scarlet fever epidemic broke out. The weeks had been a blur, sorrow heaped upon sorrow as more died. The final blow had come when they lost their homes. Maddie wasn't the only woman left with nothing but young children to care for and a burning hatred of Thaddeus Newlin to keep her going.

And today, she'd almost lost her child. Could have, if not for Scott's strength and speed in getting Josephine to the infirmary. She owed him so much.

"It has nothing to do with William."

"Is it because I work for Newlin?"

"That's part of it." A large part of it. He had no idea how large.

Scott cupped her cheek, traced circles on her skin with the pad of his thumb. It felt good. More than good. Perfect. She stiffened in an attempt to combat the effect he had on her, only to melt again.

"I won't work for him forever. Soon, very soon I hope, I'll catch the robbers."

He had only to pull her into his arms and he'd have their leader.

And then what? Once he discovered she was behind the robberies, any possibility of them being together would be destroyed.

Maddie almost burst out laughing. Who was she kidding? Be with Scott? She'd only met him less than a week ago. He worked for the man who'd ruined her life, and his assignment was to arrest her and bring her to justice.

But she didn't laugh. Because, God forgive her, being with him was what she wanted. To give herself over to his embrace, if only briefly. Let him help her forget the horrors of the day. Of the last year. Scott could do it, too. With little effort, he could make her forget her own name.

"You're incredible, Maddie Campbell. Do you know that?"

"Hardly."

"Really. You hold what amounts to two jobs, one at the store, the other here. You're raising a daughter who can't hear. And you have the grit to stand up to an awful boss and that battle-ax you call a head councilwoman."

She chuckled softly, but for some reason, it turned into a sob. She didn't want to cry again, not in front of Scott. But she was weary of the constant fight to stay in control.

"Come here."

Maddie raised her head as his hand slid around her neck. His gray eyes, two ebony pools in the silvery moonlight, bored into her. As always, his grip on her was proprietary, but not demanding. He wouldn't force her against her will. She instinctively knew that.

If she went to him, it would be because she desired it. Him. His lips on hers, claiming them, possessing them.

She stood for a moment longer, facing the open doorway where treasure or peril awaited her on the opposite side. Probably both. Was kissing Scott worth the risk? Was not kissing him something she'd always regret?

Drawing a deep breath, she walked over the threshold and into Scott's arms.

Chapter Ten

Scott kissed Maddie with the same ravenous hunger a raging forest fire consumes a pine tree, and she let him. In fact, she welcomed his assault on her mouth with an abandonment that would have made Delilah stand and applaud.

Course fabric met sensitive fingertips as Maddie's hands slid up his shirt front, seeking an anchor on which to latch. Without one, she might well be carried away in the tide of sensations washing over her. Wrapping her arms around his neck, she held on for dear life. Every thrust of his tongue, every moan of pleasure rumbling from deep inside his chest, was like a medicinal balm, soothing her pain and healing her wounds.

Don't stop, her mind cried when he paused to inhale sharply. *Don't ever stop.*

He didn't. One powerful arm circled her waist, and he bent her back. She gasped when his teeth nipped the side of her neck, shuddered when his lips ventured lower to nuzzle the hollow at the base of her throat.

He brought his mouth to hers again. "You're so beautiful. I've wanted this from the moment I first saw you in the company store."

She'd known he wanted her, had seen the passion flare in his steel gray eyes when he looked at her. Even so, she liked hearing him say it. Men had expressed desire for her before. Male customers so outnumbered female customers in the store, she received propositions on a regular basis—some honorable, most not. She'd turned every one of them down flat.

Except for Scott. Only he had broken through the barriers she'd so carefully erected after her late husband's death and Josephine's illness.

But if the council's plan to steal back the money owed the women was going to pay off, Maddie couldn't afford to become involved with a man. Any man, but especially Scott McSween.

Yet here she was, letting him kiss her, kissing him back, and thrilling to every sensual response his touch evoked.

Her entire body hummed with new life as he once again claimed her lips. Her breasts, full and aching, pressed into the firm wall of his broad chest. Warmth spread throughout her middle and cascaded downward, pooling at a place below her belly. Her heart hammered, her breath caught, and her mind emptied of all thought save him.

William had rescued her from a life she hated, fathered her child, and earned, if not her undying love, her abiding affection. She'd enjoyed their lovemaking, finding it agreeable and, on rare instances, exciting. But for all his charm and personality, he'd never given her cause to dismiss her responsibilities, defy authority, flaunt proprieties, or lose herself in his embrace to such an extent that the rest of the world ceased to exist.

If Maddie were capable of thinking clearly, she might have asked herself what made Scott different from other men, including her late husband. But her brain had quit functioning with any degree of rationality some minutes previous.

Only feeling remained. Glorious, wondrous feeling.

"I want to see you again." Scott broke off the kiss long enough to repeat his earlier request in a guttural voice not his own.

"I told you, I can't."

He didn't take no for an answer. "I have to visit the Vista Linda Mine for a few days. When I come back, I'll call on you at the store. We'll go on a buggy ride or a stroll. Have dinner at the hotel."

Maddie closed her eyes and thought several seconds before responding. The longing to say yes pulled at her stronger than she would have considered possible. For a moment, she tried to imagine Scott courting her as an ordinary man might court an ordinary woman. She found it impossible. There was nothing ordinary about either of them and any relationship they hoped to have was doomed from the start.

"I'm sorry, Scott." She paused to collect herself. How could doing the right thing be so hard? "I wish with all my heart things were different."

"No." He shook his head. "You feel something for me. I know it."

He moved closer, instantly filling her senses and proving his point. Maddie's lids lowered on a thready sigh. His hand found the small of her back. When he gently tugged her to him, she didn't resist. She might have cursed him for his damned, infuriating confidence, or herself for submitting so readily, but her mouth was otherwise occupied.

Need and desperation coursed through her, a river

rampaging in the aftermath of a downpour. It was a new and unsettling experience. If she retained any of the cleverness and resourcefulness that had sustained her during the many trying months, she'd run far and fast from Scott—and soon. But she wanted this man. So much so, she'd willingly and eagerly gone into his arms.

An understanding of her mother's addiction for whiskey suddenly dawned on Maddie as she reveled in another of Scott's bone-melting kisses. Had she realized how easy it was to develop an insatiable appetite for something destructive to one's family and friends, she might have been more tolerant and forgiving of her mother's habit.

Separating herself from him, she asked, "If I should agree to let you call on me, what then?"

"I'm not sure I understand."

"Won't you be leaving Edenville when you finish this job? A week or two, you told me. Maybe a month." She could see the truth in his eyes even before he spoke it, and her heart sank.

"Yes."

There was no room in his life for a wife and child. She'd been a fool to consider such a crazy notion, even briefly. "It might be better for us . . . for me . . . to say good-bye here and now."

"When I get back from the Vista Linda Mine, we'll talk."

Undoubtedly, but not about whether he'd come calling on her. Once he discovered there was no Irish miner named Rory O'Shea, he'd either believe her a simpleton or, more likely, suspect her of hiding something from him—which would lead to the end of their relationship, if not her arrest and incarceration.

His hand traveled a path along the curve of her shoulder and down her arm. Easing her to him, he lowered his mouth. Tonight was all they'd ever have, Maddie mused as the world receded once more. This last kiss would have to suffice for the rest of her life.

But from the first taste of his lips, it became clear one kiss wouldn't do. He didn't take her like he had before, his passion unleashed and unconstrained. Instead, he elevated their intimacy to new heights. The slow, sensual forays of his tongue into her mouth crippled her one moment and had her gliding on air the next.

More. She wanted more. His kisses, his touch, everything. It was, she knew, utter lunacy. Rising onto her tiptoes, she deepened their kiss. Her hands splayed wide, she skimmed them up his rib cage and around to his back.

He tore his mouth from hers, shifted her slightly, then wedged a leg between hers. The ridge of his arousal pressed hard against her stomach.

Maddie took an abrupt step backward and stared at Scott, seeing the same madness affecting her reflected in his eyes. It should have scared her, but didn't, an indication of just how far past the point of no return she'd ventured.

For a lingering moment, she perched on the edge of reason. Then, like a hawk launching itself from a mountainous precipice, she dove off and soared skyward. When she landed at last, she was again in Scott's arms where he made her his and his alone with yet another hot, searing kiss.

Thick, bulky pads hindered Constance's ability to balance the pot of steaming coffee as she picked her way over the uneven ground toward the infirmary. The gray swirl of early dawn didn't help. Normally, she hoarded her meager supply of coffee, reserving it for special occasions. But this morning, she'd used a few precious scoops to make the pot and didn't dare spill one drop.

She'd tossed and turned all night, unable to stop thinking about Maddie, Josephine, and that trouble-making private investigator Newlin hired. Try as she might—and oh, she had tried—she couldn't understand Maddie. What in the world had gotten into her friend lately? Maddie hadn't been acting like herself since the day that dreadful man stepped into town.

And neither, truth be told, had Constance. She'd been living in a state of perpetual dread since Maddie first mentioned Scott McSween.

Something had to be done. She and Maddie were friends. Good friends. And right now, Maddie needed her, which was why Constance had broken into her coffee supply and made them a pot. Doubtless, Maddie could use the lift. A cup of coffee would be the perfect icebreaker. It would be nice if the two of them could talk like old times, back when they'd been neighbors in the company-provided housing.

The coyote's demise had roused more people than were usually up and about at this hour. Several reported that Josephine awoke during the night and showed signs of a full recovery. The news gladdened Constance. As annoyed as she was with Maddie, her friend had endured her share of losses, as had they all, and didn't deserve another one.

Reaching the infirmary, Constance lifted the tent flap, stooped, and entered. It took several seconds in the inky interior for her eyes to adjust. Twin slumbering figures occupied the cots, one small, one large. Josephine and her mother. As much as she wanted to talk with Maddie, Constance hated to disturb her sleep. Maybe she'd stop back after daylight, in an hour or so.

Walking over to the small table, she set the pot of coffee down.

"Who's there?"

Unnerved by the strange voice, Constance jerked and gave a shriek. Her leg bumped the table, hurtling the coffeepot to the ground. It hit with a loud clatter. The lid flew off, and hot liquid splashed onto the front of her dress. Her shriek escalated as stinging pain assaulted her legs.

A figure emerged from the darkness, grabbed her by the arms, and shook her.

"Leave me alone," she yelped.

"Lord Almighty. Stop your caterwauling." It was Granny Fay.

Relief rendered Constance dizzy. "It's you."

"Who'd you think it was?"

"I honestly didn't know." Constance glared at the spreading puddle by her feet. "I spilled the coffee I brought for Maddie," she grumbled, and bent to retrieve the pot.

"She ain't here."

"No?" Constance stood, setting the empty pot on the table. "Where is she?"

At that moment, Josephine awoke and started calling for her mother in a loud, distorted voice. Granny Fay went to comfort the girl, brushing her tousled hair from her face.

"There, there, pumpkin." To Constance, Granny Fay said, "She went back to her place a little bit ago to get some sleep. The poor thing was all wrung out, so I told her I'd stay with Josephine while she took a nap."

"I see." Constance didn't really see. If her son Archie had been the one hurt, wild horses wouldn't have dragged her from his side. Her mood soured further. She hadn't slept well. Then, she spilled the coffee. And to top if off, Maddie wasn't even there when Constance most wanted to talk.

Could anything else go wrong?

Apparently so.

Josephine refused to be comforted, her cries for her mother intensifying.

"She won't settle down till she sees her ma." Granny Fay lifted a thrashing Josephine into her arms. "Would you mind going for Maddie?"

"Not at all."

On her way out the tent, Constance chided herself for overreacting. She and Maddie would have that nice chat after all while they sat with Josephine and fed her breakfast. No need to let lack of sleep and a little mishap ruin a perfectly lovely day.

The walk to Maddie's shack took only a minute or two. By the time Constance reached her destination, her good spirits had returned. At the door, she knocked. When no one answered, she knocked again, lifted the latch, and went inside.

"You awake, dear? Josephine's call—"

Enough light filtered through the cracks in the walls for Constance to see that the shack was empty and the bedroll in the corner undisturbed.

Maddie wasn't there and hadn't been all night. So where was she?

A combination of fear and dread came over Constance. Had something happened to Maddie? More than once men from town had snuck into Eden and tried to abduct unsuspecting women.

Scott McSween. His name exploded in Constance's head with the force of a cannon being fired. He'd been in the infirmary last night with Maddie—maybe he'd come back. It wouldn't surprise Constance if he had. She didn't trust the man as far as she could throw him.

She turned and bolted for the door. Outside, she began walking at a brisk pace. Something—instinct perhaps—directed her toward the gate. There, in the distance, stood Maddie. She and McSween were engaged in some sort of conversation.

Expelling a huge sigh, Constance picked up speed, her long skirt swirled about her legs, stirring up small clouds of dust. All at once she came to a grinding halt and stared at the sight before her. The greeting she'd been about to issue died in her throat as Maddie and McSween came together, their arms entwined about each other and their mouths locked in a passionate kiss.

A cry of dismay must have escaped Constance's lips, for the lovers abruptly sprang apart.

"Constance." Maddie's hand fluttered to the collar of her dress. "It's not what you th—"

"You whore!" Feelings too ugly and awful to describe welled up inside Constance. She raised an unsteady arm and pointed in the direction from where she'd come. "While your daughter lies in the infirmary, scared and calling for her mother, you're kissing *him*. Newlin's hired gun." The idea of Maddie and McSween together sickened Constance. "I hope to G—god you rot in h—h—hell. You and him b—both."

"That's enough." McSween's arm went protectively around Maddie's waist.

"Don't you *dare* speak to me like that! And take your hands off her."

He didn't budge. "I suggest you leave now, Mrs. Starkweather, before you say something else you'll regret."

Her vision blurred as tears filled her eyes. No need to tell her twice. Constance would just as soon die than remain there looking at them. Grabbing her skirts, she ran as fast as her rubbery legs would carry her.

Straight to Lavinia's tent.

* * *

There were so many things for which to feel guilty, Maddie was hard pressed to pick just one.

Not being with her daughter when she woke up and needed her. Having her daughter watch her being escorted from the infirmary by a tight-lipped guard mere minutes after she'd arrived. Disappointing a good friend. Betraying the women who trusted and depended on her. Breaking the very rule it was her job to enforce.

Kissing a man she hardly knew—a man who was Thaddeus Newlin's hired private investigator.

"What have you to say for yourself?" Lavinia's voice intruded on Maddie's thoughts, scattering them like dried leaves swept up in a dust devil.

What *could* she say for herself? Nothing excused her actions. Last night, in the cover of darkness, when loneliness and desperation were winning the constant battle she waged with them, Scott had been there, wanting and willing to protect her. Comfort her. Cherish her.

And Maddie had let him. For one of the few times in her life, she'd allowed someone else to steer her course—with disastrous results.

She didn't need to see the disapproving faces of the council members to tell her as much. One glimpse at the dark walls of her broken heart was enough.

"I'm sorry," she said at last. The apology sounded trite even to her own ears.

Lavinia evidently thought so, too, judging by her indignant "Harrumph."

Maddie stood before the council members, head lowered and hands clasped in front of her. They'd convened on the south end of Eden, away from prying eyes and eavesdropping ears. At least, thought Maddie, her reprimand and punishment wouldn't be witnessed by the entire population. Only her shame, which she'd suffer the remainder of her days.

Days that might be spent elsewhere than Eden.

"What are we going do with her?" Constance demanded. "She has to be punished."

"Banish her," someone shouted. "We don't need the likes of her here."

"Reduce her rations," suggested another, less harsh voice.

"No beans. And no meat, not that we have any. But if we get some, none for her."

Maddie looked up. She'd accept whatever punishment the council chose to mete out, but she'd accept it with her head held high.

"What in tarnation has gotten into y'all?" Dora stomped to her feet from the overturned wheelbarrow on which she'd perched. Hands on hips, mouth set in a stubborn scowl, she gave each of the council members a generous dose of see-here. "This is Maddie Campbell we're talking about."

"We know her name." Lavinia's sigh bespoke her impatience.

"Do you?" Dora asked with exaggerated surprise. "I was thinking maybe you forgot. You sure as shootin' forgot what she's done for y'all. For *everyone* here in Eden."

"No one has—"

Lavinia didn't stand a chance. Dora rolled right over her.

"Just in case some of you are saddled with shorter memories than others, let me remind you. Maddie Campbell pulled every one of our sorry hides out of the fire and gave us something to live for. We'd likely be dead without her, or near enough to starving we wished we were dead."

"We're well aware of Maddie's contribution to the community," Lavinia said.

"Patience." Dora went to stand in front of the council member in charge of food supplies. "Ain't your two daughters wearing new shoes?"

"Yes. But I don't see—"

"Where did the money come from to buy those shoes?"

Patience stated the obvious. "The robberies."

"My point exactly," Dora proclaimed to the group at large. "And Patience's ain't the only younguns in Eden wearing shoes instead of rags on their feet, thanks to Maddie."

A flurry of whispered remarks were telegraphed down a line of raised hands.

"It ain't like none of us can really blame her." Dora's tone softened. So did her countenance. "I miss having a man hold me in his arms. And I'd wager I ain't the only one here who feels likewise." Her direct gaze challenged anyone on the council to disagree.

"Thank you," Maddie mouthed. She was honored and touched to be the recipient of so much loyalty.

Dora turned to Maddie and gestured expansively. "All right. She made a mistake. A big one. But it ain't the end of the world. The sheriff didn't storm the gate to Eden and arrest us all. Lightning didn't strike and burn our homes, such as they are, to the ground. We're safe, and McSween still doesn't suspect a thing."

"You don't know that for sure," Lavinia cautioned.

"What do you bet after this morning, Maddie's the last person on earth McSween suspects?" Dora chuckled mischievously, and one or two council members joined her.

All jesting aside, Maddie hoped Dora was right.

"I admit your argument has merit," Lavinia conceded. "Only last week we voted that Maddie should encourage McSween's interest in her in order to glean information from him."

"If you look at it that way, she was just doing what we'd asked her to." Dora beamed while others nodded their agreement.

"She has to be punished!" Constance repeated with vehemence. "She consorted with the enemy."

Another, sharper, stab of regret pierced Maddie's insides. She and Constance had drifted so far apart the past week, and she had only herself to blame.

"Kissing McSween within the gates of Eden was a violation of community rules," Lavinia continued in a voice of authority. "However, as Dora says, Maddie's indiscretion may very well have removed suspicion from us."

"You didn't see them!" Constance refused to be swayed. "She can't be trusted, I tell you."

"Can't trust you, either," Dora retorted with an unpleasant sneer. "What kind of friend rats on the other?"

All eyes swung to Constance, many of them accusatory. She glowered at Dora in return.

"Please!" Maddie pressed fingertips to her throbbing temples. She hated seeing her two dear friends and partners arguing.

Lavinia rang her bell, but it proved unnecessary. Tempers were already abating. "Constance and Dora. Take your seats now and let anyone else speak who has a mind to."

Discussion continued for the next half hour. Though most sided with Dora, Constance had two vocal supporters who made a compelling case against Maddie.

During a particularly heated debate, she lost her battle with panic. She hadn't realized until now just how afraid she was of being forced to leave Eden.

Where would we go? Not back to West Virginia. Never there, so long as her stepmother resided in the family home. Besides, Maddie didn't have enough money to travel the forty miles to Tucson, much less halfway across the country.

Scott might be willing to purchase tickets for her and Josephine, but Maddie would change dirty bed linens at the Strike It Rich Saloon before she'd ask him for money. Misplaced as it might be, she had her pride.

"What are your feelings for this man?" Lavinia's tapping foot made scratching noises in the dirt as the council members waited for Maddie to respond.

How to answer? Did she even know?

"I'm grateful to him for his help with my daughter."

"Is that the extent of it?"

"Yes." But, she admitted only to herself, it might be different if Scott weren't working for Newlin.

"Is there any chance your loyalties will shift to him?"

"No, I swear it." She made a heartfelt plea. "Eden is my home, and the people here my family. My loyalties will never shift."

In the end, Constance and her two supporters were outvoted. Maddie received minor consequences for breaking a community rule; sitting in the back during Sunday sermon and a week of latrine duty. It was a compromise, one Lavinia undoubtedly made to maintain peace. Maddie didn't envy the head councilwoman her difficult job.

On route back to the infirmary, Maddie murmured a prayer of thanks. She and Josephine would remain in Eden. But the council's trust in her had been shaken and justifiably so. Regaining it wouldn't be easy.

Physically exhausted and emotionally drained, she entered the infirmary to discover Josephine wide awake and agitated. Within minutes, her behavior deteriorated. Anger at what she perceived as her mother's abandonment manifested itself in a full-blown tantrum. Maddie's guilt compounded as she struggled to reason with the enraged three-year-old. At least, Maddie told herself, she no longer worried whether her daughter would make a full recovery. As Granny Fay had predicted, Josephine was up to her old tricks.

An exceedingly long and difficult hour dragged by before Josephine wore herself out and fell into a sound slumber. Since Granny Fay had left for town in the surrey, Maddie curled up on the cot beside her daughter, something she probably should have done instead of walking Scott to the gate.

But then they wouldn't have kissed. For a few wild and reckless minutes, Maddie had imagined him rescuing her from a life of poverty and despair. It had been glorious and exhilarating—until the crash came.

Such was the pattern of her life, she thought as sleep continued to elude her. Any happiness she found was quickly snatched away and replaced with a greater misery. Why should she expect things to change now?

Scott was going away at the end of the job. He'd made as much clear during their kisses. And he hadn't asked her and Josephine to accompany him. Not that he would. If Scott were successful in capturing the robbers, and, according to him, he always was, he'd leave Edenville in the near future with Maddie behind bars.

Chapter Eleven

"Go away," Scott hollered at the person outside his hotel room door.

The knocking resumed. "Mr. McSween? Are you in?"

Damn. Scott recognized the voice. In his current sleep-deprived condition, he was in no mood to deal with Zachariah Forrester. "I said, go away."

"Mr. Newlin asks that you meet with him this morning at your earliest convenience. He'd like me to wait and accompany you."

Scott muttered a second, riper curse. He wasn't so tired or angry or frustrated that he didn't recognize an order in the guise of a request. Newlin must be really champing at the bit. The infrequency of Scott's reports was a constant sore spot with the majority partner.

"My earliest convenience isn't for another hour. Maybe two."

He couldn't avoid Newlin indefinitely. But he sure as hell could stall him. Scott prided himself on his service to his clients. In return, he required a degree of respect, refusing to be commanded like some servant.

"Mr. McSween. Is there some manner in which I can be of assistance? Order breakfast from the kitchen? Arrange for a bath to be brought to your room?"

Speaking of servants . . .

"I can get my own breakfast, Forrester."

Not that Scott wanted breakfast. His stomach wasn't much in the mood for food. The bed springs creaked under his weight as he sat up and swung his legs onto the floor.

The problem was, he actually wanted to talk to Newlin. Specifically, about making arrangements to travel to the Vista Linda Mine to check out the Irish miner Maddie had told him about. He wasn't sure whether he believed her story. He wanted to, but then, he wanted a lot of things where Maddie was concerned. None of which were feasible.

"I'll be down in thirty minutes," he told the secretary through the door.

"Very good, sir. I'll wait for you in the lobby." The sound of receding footsteps echoed down the hall.

From his place on the bed, Scott stared out the small open window. Noises drifted in from the street below. Not yet eight o'clock in the morning and already the town bustled with activity. From what he'd seen since his arrival, busy was a way of life in Edenville. Everyone, from the most prominent citizens to the lowliest miners, had the same objective in mind: make money.

Scott pushed himself to his feet. Lying in bed and mentally reliving the events of the last day succeeded only in giving him a giant headache and an equally giant case of remorse. Neither were common afflictions for him.

Scrubbing his hands over his beard-stubbled cheeks, he crossed the room to the washstand. He hadn't allowed himself to feel remorse for the last five years. Not since he'd left Galveston, convinced he'd been in the right even if the rest of the world didn't agree.

Maddie changed that. She evoked all sorts of feelings he'd fought hard to extinguish, including regret. Leaving her this morning was the hardest thing he'd done since turning in his badge. He need only close his eyes and he could recall the sensation of her lush and giving body nestled firmly against his. Taste her full, sweet lips as they molded to, then parted beneath his, giving him the entrance to her mouth he'd so desperately craved.

When was the last time anything had felt that right or good in his life?

The answer was easy. Five long, lonely years.

A fresh burst of anger exploded inside him as he remembered the scathing insults Constance Starkweather had screamed at Maddie. He should have stayed in Eden, protected her from further mistreatment. The head councilwoman, Lavinia, impressed him as a force to be reckoned with. But Maddie had insisted he go, all but tossing him out on his rear.

So he'd left, resigned that his continued presence hurt more than helped. But he couldn't stop feeling like a first-class heel for abandoning her.

Going back to check on her would be a waste of time. The guards made it clear the night before he'd be shot on sight if he stepped foot inside Eden. No small surprise they didn't shoot him dead the second Constance reported his and Maddie's indiscretion. As it was, he'd endured their eyes boring into the back of his head for what seemed like the entire ride to town.

He should probably wait to speak to Maddie again until after he returned from the Vista Linda Mine. Her movements had to be under careful scrutiny. She'd been caught dallying with the private investigator hired to capture the gang of robbers tormenting the very individuals the women held responsible for their husbands' deaths. If the women didn't consider Maddie an out-and-out traitor to their cause, they surely considered her association with him a risk.

And when he finally did speak with her, what then? Were he brutally honest with himself, Scott wasn't prepared to offer her anything beyond a casual affair. He had a job to do, and when it was over, he'd leave Edenville for the next one. There was no room in his life for a sweetheart, even one as appealing as Maddie Campbell.

Yet something about her intrigued him like no other woman. She was a fascinating mixture of plain, simple honesty and deep, dark secrets. Raw strength and shy vulnerability. Proper lady and brazen temptress.

She was also a liability, the kind Scott should avoid at all costs.

Removing his hat from the peg on the wall where it hung, he noticed the bullet hole in the crown—*really* noticed it—and let out a low whistle. Maddie had considerable skill. Four inches lower and he'd have been a dead man, shot square between the eyes.

As promised, Zachariah Forrester met Scott in the lobby. "This way, Mr. McSween." He gestured for Scott to follow him outside. "I've arranged for a buggy and horses to take us to Mr. Newlin."

Scott held out his damaged hat. "Is there a haberdashery we can stop at first?"

Forrester eyed the hat critically, then gave Scott a

curious look. "You're either a very lucky man, Mr. McSween, or your adversary had excellent aim."

"I'd say you're right on both accounts."

Scott had been half joking, but Newlin's secretary didn't laugh.

During the ride to the mining compound, Scott kept picturing Maddie as a little girl, shooting tin cans off a fence railing for money. When faced with trying circumstances, she'd shown an impressive amount of grit and resourcefulness for a youngster.

What was she capable of as an adult?

From his higher vantage point, Thaddeus Newlin watched the buggy and its two passengers ascend up the narrow and bumpy mountain road. In another few minutes, Forrester and McSween would arrive at his private observatory.

His secretary had been warned not to come alone. It pleased Newlin to see his instructions being followed to the letter. Forrester, despite his sketchy history of employment, knew how to get the job done. Besides, Newlin contemplated while puffing a fat, fragrant cigar, everyone was entitled to a few secrets. He certainly had his share.

The last hundred feet of the road were the worst. Steep and winding, with forty-foot drop-offs in some places, it was a true test for the faint of heart. The horses, a fine set of matching blacks shipped special from Tennessee, dropped their heads and pulled. Forrester had no need for the whip. Like everything and everyone under Newlin's rule, the horses knew their job and performed it obediently.

With, perhaps, the singular exception of Scott McSween.

The private investigator had tried Newlin's patience

from their first meeting, but that was about to end. Starting today, McSween would fall in line—or pack his bags and catch the next train leaving Edenville. Newlin would see to it.

Breathing hard, their sides heaving, the horses came to a stop at a level circle of ground outside the observatory entrance. Both men climbed down from the buggy, but only McSween entered the seating area. Forrester remained behind, tethering the horses to a hitching post. He would stay there unless called.

"Nice place you got here." McSween let his normally guarded gaze sweep the impressive panorama.

"Isn't it?"

Newlin didn't stand—he reserved that formality for guests, not employees. The blue smoke from his cigar drifted lazily in the slight breeze. He observed a flicker of admiration in McSween's eyes and felt one corner of his mouth lift in a smile. Even the reserved McSween was impressed. Good. Putting him at a disadvantage had been Newlin's plan from the start.

The observatory was situated on a flat ledge about two-thirds up the side of the mountain. Three stone benches, strategically arranged in a semicircle, afforded the occupants the best possible view of the entire mining operation. The different-sized buildings, with their various purposes, had been built into the side of the mountain, one on top of the other.

Directly below the mining operation was Edenville. The houses belonging to the wealthier citizens were clustered in the foothills, Newlin's home being the largest and most ostentatious. The thriving commercial district occupied midtown and on the outskirts was the company-provided housing.

Beyond that stretched endless miles of desert with another mountain range in far distance.

Even the ramshackle community of Eden, a blight on the face of the earth in Newlin's opinion, didn't detract from the spectacular scenery, a blending of both nature's and man's most significant triumphs.

Not a man, or woman for that matter, looked out from the observatory who didn't realize the extent of Newlin's power, appreciate it, and concede to it.

"I'm glad to see you're in good health this morning. I was concerned you might be dead," Newlin said as they took a seat on the benches.

McSween's head spun around. "Where did you get that idea?"

Newlin complimented himself on once again hitting the nail on the head. "You spent the night in Eden. Men have been shot for less."

"My staying in Eden doesn't concern you."

"*Everything* you do concerns me. Especially when I'm paying handsomely for your time. You missed making your daily report yesterday. I had someone check on your whereabouts and keep checking until you returned."

McSween glanced at Forrester lounging by the buggy. Newlin didn't deny or confirm what the glance implied.

"I went to Eden to follow up on a lead."

"And following up on this lead took all night," Newlin stated rather than asked.

"No."

"What did, pray tell? And don't insult my intelligence by telling me it was a good night's sleep."

"I slept some."

"You expect me to believe the women of Eden let you, a stranger, spend the night in their midst?"

"I don't recall saying I spent the night there."

"My informant told me—"

"Your informant is wrong." McSween ground out the words.

A show of emotion, Newlin thought with mild interest. He debated pushing the issue further, but let it drop. Whoever's bed McSween had shared really didn't matter.

"Tell me about your lead." Newlin listened intently as McSween filled him in on an Irish miner supposedly working at the Vista Linda Mine.

"I'd like to visit the mine," McSween said. "See what information I can dig up on this Rory O'Shea fellow."

"Naturally. I'll have Forrester make the arrangements. You can leave this afternoon."

Newlin smiled. He forgot all about forcing McSween to fall in line. He forgot all about showing him who exactly was in charge and threatening him with a sound firing if he didn't change his attitude.

Instead, Newlin thought about the robber leader with the Irish accent. The bastard hadn't settled for simply emptying Newlin's pockets of cash. No, he'd humiliated him in front of dozens of people. Not once, but twice. Hundreds more had heard the tales and dared to laugh at Newlin behind his back.

Fury at the indignation he'd suffered consumed him until it ruled his every thought and action. Fury and a powerful thirst for revenge. He could almost feel the robber's scrawny neck between his fingers, the flesh giving and the fragile bones snapping as he squeezed harder and harder.

"Whatever it takes, McSween, you find O'Shea." Newlin dropped his cigar and crushed it to a pulp with the heel of his boot. "And when you do, bring him to me. I have a score to settle with the bastard before you turn him over to the authorities."

"Get away from there, you little hoodlums!" Mr. Abernathy chased a trio of young boys away from the candy display, almost losing the sack of cornmeal he balanced on his shoulder. "If I catch you stealing again, I'll blister your hides."

The boys bolted toward the door with Mr. Abernathy hot on their heels. He stopped at the doorway long enough to grab the buggy whip he kept in an umbrella stand for just such occasions. Stepping out onto the verandah, he lifted his free arm and snapped the whip in the general direction of the fleeing boys. They scampered away, stuffing pilfered gumdrops in their mouths and poking fun at his bad aim. Lucky for them, Mr. Abernathy couldn't hit the broad side of a barn.

Maddie watched the goings on from a few feet away. She'd been bent over, cleaning the inside of a pickle barrel with a stiff brush. The barrel stunk, and slime had stained her hands a disgusting shade of greenish-brown. She silently thanked the children for creating a diversion and allowing her to straighten up and breath some fresh air—if only for a few moments.

"What are you staring at?" Mr. Abernathy barked at her. "Get back to work." He returned the buggy whip to its place in the umbrella stand, repositioned the cornmeal on his shoulder, and headed toward the counter where customers waited.

Maddie shot a murderous look at her boss's back and imagined another use for the buggy whip. He'd been a pain in her side since she'd come in to work, giving her every menial and degrading task he could think of, such as scrubbing the pickle barrel and cleaning up mouse dung in the stockroom. Punishment, she supposed, for missing work yesterday.

Despite sending word that her daughter had been injured and having Dora present herself as Maddie's temporary replacement, Mr. Abernathy remained angry and determined to take it out on her. Certainly Maddie's threat to expose his embezzling scheme to Thaddeus Newlin hadn't endeared the store owner to her.

If she didn't need her job so badly, she'd . . . what? Quit? Hardly. She *did* need her job, for the wages, paltry as they were, and for the valuable information she was able to get from eavesdropping on customers. Information that had come in handy more than once during the robberies, including the one the women had scheduled for tonight.

An impromptu visit from Levi Jacobson, one of the wealthier minority partners, had dropped opportunity in their laps. Not trusting banks, the elderly gentleman habitually carried large sums of cash and, because of his tendency to imbibe large quantities of wine, he'd proved an easy mark when the women had first robbed him some months earlier.

With Scott McSween away visiting the Vista Linda Mine, the timing couldn't be more perfect. Maddie pushed thoughts of Scott and the wild goose chase she'd sent him on to a far corner of her mind. Right now, she had to focus on the robbery.

After learning of the Jacobsons' impending arrival in Edenville yesterday and Scott's departure—both pieces of news courtesy of their secret source—Lavinia had called an emergency council meeting and plans were quickly made. The council agreed to let Maddie participate in the robbery, and for that she was glad. If all went well, and she prayed it did, she'd be back in their good graces by tomorrow.

Constance sidled up beside Maddie and whispered, "I heard Mrs. Newlin say she expected their guests to stay until ten this evening." Constance had spent considerable time waiting on Newlin's pampered wife, grinding coffee beans to her exact specifications, helping her select candles for their solid gold candelabra, and choosing after-dinner sweets guaranteed to please the most discriminating palate.

"Did she mention what time her guests were arriving for dinner?" Maddie whispered back.

"Not exactly. But she did say dinner would be served at eight."

Maddie nodded, running an imaginary scenario in her mind. "If they arrive at seven and stay until ten, they'll be drunk as skunks when they return to the hotel."

Mr. Jacobson's first wife had died several years previous. His second wife, younger than he by a good two decades, shared his penchant for wine. As long as their hosts were pouring, the Jacobsons partook.

"Did someone send a message to Gertrude?" Maddie asked.

"This morning."

The easy conversation between her and Constance was an act. They hadn't mended their fences. By mutual agreement, however, they'd set their argument aside for another day. Feeding and clothing the citizens of Eden took precedent.

"Granny Fay will bring Dora when she makes the last run to town." Constance helped Maddie turn the pickle barrel over and roll it to a place near the window to dry. "She'll have our clothes and guns with her."

Sneaking into the Jacobsons' hotel room was risky, even disguised as men. Unfortunately, Mr. Jacobson was not a trusting enough soul to leave his money in the hotel room while they were out. But it wouldn't be the first time they'd attempted such a daring feat. Gertrude Michaelson's position as a maid in the hotel had benefitted them in the past and would do so again tonight. She'd use her master key to sneak Maddie, Constance, and Dora into the Jacobsons' room after the couple had, God willing, fallen into a drunken sleep.

"Hey, you two!" Mr. Abernathy shouted from across the store. "Get back to work. Maddie, if you're done with the pickle barrel, you can sweep the cobwebs from the ceiling."

Maddie groaned and, flashing Constance a tired smile, went scouting for a long-handled broom. Last week, her friend would have commiserated and uttered encouragements. But not today, and the sorrow Maddie carried around inside her over their troubled friendship grew a little heavier.

When she came out of the supply pantry, broom in hand, she saw Constance talking to a disreputable-looking man. Maddie lifted the broom to the ceiling and started sweeping cobwebs, but she continued to cast furtive glances at Constance and her customer.

He'd been in the store before. She recognized him as one of Newlin's men and thought his name was Jonesy. The majority partner kept a group of thugs on the payroll. They did everything from running errands, to guarding important shipments, to maintaining order among the miners. And they weren't above using their fists. It was clear they felt their position afforded them certain liberties with the law and the female population. The sheriff, also on Newlin's payroll, turned a blind eye.

"What time are you finished here, darlin'?" The man leaned in closer to Constance, his lewd grin revealing a row of crooked and discolored teeth. "I figure maybe you and me could get together later."

"No, thank you." Constance made an attempt to pass him.

"Hey, where you going?" The man blocked her retreat down another aisle. "I'm just being sociable." His grin transformed from friendly to predatory. "Can't you be polite and return the favor?"

"I said no, thank you." To her credit, she put up a brave front.

Maddie wished she held a rifle instead of a broom. It infuriated her when men made inappropriate advances toward the women of Eden. They assumed the lack of husbands made them fair game.

She glanced around the store. Mr. Abernathy was busy selling garden seed to the wife of one of the German farmers who'd recently settled in the area. Not that he'd be any help. Snow would fall in hell before he'd go up against Newlin's man. No one else in the store appeared to notice or care. Maddie's infuriation compounded.

The man reached a grubby hand up to fondle Constance's cheek.

She recoiled at the brazen impropriety. "Don't touch me."

"Come on, darlin'." He cupped her chin and tilted her face to him when she tried to avert her head. "I promise you won't be sorry."

She jerked backward, her eyes huge and filled with revulsion. He frowned and grabbed her arm, hauling her to him. Maddie could see his fingers digging into Constance's flesh, and her own fingers tightened on the broom handle.

"Where are you going in such a hurry?" he crooned, putting his thick lips next to Constance's ear.

She made a sound both angry and scared and slammed her foot down hard on his. He howled and momentarily lost his balance. Constance seized the moment and fled. He caught up with her in two strides, grabbing her thick braid and using it like a lasso to reel her in.

"Get back here, you bitch."

Maddie didn't hesitate. "Let go of her!" She wielded the broom like a club and advanced, prepared to strike.

The man pivoted, took one look at her, and burst out laughing. "What do you think you're gonna do with that? Sweep me under the carpet?" He shook his head in amused disbelief, still holding on to Constance, who whimpered and pulled at his hands in a vain attempt to extricate herself.

People in the store were looking at last. Maddie could feel their stares, hear their muffled gasps, sense their shock. Yet no one attempted to intervene, proving once again just how far Newlin's arm reached in Edenville.

"I told you to let go of her, and I meant it." Maddie didn't know what she'd do with the broom, but she refused to let him intimidate her. She raised her makeshift weapon higher. If she aimed just right, and the man's reflexes were on the slow side, she might be able to incapacitate him with a blow to the side of his head.

The man swung Constance in a wide arc, his reflexes unquestionably and frighteningly quick. She cried out as she bashed into stacked dry goods and stumbled to her knees. Without thinking, Maddie rushed forward.

"Get back," he growled, and pulled Constance up sharply, using her as a shield. His other hand went for the gun he wore at his side.

At the distinct sound of a trigger being cocked, he froze. So did Maddie and Constance.

"I believe the lady made it clear she's not interested."

Scott stood just inside the open doorway of the store, his Colt revolver leveled at the man's head. The outstretched arm holding the weapon didn't so much as twitch, and his gray eyes glinted with ice-cold contempt. He appeared to grow in size with each passing second until his form completely filled the doorway.

Everything about him, from his uncompromising stance to his implacable expression, said he'd killed before—and would do so again if pushed.

Mr. Abernathy took one look at him and slunk off around a corner, having no backbone and no taste for violence.

Maddie ignored her boss. Stunned into immobility, she gaped at Scott. Was it possible this hard, inexorable man was the same one who had shown her small daughter such tenderness and compassion? The same one who had kissed her with complete abandon? Her heart found it impossible to accept what her eyes told her was true.

"Release the lady now," Scott said, his voice every bit as deadly as the gun in his hand.

"You ain't gonna shoot me." The man's mouth curled back in an ugly sneer. "Not if you want to keep your job."

Scott stepped closer. "You willing to bet your life on it?"

Evidently not. After a long moment, during which everything came to an eerie standstill, the thug released Constance, pushing her from him with an angry thrust. She dropped to the floor, gathered her braid to her chest, and crawled away. Maddie rushed toward her and when they were a safe distance from the man, helped her to her feet. Constance shook from head to toe.

"Mr. Newlin's gonna hear about this." The man righted his hat, which had been knocked sideways in the scuffle, and then wiped a line of spittle from his mouth with the back of his hand. "And he won't like it."

Scott somehow managed to convey a shrug without moving a muscle. "If I were Newlin, I wouldn't like hearing that one of my employees accosted a lady in public, either."

"Lady?" The man choked out a derisive laugh and leered at Maddie and Constance. "They're nothing but whores. The whole lot of them."

For some inexplicable reason, Maddie felt like the man knew all about her and Scott kissing. Shame filled her, and when Constance met her gaze, Maddie's cheeks burned.

Her friend's expression, however, was neither condemning nor judgmental. "Thank you for helping me," she said.

The simple statement of gratitude affected Maddie profoundly, and she gave Constance a quick hug.

"If you have no other business here, I suggest you leave and allow these ladies to return to their work." Scott had yet to holster his gun.

"We ain't done, McSween. Not by a long shot." The man rounded on Maddie and Constance, redirecting his anger and hatred at them. "And we ain't done, either. You can count on it. No two-bit whores are gonna get the better of me." He stormed off, his jangling spurs an angry accompaniment to his pounding footsteps.

Only when he was completely through the door did

Scott holster his gun. The lack of a weapon didn't make him appear any less imposing or threatening.

He was her adversary, Maddie had known that from the beginning. What she hadn't fully taken into account was the very real danger he presented. His job was to capture the robbers. And after today, it was evident he had no reservations about killing them, either. She couldn't stop her knees from knocking together beneath her skirt.

Who would take care of Josephine if anything happened to her? Not for the first time Maddie wondered whether the dangerous path she'd chosen for herself was the right one.

Scott came to her and Constance, still every inch the lawman. "Are you all right, ma'am? Did he hurt you?"

"No, I'm fine," Constance answered meekly, visibly in awe of Scott. She might dislike and distrust him, but he'd also just spared her a most loathsome ordeal—and did it by intimidating a town bully. "I . . . we . . ."

"We are indebted to you, Mr. McSween," Maddie finished for her. Then added, "Again."

"My pleasure." He gave Maddie and her broom a thorough once over. "Though I'm not sure you needed my help." Amusement tinged his voice, softening his appearance.

"You overestimate my abilities."

All amusement fled. He stared her straight in the face. "You're wrong about that."

Maddie's stomach knotted. He had to be referring to the Vista Linda Mine and the ruse she'd pulled on him. His steely eyes, which two nights ago had been bright and alive with unbridled desire, burned into her. She nearly wilted beneath them, but held her own by conjuring a picture of Josephine's innocent young face in her mind.

"All right, everyone." Mr. Abernathy came out of hiding and paraded through the store, encouraging customers to return to their shopping. "Show's over. Maddie and Constance, back to work."

Justified or not, he held them responsible for the disturbance. But he wouldn't berate them in front of Scott. The company store manager had a healthy respect for anyone with a gun.

Maddie walked with Constance and gave an imperceptible nod toward the stockroom. It was where they met when they needed a few minutes' privacy at work. Scott's early return from the Vista Linda Mine had impacted their plans for robbing the Jacobsons tonight, and a discussion was in order.

"Maddie," Scott said from behind them. "Do you have a minute?"

She jerked to a stop, as did Constance. They exchanged worried glances from beneath lowered lashes before Maddie silently urged Constance to move ahead.

"Are you sure? I can stay."

"I'll be fine."

Maddie waited several moments, as much for her friend to get out of earshot as to bolster her courage.

Scott had found her out. What other reason could he have for wanting to talk to her?

Polite smile firmly in place, she spun around to find him standing directly behind her. She didn't remember him following her.

Swallowing down a surge of sudden panic, she said, "Yes?"

Chapter Twelve

Beef stew, corn bread lathered with butter, and applesauce. Maddie stared at the untouched bounty before her. If there were such a thing as ambrosia for the gods, this was surely it. She hesitated, spoon in hand. Consuming such a magnificent meal didn't seem right, not when so many others in Eden were going hungry.

"Hurry up and eat before your food gets cold." Delilah hovered near the table where Maddie, Constance, and Dora sat taking their supper. It stood in the center of Delilah's parlor, one of three rooms in her suite at the Strike It Rich Saloon. The town madam must have read Maddie's mind, for she chided, "If you don't, the maid will just toss it out. And you'd hate for that to happen."

Maddie *would* hate seeing food go to waste. She dipped her spoon into the rich stew and tried to remember the last time she'd eaten beef stew. Not since the accident, before the scarlet fever epidemic struck. Friends and neighbors had dropped by her and

William's small house to offer their condolences, many of them bringing food. Her entire kitchen table had been laden to overflowing. What she would give to have even half that food now . . .

"Eat," Delilah coaxed again.

Dora was the first to surrender. She took a large bite of stew and chewed, slowly at first, then hungrily. "Oh, dear Lord. Thank you, thank you." In the middle of her second spoonful, she began to cry. "This is good, Delilah. Really good." She ignored her tears in favor of trying the applesauce. "I swear, I've died and gone to heaven."

"I'm glad you like it." Delilah smiled fondly at her guests. "Cook is quite good, actually. I hear he trained in New Orleans. Lulu," she said, "fetch our guests some whiskey."

The former Eden resident rose from lounging on the velvet upholstered settee and sashayed over to the side table where a variety of liquors were stored in crystal decanters. Her hair had been artfully pinned atop her head, and her silk gown clung seductively as she walked.

"I need to go downstairs soon," Lulu said. "Customers are waiting and Fat Mike'll be mad if I don't hurry."

It was an excuse. Maddie could hear it in Lulu's voice. *She doesn't want to be here with us.*

Lulu had changed so much in the last year. She was nothing like the sweet, timid thing who had once bubbled with joy at the prospect of being newly married and expecting her first baby. She'd lost both husband and baby within weeks of each other. Working at the Strike It Rich wasn't the life Maddie would have chosen, but she couldn't be too harsh on poor Lulu. Everyone dealt with grief in their own fashion.

And Maddie was in no position to cast stones. Lulu might have turned to a life of prostitution, but Maddie had turned to a life of crime.

"We should save some," Constance said. She and Maddie had both started on their meals, savoring every bite. "For the children."

Delilah had informed Fat Mike that she was entertaining a gentleman in her rooms and to have supper sent up. She was, in fact, entertaining three gentlemen. Maddie, Constance, and Dora had changed into their disguises shortly after being snuck into Delilah's rooms.

"Assuming you were able to get the food to Eden, how many would it feed?" Delilah asked. "There's barely enough for the three of you." Taking the decanter from Lulu, she poured generous dollops of whiskey into the women's cups of hot tea. Real tea from China, nothing like the bitter homemade brews Maddie and the others were accustomed to drinking.

"It's not right," Constance protested.

"Nonsense." Delilah wasn't being mean, just practical. "You need your strength for tonight. I'm sure no one in Eden will begrudge you a decent supper, particularly when you bring them home a bundle of cash."

"I'm not so sure we should go through with the robbery." Maddie said. She was surprised to look down and see half her meal gone. Had she even bothered to pause between mouthfuls?

"Why not?" Dora demanded. Her tears had ceased, though her cheeks remained wet and bits of food clung to the corners of her mouth. She was evidently too busy eating to bother with trivial matters such as wiping her face.

"McSween returned early from his trip to the Vista Linda Mine," Maddie explained. "When we first planned this robbery, it was with the understanding he'd be out of town."

"I don't see what difference it makes."

"He'll be watching the Jacobsons." Maddie used the last morsel of corn bread to sop her bowl clean. "That's his job."

"Does he even know the Jacobsons are dining with the Newlins tonight?" Dora asked. "Seeing as he just got back this afternoon."

"He does if he's any good."

"He *is* good." Constance twirled her spoon. "We have to be careful."

Maddie studied Constance from behind her cup of tea and whiskey. What was her friend thinking about? The incident at the company store earlier that afternoon, or when Scott had visited Eden and stayed all night? Both? Constance was right to advocate caution. Scott had proved more than once how dangerous he could be—and not just with a gun.

"What did he say to you in the company store?" Delilah asked Maddie. She glided over to the side table and poured herself a whiskey. Straight. No tea.

Lulu had again retired to the settee. She seemed distracted and more melancholy than usual. She'd also been drinking heavily. Did being with her old friends bring back too many unhappy memories? Perhaps she felt the wide chasm that had grown between them as sharply as Maddie did.

Delilah tapped Maddie on the shoulder and repeated herself. "What did McSween say to you in the company store?"

"He . . . ah . . ." She blinked and shook her head. "He apologized."

"For what?"

"Causing problems the other day at Eden."

"Really? What kind of problems?" Delilah's face lit with curiosity. "And what was he doing at Eden? Is he on to you?"

Maddie suddenly found her empty stew bowl fascinating. She recalled her brief conversation with Scott at the store. It had been nothing like what she'd expected, and she was still reeling inside from the aftereffects. She'd assumed he'd uncovered her deception about the Irish miner and intended to confront her. But he hadn't. He'd merely said he was sorry for taking advantage of her and promised it wouldn't happen again.

After a long moment, during which she'd died any number of small deaths, she stupidly mumbled, "Is that all?"

In reply, he'd given her a curious look and said, "What else is there?"

Everything afterward had been a blur. She must have excused herself, or he did, for the next thing Maddie remembered, they were bidding farewell at the store entrance. The thought that he wasn't going to expose her should have reassured her, but it had the opposite effect.

Scott McSween did nothing without good reason.

She tried to push her worries aside and concentrate on Delilah's question. "If he's suspicious of us, he didn't give any indication."

"Why was he at Eden?"

"The sheriff told him William spoke with an Irish accent, and McSween came to see if there was a connection between him and the Irish robber. I concocted a story about another miner, also from Ireland, who worked at the Vista Linda Mine."

"And then McSween left?"

"Yes."

Constance and Dora didn't offer to elaborate on Maddie's tale, for which she was grateful.

"And he felt he needed to apologize for this?" Delilah was a busybody by nature and not one to be sidetracked.

"Apparently."

She huffed indignantly. "You don't expect me to believe—"

The clock on the fireplace mantel chimed, sparing Maddie further interrogation.

"It's ten o'clock," Constance said. "We should hurry. Gertrude's waiting to let us into the Jacobsons' room."

The women's plan was to bind and gag the Jacobsons and leave them for the maid to find in the morning, unhurt and many hundred, if not thousand, dollars poorer.

After the robbery, Gertrude would escort the women back to the vacant room where she'd hidden their clothes. There, they'd change into their dresses and escape to Eden on foot. Maddie didn't much like the idea of the three of them walking first through town and then the mile across the desert in the middle of the night—alone and carrying a substantial sum of cash. But using the surrey was out of the question. And, Maddie reminded herself, they'd be well armed.

"Are you sure we should go through with this?" Maddie asked. Since encountering Scott in the company store and realizing he'd returned early from his trip, she'd been plagued with an unshakable and dire sense of foreboding. "It's not too late to back out."

"This is our only chance." Dora stood, yanking on the rope belt holding up her too-large pants. "The Jacobsons are leaving tomorrow for California."

"I agree." Constance also stood.

Only Maddie remained seated.

"You all right, love?" Delilah asked.

"I'm fine."

But she wasn't. The food she'd eaten, which had tasted so good going down, sat like a lead weight in her stomach.

Scott *must* have uncovered the truth about the Irish miner. Why else would he have returned a day early? And why hadn't he'd hauled her in to the sheriff's office for questioning like any other suspect?

He was up to something, he had to be. And not knowing what—was killing Maddie.

"Sweet Lord in heaven," Dora proclaimed in a hushed whisper. "That man can snore." She'd recently finished tying Mr. Jacobson's ankles together and stood at the foot of the bed, inspecting her handiwork. "How do you reckon his wife gets any sleep?"

"Shhh." Constance jerked her head toward Mrs. Jacobson, whose scared eyes followed their every move.

"Sorry," Dora muttered through the kerchief covering her face.

Mrs. Jacobson lay on the bed next to her husband. They were both fully clothed, hog-tied, and gagged. Mr. Jacobson had passed out cold some minutes earlier, the victim of a drunken stupor. He'd put up little resistance when faced with the business end of Maddie's Colt pistol, handing over his money as if he'd fully expected to be robbed.

For a change, his wife had imbibed considerably less than her usual. She was more alert than they had expected and hence, more dangerous. When Mrs. Jacobson had started to scream, Constance had no choice but to quiet her with a swift right hook to the chin.

The minority partner's wife had roused a few minutes later, a rag stuffed in her mouth and ropes binding her wrists and ankles. But being unable to move or speak didn't stop her from watching them and listening to their every word.

"Blindfold her," Constance ordered in a gruff masculine-sounding voice.

Locating a scarf in Mrs. Jacobson's trunk, Dora carried out Constance's instructions, chiding herself for not thinking of blindfolding Mrs. Jacobson first. She sometimes doubted she'd ever get the hang of being a real criminal. It baffled her sometimes why Maddie had recruited her in the first place. Now *there* was someone with a whole heap of natural talent.

"How much we get?" Dora asked Constance. She was careful to disguise her voice, too.

Constance carefully folded the money they'd taken from Mr. Jacobson and put it in the leather pouch tied to her belt. "Two hundred and eighteen dollars," she whispered.

"Is that all!"

Constance shot Dora a look that said she'd be the next one gagged if she didn't shut up.

Dora grimaced apologetically. She hadn't meant to be so loud. But the money wasn't nearly as much as they'd hoped for and less than half of the amount they'd taken the first time they robbed Mr. Jacobson. Maybe, thought Dora, his spoiled wife had spent the money that afternoon on a fancy new dress or new shoes.

Still, $218 would buy bolts of chambray and wool, buttons, needles, and thread. All things the women desperately needed. Being dirt poor, thought Dora, had no effect on the rate at which children grew. They sprouted up like cornstalks and were always needing new clothes to replace the ones they'd outgrown. Even the hand-me-downs were in short supply.

"Hurry," Maddie growled. She guarded the door, her spine ramrod straight and her pistol raised, ready to shoot if someone should burst into the room.

It didn't take one of them gypsy fortune-tellers to see something had been bothering Maddie all night. She flinched at the least little noise and twice let out a gasp when Dora accidentally bumped into her.

It was no wonder why she was jumpier than usual about pulling off this robbery. Dora knew how much Maddie wanted to prove herself and regain the council's trust. Or, more likely, it was that private investigator, Scott McSween.

Though Dora had defended Maddie at the council meeting, she wasn't altogether sure she'd have done the same thing in her friend's place. McSween was a handsome devil, no argument there. But if he weren't trouble with a capital *T*, Dora would eat Mrs. Jacobson's lace-trimmed slippers for breakfast.

"I wish 'you know who' would hurry up and get here," Dora whispered. She stowed the rags and rope they hadn't needed in the burlap sack she'd brought with her from Eden.

"Quiet." Constance jabbed Dora with her elbow.

She sighed. They had to wait for Gertrude to fetch them. If met in the hall by the hotel's night manager, she could always claim a patron had summoned her for some menial task. But three strange men walking about at eleven o'clock at night would, without a doubt, garner attention.

At a loud thud, they all spun in the direction of the bed. Maddie raised her gun, finger poised on the trigger.

Constance held up a hand, signaling them to wait. She took a step forward.

Mrs. Jacobson lay on the floor beside the bed. She wriggled, the heels of her shoes scraping the wood floor and making enough noise for a small crowd.

Maddie wasn't so rattled she couldn't be counted on to do her job. She flew across the room and went down beside Mrs. Jacobson, pressing the barrel of her gun to the woman's forehead. In her late husband's Irish accent, she hissed, "Quit yer moving right this second, or I'll blow yer brains out."

Well, thought Dora, *that did the trick.*

Mrs. Jacobson went immediately still and uttered a series of squeaks, which Dora took the liberty of translating to mean, "Don't shoot, I'll be good."

The woman needn't worry—Maddie wasn't going to kill her. A gunshot would bring people running. The last thing Maddie, Constance, and Dora wanted was a lot of people anywhere near the Jacobsons' room. But they weren't about to tell that to Mrs. Jacobson.

Grabbing her by her dress collar, Maddie hauled the other woman to her knees. Not an easy feat, considering Mrs. Jacobson's wrists and ankles were bound.

At a rap on the door, time and motion came to a stop for everyone—the possible exception being Mr. Jacobson who continued to snore in blithe ignorance. Dora, Maddie, and Constance exchanged frantic glances. Who could it be? Not Gertrude. Not this soon.

The knock came again, stronger and sharper.

Fear pulsated through Dora, and the burlap sack fell from her limp fingers. She scrambled to retrieve it, biting the inside of her mouth to prevent herself from blurting an apology.

"It's Scott McSween, Mr. and Mrs. Jacobson," came a voice through the door.

Holy mother of Jesus! What were they going to do?

"Are you all right?" he said. "I heard a noise."

The brass doorknob turned and jiggled. Dora's heart knocked against the insides of her ribs.

They'd secured the lock, hadn't they? She couldn't remember, her mind having gone completely blank. Her gaze sought Maddie's. She was their leader, she must know what to do.

And, thank God, she did.

Maddie hoisted Mrs. Jacobson to her feet, the pistol still shoved in the side of her head. Unfortunately, they made considerable noise in the process.

"Mr. and Mrs. Jacobson!" McSween's voice increased in volume, and he jiggled the doorknob again. Harder. "Answer me, please."

For one awful second, Dora was convinced he'd kick down the door. Then where would they be? If one of them didn't do something fast . . .

"Tell him ye and yer darling husband are simply lovely," Maddie hissed in Mrs. Jacobson's ear while working the knot on her gag.

"Please," Mrs. Jacobson whimpered when she could finally talk. "Don—"

Maddie silenced her with a hard yank on her hair and a jab in the back of her neck with the pistol. "Tell McSween yer fine, or I'll pull the trigger," she said in a threatening voice that raised goose bumps on Dora's arms.

Mrs. Jacobson promptly slumped into a dead faint. Maddie couldn't support the other woman, and she slid to the floor, taking Maddie along with her.

The door shook and groaned as if someone—a big, strong someone—had thrust their shoulder into it.

McSween!

"Ah . . . ah . . . y-y-yes. We're . . . f-fine." Dora couldn't believe her own ears. Was that her speaking? The words, their pitch unnaturally high and thin, had erupted from her mouth without conscious thought. "Th-thank you, Mr. McSween, for checking on us."

She pulled down her kerchief and inched toward the door, looking to her cohorts for guidance. An owl-eyed Constance gawked at Dora, offering no help. Maddie, in the process of untangling herself from an unconscious Mrs. Jacobson, nodded her approval, bolstering Dora's flagging courage.

"Are you sure?" McSween was no dunce. His uncertainty penetrated the barrier of the wooden door loud and clear.

Dora cleared her throat and endeavored to sound more like the refined Mrs. Jacobson.

"Of course," she trilled. "We had a slight mishap is all. Mr. Jacobson . . . uh . . . overindulged this evening. He does like his wine. We were . . . He . . . ah . . . Well, let's just say his ambitions exceeded his abilities," she added with a bright laugh. "I'm afraid he accidentally tumbled out of bed."

Constance covered her mouth with her arm and buried a cough in her shirt sleeve while Maddie grinned.

"All right," McSween said with a noticeable lack of conviction.

"I'll be sure to inform Mr. Newlin of your concern for our well being."

"If you need anything, just holler. I'm right across the hall."

Across the hall! If Dora weren't such a God-fearing Christian, she'd have let loose with a string of curses.

After several false starts, she managed a frail, "Thank you. It is truly a comfort knowing you're so close."

"Good night, ma'am."

"Good night."

Dora pressed a palm to her forehead. It was damp with perspiration. So were her underarms. In a delayed reaction, the bones in her legs turned to jelly.

"Well done," Maddie whispered.

Constance reached out and jostled Dora's arm. Her expression asked, *Are you crazy?*

"It worked, didn't it? He's gone." Suddenly giddy, Dora could have laughed with relief. Maybe she *was* cut out to be a criminal at that.

Mrs. Jacobson came slowly awake, her whimpers bringing a fast end to the argument.

Maddie lowered her head close to Mrs. Jacobson's. "Shut yer trap."

She delivered a warning shove to Mrs. Jacobson with the point of her gun before holstering it and climbing to her feet. She left their prisoner where she lay on the floor and gathered Dora and Constance into a huddle on the opposite side of the small room.

"We can't afford to wait for Gertrude," she whispered. "Not with McSween across the hall. Rest assured he's listening for anything out of the ordinary."

"What'd'ya reckon we do?" Dora asked. "Climb out the window?" She didn't much like heights, but she'd gladly do what was required of her.

Maddie's glance darted from Constance to Dora and back again. "I'll distract him," she finally said. "Keep him busy while you two get away with Gertrude and the money."

"No," Constance stammered.

"Yes. It's our only chance."

"Too risky." She shook her head insistently.

"I can handle McSween."

Dora didn't dispute that.

"He's already suspicious," Constance pressed. "If he

decides to check on the Jacobsons, he might put two and two together and have you arrested."

"Let him. While the sheriff is questioning me, you two and Gertrude can escape."

"Mrs. Jacobson will tell the sheriff about us."

"Mrs. Jacobson will tell the sheriff three men robbed her and her husband."

"I . . ." Constance prodded a deep gouge in the wooden floor with the toe of her boot. "I'd hate for something to happen to you."

"I'll be fine," Maddie gently assured her. "I swear."

Dora couldn't help grinning. She sent a silent prayer heavenward, thankful at having witnessed the beginnings of a reconciliation between her two friends.

"How you going to distract McSween?" she asked Maddie after a moment. "One look at you in that getup, and he'll figure out right quick things ain't what they should be."

"I think Mrs. Jacobson can help us with that particular problem." Maddie evaluated their hostage, one eyebrow raised and her mouth pursed. "She and I are about the same dress size, wouldn't you say?"

"Yes." Dora's grin deepened. She had caught on to what her partner was implying and approved. God forgive her, but she really was getting quite good at being a criminal.

Maddie had never handled such a beautiful dress, much less worn one. The lavender material, light and airy and incredibly soft, felt like it had been woven from clouds. Ironically, the dress she'd selected to wear was by far the plainest one in Mrs. Jacobson's trunk. Yet, compared to Maddie's course homespun garments, it was fit for a princess.

The waist was large, the hemline short, and the bodice more than a little snug. The multitude of tiny buttons down the front had not quite closed over her breasts, and three were left undone. A search of the Jacobson's hotel room produced a fringed cotton shawl which, when carefully arranged, hid the opening.

"How's Mrs. Jacobson?" Maddie asked in a whisper, slipping into a pair of the woman's shoes that, by some miracle, fit. The leather was the softest, most supple Maddie's toes ever had the good fortune to nestle against.

"Quiet as a church mouse." Dora winked impishly.

After considerable debate, they'd settled on shoving the blindfolded and gagged minority partner's wife under the bed. For his part, Mr. Jacobson continued to oblige them. Stretched out from one end of the mattress to the other, he snored loud enough to rattle the glass globe on the dimly burning lantern. It was unlikely Mrs. Jacobson could hear much of anything over her husband's nighttime serenade. Still, they spoke softly.

It hadn't been the easiest of robberies, and Maddie prayed their luck would hold out just a little longer.

A rapping on the hotel room door had the three of them jerking in surprise.

They breathed a collective sigh of relief when the rap was followed by several more. It was Gertrude, using a prearranged series of knocks to identify herself. Maddie moved toward the door, but Constance intercepted her.

"Better let me answer it," she whispered. "No telling what she might do when she sees you in that dress."

Maddie stepped aside. The material of the dress floated around her legs, and she couldn't resist smoothing the generous folds with her hand. What would it be like to wear such finery every day? She could only imagine.

Cracking open the door, Constance peered out, then eased it just wide enough for Gertrude to slip inside the room. Fulfilling Constance's prediction, Gertrude got one look at Maddie and uttered a bewildered, "Oh, my!"

"Hush," Constance warned her, then went on to explain in a low voice. "We've had a change of plans. McSween is staying in the room across the hall."

"I know." Solid and sturdy and a full head taller than anyone else in the room, Gertrude could, and had, licked many a man. The rest, she scared off with a well-practiced scowl. Beneath her imposing exterior, however, existed a kind and generous spirit. "He switched rooms tonight to be near the Jacobsons. There was no way to send you a message, or I would have. Did he see you?"

"Not exactly." Maddie stepped forward so that their conversation could be conducted more discretely. "He came to the door earlier. Dora pretended to be Mrs. Jacobson and sent him away."

"That's good."

"He'll be back. It's his job to protect the Jacobsons." She tugged on the shawl, which had slipped from her shoulder. "I'm going to distract him while you, Constance, and Dora get away as planned."

"Maddie, no! The council—"

"I'll be fine." She clasped Gertrude by the shoulders. "You just get them and the money to safety. I'm depending on you. So is everyone else."

"All right."

Maddie steeled her resolve as she had a thousand

times previously in her twenty-three years and headed toward the door. Agitation built inside her, not all of it from the robbery. In a matter of minutes, she would be alone with Scott in his hotel room. That, and the fact she'd make any sacrifice necessary to safeguard her friends and the money, was enough to start her pulse racing.

"Take care," Constance cautioned. "Don't think you have to place yourself in . . . a compromising position to save us. We'll be all right."

Maddie nodded. "I'll be fine. Trust me."

"I do."

She cleared her throat, a rush of emotions at Constance's declaration of faith in her having clogged it. "Wait until I've been gone at least a quarter hour before you leave," she instructed them. "That should give me enough time."

"Time for what?" Dora asked.

"I'm not sure yet." And she had only the minute it took to walk across the hall to Scott's room to think of something.

Chapter Thirteen

"Maddie. What are you doing here?" Scott stood in the doorway of his hotel room, wide awake and fully dressed except for his hat, casually confident as always. Behind him, a lantern on the bedside table glowed softly.

He hadn't been sleeping.

She'd assumed as much, yet seeing him sent a burst of adrenaline coursing through her.

"Do you have any idea how late it is?" he asked.

His expression revealed little, least of all surprise at seeing her. Was he used to women showing up at his door, or had he been expecting her? Maddie didn't like either possibility.

"Did I disturb you?"

"Not at all," he replied.

He extended no invitation for her to enter, and Maddie couldn't afford to wait much longer. Scott mustn't see Constance, Dora, and Gertrude leaving. She had to get him inside and quickly.

"Are you . . . alone?" she asked.

"Yes." He still didn't move, forcing her to be blunt.

"May I come in?"

"Maddie . . ."

He didn't say it, but she could hear the unspoken admonition nonetheless. Proper ladies didn't visit gentlemen in their hotel rooms, especially unchaperoned and late at night. Well, Maddie wasn't proper and hadn't been for quite some time. Not since Thaddeus Newlin refused to pay the death benefits and back wages for the men who died in his mine. Fighting every day solely to survive didn't leave room for proprieties.

"Please," she implored. There was so much at stake. Money and lives. Hundreds of lives, including her daughter's and those of her three friends across the hall.

His eyebrows shot up at her entreaty. For one anxious moment, she thought he was going to refuse. Fear rippled through her. Then he stepped aside, his expression again schooled to reveal nothing. "By all means, come in."

Air rushed from her lungs as she stepped over the threshold. The door closed behind her with an unnaturally loud click.

Scott was tidy for a man, she noted as she surveyed his room. Like her father. Her late husband William had been born without a single neat inclination, and she'd been forever picking up after him. Stopping abruptly, she chided herself for comparing Scott to the men in her life.

"Why are you here?" he asked.

She started. As before, he'd snuck up behind her undetected.

"I, ah, wanted to talk to you." He was so close. If she

leaned back, she'd be supported by his broad, muscular chest.

Would he envelop her in his arms? Send her good judgment packing again? Make her feel cherished and treasured and, heaven help her, desired? Would he try to kiss her?

"It must be important." He inched closer, his fingertips toying with a wisp of loose hair by her ear.

Her skin tingled and heated in response. "Why do you say that?"

"You took quite a risk coming here."

He had no idea.

"I was careful. No one saw me leave." And no one had, Gertrude made sure of it.

"Good. I wouldn't want you to get in any more trouble."

He smelled nice, clean and faintly of shaving cream. Not sweaty and rank like some. Nor did he douse himself in bay rum. Mr. Jacobson, the old goat, reeked as if he swam in the stuff. The dirty kerchief Maddie had worn over her face hadn't kept the suffocating odor from reaching her nostrils.

"How's Josephine?" he asked.

"She's fine. Fully recovered. And ornery as they come."

Her daughter's sour mood of the last few days hadn't improved, and Maddie was at her wits' end. Another night of leaving her daughter in Granny Fay's custody so soon after the last one hadn't helped, either. Poor little Josephine, always abandoned. If there were any other way . . .

But there wasn't. And Maddie didn't know how to explain, using only gestures and simple words, that she had to leave. Everything Maddie did, she did for

Josephine. Her job at the company store. The robberies. Patrolling Eden. But somehow, providing for and protecting the one person she loved most in the world disappointed and hurt that very same person.

Maddie mentally added selfishness to her growing list of failures. Some days all she wanted was to be unburdened of the heavy responsibilities constantly weighing on her if only for an hour. In the few minutes of Scott's embrace, she had found that freedom.

A noise, the creaking of a door opening perhaps, roused her from her reflections and set her pulse to racing. Had Scott heard it, too? Was her overactive imagination at fault?

Another creak reached her ears, muffled and distant, but unmistakable. Scott stiffened and eased away from her.

No!

She reeled around, so fast he had to catch her to stop her from crashing into him.

"Whoa, there." He stilled her with his strong, capable, and when circumstances required it, deadly hands. "What's the matter?"

"I . . . I . . ."

His thumbs kneaded her flesh, pressing sensual circles into her skin. She had to remind herself he was her enemy, bent on destroying her and all she held dear. She should have recoiled at his touch, but didn't. If anything, she reveled in it.

"Why did you really come here, Maddie? What did you want to talk to me about?"

His hands journeyed down her arms and back up, more comforting than sexual, though that could quickly change. The shawl she'd borrowed from Mrs. Jacobson slid off her shoulders to drape from the crook of her elbows. His gaze, impossibly hot yet cool at the same time, fell to the lace trim at her throat. Maddie lifted her chin, her fingers automatically going to where his stare rested. Scott's jaw clenched in response.

A footstep softly padded outside in the hall. Then another.

The noise reverberated in Maddie's ears like gunfire at close range.

Her mission was to distract him, she reminded herself, refusing to panic. Engage his attention so her friends could escape with the money. Nothing else mattered and no sacrifice required of her was too great.

She threw herself at him and kissed him with a haste bordering on frantic.

He, thank God, responded with similar abandon, lifting her off her feet and into his arms. Her lips instantly parted, and his tongue plunged deep inside her mouth. A groan of desperation, or perhaps satisfaction, rumbled from deep in his chest.

Maddie heard nothing after that save the cadence of Scott's heart as it matched rhythm with hers, and she doubted he did either.

The shawl slithered to the floor and puddled at her feet as she looped her arms around his waist. He tore his mouth from hers to bury his face in her neck. He planted hungry kisses beneath her ear and along the length of her collarbone. With one hand, he pulled her closer so that their hips were intimately aligned. His erection was unmistakable. With his other hand, he cupped her breast and began slowly stroking. Maddie's head fell back, and she uttered a sound of pure delight.

Her head snapped upright when he encountered the opening of her dress.

"What's this?" He pulled back, rolling an undone button between his index finger and thumb.

It was carved from ivory and considerably finer than anything Maddie could ever afford. His free hand climbed the length of her spine, and the clearly expensive fabric rustled beneath his fingers.

Curiosity suddenly replaced the light of passion that had been burning brightly in Scott's eyes.

"Where did you get this dress?" he asked.

Maddie fought the urge to shy away from him. Doing so would make her appear guilty. Instead, she distracted him again, employing wiles she'd learned from watching Delilah.

"I borrowed it." She stood on tiptoes and dropped tiny kisses on his chin and cheeks. "I wanted to look pretty for you." Neither statement was an outright lie, though returning the dress to Mrs. Jacobson might prove to be problematic.

"Maddie—"

He promptly shut up when she licked his bottom lip. Maddie smiled inwardly.

Her success was quickly forgotten as she gave herself over to the magical splendor of his kisses. Soon, she was utterly and completely lost—to the world, herself, and to him. Scott McSween. Her enemy and the man she should rightfully hate.

Only she didn't.

When he scooped her up into his arms and carried her to the bed, she didn't object. Somewhere in the back of her mind, she'd known the night would come to this. A woman didn't throw herself at a man and not expect him to reach certain conclusions.

But they didn't have to make love. Her friends had escaped; she'd heard no incriminating sounds for several minutes. She could stop this charade with a single protestation. Scott wouldn't force her despite her leading him on; she was absolutely certain of that.

But she *wanted* to make love with Scott, and damn the consequences.

Her logic was admittedly flawed, yet she couldn't help her feelings. It had been more than a year since she'd savored a man's touch—a long, difficult, lonely year.

Yet that wasn't the reason she sought comfort in Scott's arms and pleasure in his bed. Her need to join with him was as powerful and compelling as any hunger she'd ever felt. And like food—she thought she'd waste away from lack of him.

Tomorrow, or the day after, Scott might uncover the truth about her and hate her for the rest of her life. If by some miracle he didn't, he'd be leaving soon for his next assignment. Either way, they had only tonight, and she didn't want to waste a moment of it.

Having reached her decision, she gazed into his handsome face. He smiled at her, so warm and tender, she feared she might start to cry. She vowed to always remember him as he was tonight, despite what the future brought. It could very well be the only thing she'd have left of him.

Scott covered the remaining few feet to the bed in two quick strides. There, he stopped, his gaze taking her in from head to toe, resting longest on the opening in the front of her dress.

"Are you sure?" he asked. "I don't want to—"

"Shh."

"What if you get pregnant?"

She shook her head. "I don't think that will happen."

"I'll take care of you and the baby if it does."

She silenced him by pressing a finger to his mouth. When he said no more, she tickled the tuft of black chest hair peeking out from the neck opening of his shirt. "If you're stalling because you've changed you mind . . ."

Scott laughed. "No chance of that." His mind had been made up the instant she'd licked his lip.

He once thought of her as being both a proper lady and a brazen temptress. She'd shown his assessment to be one hundred percent correct. Maddie was no timid virgin, yet there was an air of inexperience and naivety about her. The combination had an incredibly powerful effect on him, one she'd have to be blind not to notice.

He was glad she wanted him with the same intensity he did her. Though he couldn't say where it would lead, this was much more than a casual affair for him and, he hoped, for her too.

What, he asked himself, was so special about Maddie? Others before her had tried to reach the murky side of his soul and failed. Why her? And why now, when he should be focusing all his attention on capturing the robbers?

Turning sideways, he reached for the knob on the side of the lantern.

"No," she said, her voice low and seductive. "Leave it on."

He went stone still, unable to draw a decent breath. The idea of undressing Maddie by lantern light, of watching her expression change from surprise to delight when he entered her, had caused an invisible band to wrap clean around his chest and cut off his air supply.

Tumbling onto the bed, he took her with him. Midway there, their lips came together in a searing kiss, hitting him like a slug of potent whiskey.

"You're breathtaking." He rolled her onto her side, drinking in each curve of her lovely figure. "Everything a man could possibly want."

"It's just you I want to please."

He groaned, near crazy with wanting her, and attempted to kick off his boots. The already awkward undertaking was further complicated when she linked her arms around his neck and dragged him down for another kiss. No sooner had his boots hit the floor then she attacked the buttons on his shirt, fumbling in her hurry to unfasten them.

He'd meant to savor their undressing, drawing it out until they were both wild with desire. Such was not the case. Their clothes were removed and discarded with lightning speed. His first. Propped up on one elbow, he lay naked beside her and fully aroused. Maddie wore only her chemise and not for long if her busy hands were any indication.

Scott was determined to take this last part of her disrobing at a less frenzied pace.

"Let me," he said, and brushing her hand aside, tugged on the pink silk ribbon securing the front of her silk chemise. It was a pretty piece of finery, and he briefly wondered if she'd borrowed it along with the dress. Then he stopped dwelling on clothes entirely.

With a soft swoosh, the material came loose. The opening revealed a deep V of smooth, creamy skin. Scott followed the outline of the V with fingers not quite steady.

Maddie sat partway up, and he eased the cap sleeves off her pale shoulders. She freed her arms from the confining garment, baring her full, lush breasts. He stared, then bent his head to gently tug one rosy nipple into his mouth and swirl his tongue around the taut peak.

She tasted sweet. Honey, fresh from the hive. Scott suckled harder, and she arched beneath him, holding his head to her and sighing his name. His hand went to the chemise tangled at her waist and pulled. She lifted her hips, and the chemise sailed through the air to join the rest of their clothes on the floor.

Scott trailed kisses from one breast to the other. She moaned, her silky body rolling from side to side.

Alarmed he might have gotten carried away, he raised his head and asked, "Did I hurt you?"

"Not at all." She gave a seductive chuckle. "I want more of the same. A lot more."

Scott loved how she talked. Straightforward and honest. In bed, at least. Out of bed was another story, but he wasn't in the mood to ponder that paradox right now. Not when she was removing the pins from her hair. He'd spent the better part of the past four nights dreaming about Maddie with her hair falling in waves around her bare breasts.

"Let me. Please." He was prepared to beg if she denied him.

"All right." She tilted her head to give him better access to the knot of tightly coiled hair atop her head.

With the removal of the last pin, her golden tresses spilled loose. Smiling, she lay back on the bed and opened her arms, beckoning him to join her.

Scott couldn't have moved if his life depended on it.

If he were to imagine a vision of female perfection, it would be Maddie as she was in that moment. Unclothed, flushed with desire, her hair fanned out on the pillow.

"You're stunning," he said in a raspy whisper. "Some artist should immortalize you on canvas."

"Keep complimenting me like you are, Mr. McSween, and I'll eventually believe it."

"Believe it."

Scott lay down beside her, his fingertips wandering in search of new territory.

"What's this?" He traced a thin white scar between the center of her breasts to her belly.

"I told you about my mother being attacked by Confederate soldiers when I was a baby." At his nod, she continued, her green eyes locking with and holding his. "She fought them at first. Until they cut me. And my brother, too. On his face. He has a scar, too."

"Jesus, Maddie." Scott wanted to be sick. What sort of monsters maimed innocent children?

"It's all right." She dispelled the ugly images in his mind by kissing the inside of his hand and then placing it on her stomach. "Make love to me, Scott."

He could hardly refuse. His fingers traversed the smooth span of her belly, continuing until they came to the patch of curls at the junction of her legs. Maddie shifted, opening her legs in subtle invitation. Scott responded by finding and exploring her feminine folds. Her gasp of delight was cut short when his mouth came crashing down on hers.

He wanted to bring her pleasure, wanted to watch her peak as he continued to caress her. Maddie was his and she would know fulfillment at his touch. He took tremendous satisfaction in her every sharp inhalation and ragged moan of ecstacy.

Sooner than he might have expected, her hips bucked and the muscles surrounding his fingers began to clench. She was close. So close.

Scott moved to kneel between her legs. But instead of entering her as she seemed to expect, he kissed the deliciously scented valley between her breasts. Next, he followed the line of her scar all the way down her belly. Then he kissed the slight indentations by each hip. Lastly, he brushed his lips over her thatch of downy curls.

God, she was so beautiful.

"What are you doing?" she gasped, rising onto her elbows.

"I'm finishing what I started."

"I thought—"

Gently easing her thighs apart, he placed his mouth directly on the very center of her womanhood, kissing her there with the same skill and fervor he'd kissed her mouth.

"Scott!"

Her startled reaction told him this type of lovemaking was new to her. Her subsequent melting and long drawn-out "Oh," told him she liked what he was doing. It gave his confidence a boost to know that he was the first to satisfy her in this manner.

Maddie showed herself to be an apt student, and Scott was a patient teacher.

As soon as the first small tremor hit her, he raised himself above her and entered her in one swift thrust—and found heaven.

He abandoned all hope of going slow when she grabbed his buttocks, wrapped her legs around his waist, and urged him more deeply inside her. He couldn't have delayed for all the riches buried in the Edenville Mine.

"Maddie." He kissed her hard before losing complete control.

Afterward, they lay together, her back to his front, his arm draped possessively over her waist, and her head tucked beneath his chin. There was so much he wanted to tell her, but he didn't know where to start. She seemed happy just to be with him and in no great hurry to hear the jumble of words filling his heart.

After a while, Scott got out of bed and went to the washstand in the corner of the room. Pouring fresh water from the pitcher into the basin, he wet a clean cloth, wrung it out, and took it back to the bed.

Maddie put her hand out. "Thank you."

"This isn't for you." Scott sat on the edge of the bed. "It's for me."

Starting with her breasts, he proceeded to wash every inch of her using slow, firm strokes. Her arms. Her legs. The insides of her thighs.

"You're spoiling me," she purred. "First my pins and now this."

"You deserve a little spoiling. I'm happy to oblige."

A hint of distress flitted across her face. Or was it merely a shadow from the flickering lantern? Scott couldn't be sure.

Having finished, he returned to the washstand. Rewetting the cloth, he cleaned himself.

"It'll be dawn in about three hours," he said walking back to the bed. "We should get you back to Eden before everyone wakes up." He extended his hand to help her from the bed. "We can take my horse."

"Yes," she answered lazily, gazing at him through slitted eyes. "But not yet."

She pulled, and he landed on top of her. Rolling him over onto his back, she took him in her palms, her bold strokes making him quickly hard. The thought of leaving for Eden became a distant memory as she straddled his middle and guided him inside her.

"What's this?" With butterfly-like strokes, she touched the circular scar on his chest.

"A souvenir from my days as a U.S. Marshal." He didn't want to discuss the shooting, certainly not when he had Maddie, naked and willing, sitting astride his hips.

"It's so close to your heart. You're lucky to be alive."

He was, if only for this night with her.

She lowered her head and kissed his scar in much the same manner he had hers.

Her long blond tresses fell in a curtain around their heads, making it easy for Scott to block out everything and everyone. He didn't want to think. Not yet. There would be sufficient time for that later.

Their second coupling was no less frantic and no less gratifying than the first. When it was over and their passion spent, they clung tightly, recuperating in comfortable silence. One minute lengthened into five, then ten. Scott's eyelids became increasingly heavy, and Maddie hadn't moved for some time. If they didn't soon rise and get dressed, they'd fall asleep, and that would cause trouble for him and Maddie. She had to contend with enough difficulties in her life without him adding to it.

But he couldn't recall a time he'd felt so content after making love. More than content, he was at peace for the first time in five years.

Stroking Maddie's arm, he said, "Come on, sweetheart. We have to go."

"I suppose you're right."

She pushed herself up to a sitting position. So did he, and they enjoyed one final kiss before leaving the bed.

Scott watched her dress as he did the same, admiring her figure once again. He'd not been without the company of women in the years since the lynching attempt and his fiancée's desertion. But those temporary unions had been nothing more than a means to a mutually agreeable end. The same, however, couldn't be said about tonight. Not by a long shot.

But if not an affair, what was Maddie to him?

The answer came like a gentle breeze blowing softly in his ear.

She's more. Much, much more.

Which made her lying about her involvement in the robberies increasingly sticky.

Chapter Fourteen

The horse picked his way down the mile-long dirt road to Eden quite well, thought Maddie, considering it was black as pitch outside and he was carrying two passengers. She rode behind Scott, her fingers resting lightly on his belt. Anyone watching them would never guess that less than an hour earlier, they'd lain in bed together, naked and more intimate than many married couples. Certainly more intimate than Maddie and William had ever been.

She and Scott had hardly spoken since leaving the hotel. She sensed his withdrawal, and her emotions plummeted.

What else had she expected? That he would declare his undying devotion to her? Hardly. Not after she'd practically seduced him. No, *did* seduce him. And while she could attempt to justify her actions, claiming she made love with him to aid her friends' escape, the truth was their coupling had meant something to her. She thought it had meant something to Scott, too, which was why his current mood saddened and confused her.

Well, so be it. She'd made her choice back in the Jacobson's hotel room and was prepared to live with the consequences, whatever they might be. The money, though not as much as they'd hoped for, was what really mattered. Not whether she and Scott had a nice chat on the ride home.

"Will anyone be waiting up for you?"

His abrupt question jarred her and made her glad he couldn't see her face. Lying still didn't come easily to her. Her brother, on the other hand, could lie with the best of them and had since embarked on a thriving career, using his talent to the utmost. She couldn't condemn him, not when his ability to bend the truth had helped them throughout their childhood and, she was sorry to say, their adulthood, too.

"No. No one will be waiting for me." A fairly convincing falsehood, she told herself. Her brother would be proud.

In actuality, several people were probably waiting up for her. Dora, a born worrier, might be in bed, but she wouldn't be sleeping. The same for Lavinia. In spite of her gruffness, the council leader was a mother hen and couldn't rest until her charges were home, safe and secure. A few others, too. Granny Fay, most likely. And Constance.

The gate to Eden came into view, a large inky shadow against an inkier night sky. An owl sat atop the squared arch. With a warning hoot to the intruders, he spread his wings and took flight, disappearing almost instantly. Upon seeing the gate, Maddie was reminded of her and Scott's first kiss. It seemed as if this place was going to be the scene of more than one good-bye for them.

Would this be their last one? Maddie's emotions plummeted further at the prospect of not seeing Scott again. Yet, what future did they have? A bleak one at most.

He pulled his horse to a stop just in front of the gate. "No shooting?"

"I beg your pardon?"

"Where are the guards?"

"Ah . . ."

Maddie cursed herself for being preoccupied with her own thoughts and forgetting about the guards. She assumed they'd been informed of her delay and the reason for it. They were probably also told about Scott and the possibility he might accompany Maddie to Eden.

"Don't they patrol at night?" he asked.

"Yes." She needed another lie, but wasn't yet apt enough to manufacture them on the spot, leastwise a decent one. "But as long as you don't enter Eden," she said, grasping at straws, "you're safe."

Dismounting with ease, Scott left Maddie alone on the horse. "I wasn't safe last week when I rode here in broad daylight."

Damn, but he was tenacious. "I honestly don't know where the guards are." She feigned ignorance. "I guess we should just consider ourselves lucky and leave it at that."

Her silent pleas were answered when he didn't pursue the subject. Holding the horse's reins with one hand, he helped her down with the other—and right into his arms.

"Oh!"

Hooking an arm around her waist, he lifted her hard against his chest. "Don't leave yet."

As if she could. When Scott McSween had it in his head to hold on to someone, he or she was pretty much stuck until he decided otherwise.

"I want to talk," he said.

"Now?" she asked, her voice a little too loud and high-pitched. "Why not on the ride here? We couldn't talk then?"

"I was busy thinking." His expression was a mixture of shadows and, as usual, revealed nothing.

"You have a lot of nerve." She made a token effort to disengage herself from his grasp, to no avail. Being trapped fueled her annoyance. "You didn't speak one word the entire ride here, leaving me to conclude all manner of terrible things."

A slow, sexy grin played around the corners of his mouth. "And what terrible things did you conclude?" He dropped the reins he'd been holding and cupped the side of her face. The pad of his thumb stroked her jaw.

Were she not so riled, she would have yielded unconditionally.

"I'm not telling you." She realized her behavior bordered on childish, but he'd hurt her. In the span of a few minutes he'd gone from making exquisite and passionate love to her to not speaking.

"All right." His eyes never wavered from hers, and his half grin remained fixed. "Then why don't you tell me about Rory O'Shea. Or, should I say, *the fictitious* Rory O'Shea?"

It was lucky he held her so tightly because her muscles had turned to mush. She should have seen this coming, and scolded herself for being caught unawares.

"Your horse is getting away," she said, hoping to stall him and buy herself some time to collect her thoughts.

No longer restrained, the animal had immediately

lowered his head to the ground and meandered off, presumably in search of food.

"He won't go far."

Granted, the horse didn't appear the sort to stampede.

"The guards will probably be here any second. You'd better leave before they start firing."

"Maddie." He was doing a much better job of sidetracking her than she was him. His thumb continued its maddening stroking, going from the sensitive spot beneath her ear to the delicate skin under her chin. "I'm worried for your safety."

"My safety?" She laughed nervously. "I'm fine."

"You're not," he said with disturbing conviction. "You're in danger. Serious danger. I know you're helping the robbers and that you made up this Rory O'Shea character to steer me away from them."

He was absolutely right, he just had no idea how right. Not three hours earlier, while he'd bedded the leader, the remaining robbers escaped.

"I did make him up." She sighed, relieved to be telling the truth for once. "Can you blame me?"

"No." He released her then and took a step back. "I understand why you did it."

Somehow she doubted he did. "Do you really?"

"More than you think."

She hugged herself, feeling strangely isolated without his arm around her and angry at his ability to affect her so profoundly. In retaliation, she lashed out with sarcasm. "You've lost someone you loved because of an evil, greedy man who cared only about his own twisted needs?"

"Yes. My fiancée and my family."

Maddie swayed slightly from the emotional avalanche of his unexpected admission. "You were engaged to be married?"

"Five years ago. Elizabeth left me a month before the wedding."

"I'm sorry." And she was. Though he tried to hide it, the sorrow was there in his eyes, and Maddie sympathized. "Why? If you don't mind me asking."

"I killed two innocent men while protecting a guilty one."

She clamped a hand over her mouth to stifle a gasp. "Sorry."

His abrupt laugh contained no mirth. "Believe me, that was nothing. I've been slapped, sucker punched, shot at, spit on, and ignored."

Maddie stared at him, speechless. She'd always known Scott was capable of killing. But two innocent men in cold blood?

"I was charged with protecting a killer while he awaited trial," he continued in a monotone. "The bastard raped, mutilated, and then murdered the daughter of one of the town's leading families. No doubt he did it. He was caught red-handed by the girl's father and two of his employees. She was a beautiful young girl, sweet and innocent. Only sixteen. Her father went into a rage when he found them in the stables . . . saw the perverted manner in which she'd been violated. If not for the two employees restraining him, there'd have been a second murder that day."

Maddie shuddered. The early morning darkness made it easy for her to picture the horrific story as it unfolded.

"The whole town was up in arms. Folks wanted to see her killer dead for what he'd done. There was talk going around that he'd wind up serving a life sentence in prison instead of being executed as he deserved. Weeks went by and still there was no trial. With each new delay, tempers flared and more trouble broke out.

I must have made six different arrests for public brawling alone.

"One night, a bunch of fellows got liquored up in the saloon and decided they'd do the world a favor and at the same time save the taxpayers some money. The man leading the lynching was the dead girl's sweetheart and only twenty years old himself. Still a kid, really. He was studying to be a lawyer."

Scott's voice wavered momentarily. When he resumed speaking, it was again in a monotone.

"Nobody wanted to see that poor girl's killer punished more than I did. The whole time he was in jail, I had to listen to him brag about what he'd done to her and the different ways he'd used her. But I was a U.S. Marshal, and my duty was clear. Enforce the law and do what was necessary to ensure the prisoner survived until his trial.

"Someone warned me minutes before the mob stormed the jail. My deputy and I barricaded the door, but it was no match for two dozen liquored-up hotheads determined to take justice into their own hands. I tried to make them understand they'd be arrested for murder if they went through with the lynching. They refused to listen. Threats began flying back and forth. Guns were drawn. I ordered them to cease and desist. They threatened to kill me if I didn't stand aside."

"And you didn't?"

He appeared not to hear her. "They were good men. Just angry, and rightfully so. I raised my gun and fired a warning shot at the ceiling. Then another. It's funny the little details you remember. Bits of sawdust fell down like snow and landed on the men standing closest to me. I can still see them, clear as if it happened yesterday." He paused, tilting his head to one side, his gaze directed inward. "I just wanted to scare some sense into them. Get them to back off and go home where they belonged. But they didn't back off, and they sure as hell weren't scared.

"I turned to give my deputy an order and must have lowered my gun. Somebody yelled 'watch out.' Next thing I knew my ears were ringing and my chest felt like it had been ripped open. I was thrown back against my desk, and my gun went off. From the impact, I suppose. Or else I instinctively shot back. There was a lot of confusion, and the pain . . ."

He reached up and absently rubbed the right side of his chest. Maddie's fingertips tingled, remembering the rough feel of his scar.

"You're fortunate the shot wasn't fatal."

He gazed at her with vacant eyes. "That's debatable."

"How can you say that?" Maddie's shock ran deep. "It was self-defense. You were doing your job."

"Not according to some." He shrugged off her argument as if it made not a lick of difference to him. "The lynching attempt ended then and there, or so I was told. I blacked out and didn't wake up for three days. When I finally did, it was to learn I'd killed two men, one of them the sweetheart of the murdered girl. His father came to the house to tell me." He faced Maddie, his expression no longer blank. Misery and self-loathing emanated from him in waves. "My uncle."

It took several seconds for understanding to dawn and when it did, Maddie let out a strangled cry. "You shot your own cousin?"

"His name was Michael. From the time he was born, everybody called him Mick." Scott stared into space, reliving a horror far exceeding her ability to comprehend.

"Oh, Scott."

She pitied the awful burden he'd carried with him all these years. Easing nearer, she offered comfort and compassion with a light touch of her hand on his arm.

He didn't respond at first. Just when she'd abandoned hope, he found her fingers and folded them inside his.

"That same day, my fiancée informed me she had no desire to marry a murderer. I didn't blame her for breaking our engagement, seeing as my family had little use for me either. My mother visited me daily during my convalescence and not once failed to remind me I'd ruined the family name. The minute I was cleared of all charges, I resigned as marshal and left Galveston. For good."

Maddie didn't blame him. The law had determined the two men's deaths were accidental. It seemed Scott wasn't sure he deserved to be absolved.

"The line between right and wrong is often blurred," she said.

He looked at her then. Really looked at her. "You would know, I suppose, better than most."

She stiffened. "So, we're back to the robbers." When she would have removed her fingers from his, he held fast.

"I understand why you're helping them, and it doesn't alter my feelings for you. What Newlin did to you, to all the widows in Eden, was wrong. He should be made to pay the death benefits and back wages. But trust me, taking the law into your own hands isn't the solution. Trouble is going to come to the robbers and anyone associated with them. Newlin will see to it." His grip tightened, verging on desperate. "I don't want to lose somebody else I care about."

"What are you saying?" In her current emotional state, she didn't trust her own ears.

"I don't know how much longer I'll be in Edenville." He dropped her hand to take her in his arms. "But while I'm here, I'd like for us to see each other again."

"See each other again while you're here," she repeated dully, her heart aching.

He didn't care about her, not really, not like he'd said. He only wanted someone to warm his bed during the remainder of his stay. And she had no one to blame but herself. Hadn't she thrown herself at him? Made love to him with complete abandonment and without an ounce of shame? Or, worse, his motives might be connected to his hunt for the robbers. She was involved, after all, and maybe he thought she might lead him to their hideout.

Apparently sensing her withdrawal, he increased the pressure of his hands and said, "I want to court you, Maddie. Take you to dinner and Sunday afternoon church socials. You and Josephine both. I won't say I didn't enjoy our lovemaking tonight, and if you choose to come to me again, I won't send you away. If you chose not to, I'll understand and accept it. That's not the reason I want to see you again."

"I . . . can't."

The idea of Scott courting her was so impossible, Maddie couldn't begin to consider it. What would he do if he found out she was behind the robberies? What would the women of Eden think? That she'd betrayed or abandoned them? What would happen when it came time for him to leave? And he *would* leave. Men like Scott McSween didn't stay rooted in once place.

"Why?" Tension crept into his voice. "Is it because I killed my cousin?"

"God, no! That was an accident. One you've paid for over and over, I'm sure."

Her lower lip began to tremble, and she bit it to stop herself from crying. The long night had taken its toll on her. Starting with the meal in Delilah's rooms, then the robbery, wearing Mrs. Jacobson's dress, making love with Scott, and ending with his unexpected request to court her. It was more than she could endure.

"I have feelings for you. You can't doubt that. Just like I don't doubt you have feelings for me." He pressed the side of her face to his chest in an endearing gesture and spoke into her hair. "I'm not an easy man to know. I tend to push people away. It's different with you, Maddie. I'm not afraid to let you get close to me. I trust you."

She did cry then, softly and to herself.

He bent and kissed her cheek, her ear, the underside of her jaw. Maddie tried to resist, but her body responded with a mind of its own and snuggled against him.

"You don't have to agree right now. Just promise me you'll think about it."

"I promise." Had she really said that? Some fragment of reason penetrated her foggy brain.

"Good." Smiling, he relaxed his hold on her and eased her away from him. "Are you working at the company store today?"

"No. It's my day off." Thank goodness. She was in no condition to deal with Mr. Abernathy on top of everything else. "I go in tomorrow."

"I'll stop by in the afternoon to check on you."

They had no future together. Common sense dictated she discourage him. But what she said to him was, "All right."

A thin ribbon of pink edged the eastern horizon as Scott rode off. It would be dawn soon. Maddie stood and watched him until the pounding of his horse's hooves were a distant echo.

Wrapping Mrs. Jacobson's shawl more snugly around her, Maddie walked into Eden and the short distance to her shack. She pushed open the door, making as little noise as possible so as not to wake the occupants.

"You're home finally." A gravely voice floated to her from the recesses of the dark interior. It was followed by a scuffling sound and the painful creaking of knee joints.

"Yes." Granny Fay was awake and waiting for her. "How's Josephine?"

"Fine. She woke only once and went right back to sleep."

A small, quiet bundle remained in the bedroll. Josephine. Maddie eased by a stretching and yawning Granny Fay to kneel beside her daughter and place a loving kiss on the little girl's forehead. Josephine stirred, murmured something, then drifted back to sleep.

Stricken with a fresh wave of guilt at leaving her child too often in the care of others, Maddie whispered a promise to take her daughter out later in the day to pick flowers. First, however, a short nap was in order. The brief one in Scott's bed wouldn't sustain her through the coming day.

"Thank you for watching Josephine." Bracing a hand on the old trunk, Maddie pushed herself to her feet. Lord, she was tired. "I don't know what I'd do—"

Tears abruptly filled her eyes. She blotted them away, hoping Granny Fay didn't notice.

"Tough night?"

The old nurse could either see in the dark or was very astute. Both probably.

"Yes."

"Did McSween hurt you? If he did—"

"Heavens, no!" If anything, she'd hurt him by refusing his request to come courting. "He's really very kind."

"For someone out to get you, I reckon he is."

"It's not like that."

"So you say." Granny Fay pressed a kerchief into Maddie's palm. "It ain't none of my business, but you were gone a mighty long time."

"Didn't Dora tell you where I was and . . . and why?"

"She did. And like I said, you were gone a mighty long time. Must have been some powerful distracting you were doing on that man."

Maddie had no answer, so she offered none. "Good night, Granny Fay."

The older woman cackled. "Guess I'll just be moseying along then."

"You're a good friend," Maddie said at the door.

"You have a lot of good friends in Eden."

"That I do." Which was one of the reasons she couldn't consider seeing Scott.

"I'll talk to you in—" Granny Fay squinted at something in the distance. "What in blue tarnation is that!"

A far-off shout came. Then another, and another. At first, the words were unintelligible. Then, as an unholy apparition took shape in the distance, they became discernable.

Fire!

A tower of flames twelve feet high rose up from the center of Eden, lighting the sky like a second sun.

"Good God!" Granny Fay squawked.

"Fire! Fire!" People poured from their tents and shacks in various stages of dress and undress, shouting and scurrying in every directions.

"Grab blankets and shovels," someone yelled, running past them. "Anything you can find to fight the fire."

Granny Fay started after them.

"No!" Maddie grabbed her and pulled her back through the door. "I'll go. You stay with Josephine." Her tone invited no argument. "If the fire comes within a hundred feet of here, you take her and you run. All the way to Edenville if you have to. You understand? Don't let anything happen to my baby."

"I won't. Now you git."

Maddie automatically reached for her rifle behind the door before tearing off at a dead run. In the single minute she and Granny Fay talked, the fire had almost doubled.

"Look!" Constance appeared amongst the stream of people, intercepting Maddie midway to the fire. "He's getting away."

Maddie turned in the direction Constance pointed and saw a lone figure hightailing it toward the outskirts of Eden. She recognized him instantly.

It was Jonesy, the man from the company store who'd accosted Constance. Thaddeus Newlin's hired goon.

"He set the fire," Constance cried. "Don't let him get away."

Without hesitation, Maddie raised her rifle to her shoulder, took aim, and squeezed the trigger.

Chapter Fifteen

The bullet hit its mark, but not in a vital location.

Maddie watched Jonesy jerk violently, then topple face first into the dirt. He lay there a moment before struggling to his feet. After a few faltering steps, he reached around to hold his shoulder and lumbered away. A dark patch stained the back of his shirt.

She debated the merits of firing again and took aim.

"Hurry, Maddie!" Patience Carmichael and her two daughters beckoned Maddie. They all carried blankets. The little girls clung to each other, clearly scared to pieces.

"I guess it's your lucky day," Maddie muttered to the fleeing man.

Lowering her rifle, she hurried after the Carmichaels. The fire presented the more pressing problem. If it spread, the residents of Eden would lose what little they had.

Heat stung her face and throat, and smoked filled

her nostrils as she approached the tower of flames—and yet her blood ran cold.

The supply tent!

She wished now she'd killed the bastard. He'd picked the most important structure in Eden to set ablaze. Their entire food store was being destroyed . . . *had* been destroyed, for the fire moved quickly, consuming everything inside the tent with frightening speed.

Those with blankets beat at the fire, and those with shovels heaped dirt upon it. Even the older children helped by clearing the area and carting off anything of value. The younger ones were herded from harm's way to the far side of Eden.

"Over here, Maddie," shouted Dora. Several women were lugging buckets filled with water from nearby rain barrels as fast as their legs could carry them.

Handing off her rifle to one of the older boys for safekeeping, Maddie grabbed a bucket and fell into line. Thank God the supply tent was situated in a spot by itself. With a little luck, the fire's hungry flames would die out before consuming the rest of Eden.

What the women lacked in skill they made up for in numbers. Twenty minutes later, the battle came to a weary and bitter end, the fire reduced to a smouldering, sodden heap. Eden had been spared, but the supply tent and all its contents were lost.

Constance turned away from the group, covering her eyes with her hand. Her body began to shake. "I never should have made him angry. He said he was going to get back at us."

Maddie laid an arm across her friend's shoulder. "Don't blame yourself, you hear me? You *aren't* at fault. *No one* is. He's an evil, spiteful man who hurts innocent people when they don't do what he wants."

"I'm sorry." Constance turned into the hug Maddie offered.

Lavinia sniffed and prodded a blackened tin can with the tip of her shovel. Whatever food it had once held was no longer fit to eat. "At least no one was hurt bad."

"Praise God for that," chimed another.

They had a lot to be thankful for, thought Maddie, releasing a teary Constance. They were alive, and they still had roofs over their heads. But as she studied the smudged and haunted faces around her, every one reflected the same fear and misery she felt.

"What're we gonna eat now?" a scared voice asked.

What indeed?

"I'm calling a council meeting." Lavinia glanced at her late husband's pocket watch, which she wore on a ribbon around her neck. "We'll meet in two hours. Pass the word." She sought out Maddie. "See if Granny Fay can drive into town and bring Delilah. We're going to need her help again."

After most of the council members had been notified of the meeting, Maddie returned to her shack to deliver Lavinia's instructions and check on Josephine. Granny Fay had already gotten the whole story on the fire. They spoke briefly of the repercussions, then parted. There were a few minor injuries Granny Fay needed to tend before leaving for Edenville.

When Maddie was alone, she washed up as best she could with a wet towel. She didn't think her hair would ever smell the same again.

With a lump in her throat, she stripped off Mrs. Jacobson's ruined dress and dropped it in a heap by the door. Though guilt would have prevented her from wearing it again, she hated seeing something so lovely turned into a worthless rag.

"Maw, Maw."

Josephine, who didn't fully understand what had happened, pestered for attention. Needing a little reassurance herself, Maddie lifted her daughter into her arms.

"Ew!" Josephine wrinkled her face and held her nose.

"Yes, your mother stinks." Maddie laughed at her daughter's antics and her spirits rose a little. She even managed a short rest. Too soon, she had to rise and change clothes in preparation for the meeting.

"Archie!"

After scouring Eden for a good half hour beneath a sweltering midmorning sun, Maddie had finally located the young man. He and a few of the older boys were at the site of the fire, shoveling debris into a wheelbarrow. She should have guessed they'd be right in the thick of things. How they could tolerate the acrid odor lingering in the air without getting headaches, she didn't know.

"Howdy, Miz Campbell."

"I hate to bother you, but could you watch Josephine while I'm at the council meeting? It's supposed to start any minute." While looking for Archie, Maddie had caught sight of Granny Fay and Delilah arriving in the surrey.

"Sure." He set his shovel down and propped an elbow on the handle. "But I can't guarantee she'll stay clean."

Maddie sighed and released Josephine's hand. "As long as she doesn't get hurt."

The little girl ran pell-mell toward Archie. Within five seconds, she was covered with filth from toes to knees and giggling up a storm.

Maddie bit her tongue. She reasoned that a happy, dirty child was better than a sad, tidy one.

The council convened in its customary spot. The general mood of the assembly was decidedly glum.

Delilah strolled over to stand beside Maddie. "Are you all right, love? You look like hell."

"Quite honestly, I feel like it, too."

"I admit, I'm glad to see you free and in one piece. I heard from Gertrude about the problems you encountered last night with Mrs. Jacobson and McSween."

"We had a couple of close calls. I'll tell you about them later."

"I'd rather hear how you distracted our very handsome and impressively virile private investigator."

At Maddie's slack jaw, Delilah gave a throaty chuckle.

Lavinia rang her bell, calling the meeting to order and sparing Maddie further embarrassment.

"First things first," the council leader said. "What, if anything, remains of our food supplies?"

Patience Carmichael, keeper of their food stores, stepped forward. "We lost everything in the supply tent." She choked back a sob. "A good two months' worth of flour and beans as well as some canned goods, cornmeal, salt, and lard."

"What else is left?"

"A few of us have small personal stores of food for the children. Not more than a meal or two." She dabbed at the tears collecting in her eyes. "There are over a hundred chickens. We've been getting about five or six dozen eggs a day."

"Five or six dozen eggs ain't gonna feed three hundred of us fer long," someone grumbled. "Let's kill the chickens and eat them."

"No!" Patience wailed, her affection for her feathered charges apparent. "We need those eggs. The hens will lay more when the weather cools off."

"We can buy more damn chickens when the weather cools off, too."

"That'll do," Lavinia warned. "We're not killing any

chickens just yet. Not until we examine all our options." She addressed the council member in charge of the treasury. "Cora, how much money do we have?"

Cora squared her shoulders and in a prim voice, said, "Including the money obtained in the Jacobson robbery last night, we have a total of three hundred twenty-seven dollars and eighteen cents."

Maddie cringed. Slightly more than a dollar a head. They could maybe afford enough food to last a week if they scrimped. Mining towns were notorious for high prices, and Edenville was no exception.

"We're gonna starve to death," someone lamented and in the next moment, chaos erupted.

"We are not going to starve to death," Lavinia said sharply and rang her bell. When order resumed, she sent a stern look to every member of the council. "I won't tolerate any more talk of starving. You got that? We'll survive this tragedy, just like before."

"How?" Constance asked, her tone more curious than critical.

Lavinia turned to the town madam. "Delilah? Have you any suggestions?"

Delilah shrugged, though she was anything but nonchalant. Her illegitimate son, Henry, and his well being were at stake. "You know I'll help. I have a little money set aside, but not much, I'm afraid."

"You've given us plenty already. We hate to ask for more. Nonetheless, we'd be grateful for whatever you can spare. Is anyone in town hiring help? Waitresses? Cooks? Laundresses?"

"I'll check." She tilted her head to one side. "Fat Mike can always use another girl or two."

No one volunteered.

"What about the Ladies' Aid Society?" Patience asked. Twice in the past, the kindly members had taken up a food collection on behalf of the widows and children. "And there's always the Methodist Church."

"Yes." Lavinia nodded thoughtfully. "They might help, too."

"I heard Hammond Brubaker is coming to town next week," Delilah said. "He's touring all three mines, stopping first at the Pinnacle and then the Vista Linda."

Every head shot up at the mention of the fourth minority partner's name.

"Do you know how long he's staying in Edenville?" Lavinia asked.

"Several days, I'm sure. He likes to take treatments at the mineral spring." Delilah pursed her mouth in contemplation. "You know, the mineral spring isn't far. It might make a perfect location to ambush him."

"I won't do it!" Constance jumped to her feet. "We agreed when we began all this we were going to leave the Brubakers out of it."

"I side with Constance." Maddie moved to the center of the group, tamping down a surge of indignation. "They're decent folk and have suffered as much as any of us."

Hammond Brubaker and his oldest son had been in the main shaft on a routine inspection during the mining accident. The fallout from the explosion killed his son and left Brubaker severely injured. A year later, he still hadn't fully recovered, hence his periodic visits to the mineral spring. Located on the other side of the Edenville Mountain, it was reputed to have healing properties.

When Newlin refused to pay the back wages and death benefits to the widows, Hammond Brubaker had fought him tooth and nail from his hospital bed while his wife, putting aside her own grief, helped nurse the children stricken with scarlet fever.

Even if Brubaker had been able to convince the other two minority partners to pay out the money, their combined votes couldn't have beaten Newlin's one.

Because of his son's death, his wife's selflessness, his own injuries, and his stand against Newlin on their behalf, the women had unanimously agreed to exclude Hammond Brubaker and his family from the robberies.

But, Maddie worried, that might have come to an end.

"The Brubakers *are* decent folk," Delilah agreed, "but you have to admit, as part owner of the mines, they've profited from the money that rightfully belongs to you."

"Hear, hear," someone shouted. "We're bickering over a few measly eggs while they're slicing a fat hog."

"Maybe we could speak to Mr. Brubaker when he arrives," Maddie suggested. "He might be willing to help us."

"Like he did before?" Delilah asked.

"He tried."

"And failed. He can't outvote Newlin, and that snake won't give you a dime."

"None of which justifies stealing from him. Let's face it, we're criminals." Maddie had never before argued with Delilah, and she didn't like it. Why was she at odds lately with those closest to her?

"Delilah's right," Lavinia interjected. "Mr. Brubaker may be willing to help us, but the fact is, he can't."

"Have you no pity?" Constance joined Maddie in the center of the group. "The man's son died, for crying out loud."

Maddie understood Constance's objection to robbing the Brubakers. They shared a common loss, that of a child.

"What about Scott McSween? He already believes we're helping the robbers, he told me this m—" She stopped herself before revealing too much. "He told me just recently."

"Which means," Dora added, "he'll be watching us *and* the Brubakers very closely. Especially after last night. He's probably questioning the Jacobsons as we speak."

Maddie hugged her waist, fighting an attack of anxiety. Since leaving Scott at the gate, she hadn't had a free moment to consider the ramifications of what would happen when he returned to town and learned about the Jacobsons. It wouldn't surprise her in the least to find her name next on his list of suspects.

"He is a problem." Lavinia drummed her fingers absently. "But one we can overcome if we put our heads together."

"Mrs. Brubaker always goes with her husband to the mineral spring." A gleam lit the speaker's eyes. "Heard tell she wears some pretty fancy jewelry."

"We can't sell stolen jewelry without someone tracing it back to us."

"I know of a man in Tucson," Delilah said. "He won't give you what the jewelry's worth, but he won't ask any questions either."

"We have no way of getting the jewelry there."

"I can help with that."

"Wait just a fool minute." Constance put herself between where Lavinia sat and Delilah stood. "You're talking like robbing the Brubakers is a done deal. Don't the rest of us get a chance to vote on it?"

Lavinia held up a hand. "We are simply discussing alternatives."

And discuss alternatives, they did, for the next hour and a half. In great detail. Opinions varied, some heated, others cool. When the vote was finally taken, those who favored robbing the Brubakers prevailed by a slim margin. Fear of starvation, Maddie thought, played the largest part in the final outcome. They all remembered that first dreadful winter in Eden.

"Let's refuse," Constance said to Maddie under her breath. "The council can't force us to rob the Brubakers if we don't want to. And what do you bet, without us, they don't do it?"

Maddie felt like her heart was being torn in two. She'd prided herself on her loyalty and commitment to the women of Eden. And now that the time had come to prove it, she was considering refusing.

Without money, they couldn't buy food. Some of them might die. But if she consented to the robbery, the Brubakers, kindly people who had tried to help them, would suffer. True, they were well-off, but robbing them still went against her better judgment. Besides, Scott was too close on their tails to risk another robbery so soon after the last one.

"No good is going to come of this," Constance mumbled.

Maddie couldn't have agreed more.

"This is entirely unacceptable!" Mrs. Jacobson's shrill voice increased in volume with each punctuated syllable, filling the small hotel room until Scott's eardrums were ready to burst. "We are the victims, Sheriff Lunsford, not the villains, and we won't tolerate being spoken to in such a demeaning tone by the likes of *him!*"

"He's only trying to help you, Mrs. Jacobson," Tom Lunsford replied, his store of patience with the minority partner's pampered wife considerably larger than Scott's. "Mr. McSween is a respected private investigator. One of the best, which is why Mr. Newlin hired him."

"He's rude."

Scott had been called worse.

"You do want to see these criminals caught and put behind bars?" Lunsford asked.

The withering look she sent him left no doubt as to her opinion of his intelligence—or lack of it. "After what they did to Levi and me? Of course I want them caught."

"Cooperating with Mr. McSween will help to accomplish that end. His purpose isn't to pry into your and Mr. Jacobson's private . . . marital relations." The sheriff's ruddy cheeks darkened.

Watching Tom Lunsford cajole Mrs. Jacobson reminded Scott of the one aspect he'd disliked most about being a lawman. Diplomacy and politics weren't his strengths.

"Here, give me that." Unappeased, Mrs. Jacobson ripped a white frilly garment from the hands of the hotel maid helping her pack. "The fabric is much too delicate for your clumsy paws." She folded the garment as if it were a treasured possession and carefully tucked it in the open trunk.

Scott lingered by the window, his attention shifting between the street below and the occupants in the room. Mrs. Jacobson didn't intimidate him, but he had grown weary of being a target for her wrath. The elderly Mr. Jacobson sat in a chair not far from Scott. Judging from his frequent tired sighs, he and Scott were of similar mind when it came to his spoiled young wife.

To her credit, the hotel maid tolerated Mrs. Jacobson's tirade with stoic calm. Tall and large boned, she didn't once glance away from her task of packing Mrs. Jacobson's belongings. When Scott had questioned her earlier, she informed him her name was Gertrude Michaelson and that she lived in Eden. She also admitted to being on duty for part of last night, but saw or heard nothing unusual, a story collaborated by the hotel's night manager.

It appeared Gertrude Michaelson had nothing to do with the robbery. He couldn't, however, say the same about Maddie.

Scott ground his teeth, something he'd been doing a lot since returning to the hotel that morning and coming face-to-face with Tom Lunsford's accusing scowl. Scott hadn't responded when Lunsford told him about the Jacobsons and asked him where he'd been. He was glad now he'd remained silent. Maddie was clearly in cahoots with the robbers. Until he learned how deep, the last person he wanted nosing around his personal life was the sheriff.

From the account the Jacobsons had given him, which was sketchy in places and riddled with inconsistencies, Maddie knocked on his door at roughly the same time they were being held at gunpoint. It was a coincidence too big and too incriminating for Scott to ignore.

Had she come to his room solely for the purpose of keeping him busy while the Jacobsons were being robbed? Or, as she'd told him last night, to talk? Scott was no romantic, but he rebelled at being tricked, if that was indeed what Maddie had done. What he needed was positive proof, and he wouldn't rest until he had it.

Gripping the window ledge, he closed his eyes, and squeezed.

She'd gotten to him, and not because they'd slept together. It was crazy. Ridiculous. Yet he wanted her, in his bed *and* by his side. Hell, he still did even after her apparent deception, which only made him angrier.

The window ledge continued to bear the brunt of his frustration.

"Where's my dress?" Mrs. Jacobson twirled in a circle, her eagle-eye gaze surveying every inch of the room.

"Which dress, my dear?" Mr. Jacobson asked, only half listening. The vast quantities of wine he'd freely admitted to drinking the previous evening had left him a bit green around the gills.

"The lavender one with ivory buttons down the front. You remember, you bought it for me in Phoenix." She frowned. "It was here yesterday. What did you do with my dress?" she abruptly demanded of Gertrude Michaelson. "So help me, if you stole it, I'll see that you're fired."

Scott turned from the window, his full attention on Mrs. Jacobson and the maid. The back of his neck had begun to tingle in a way he didn't like, and he rubbed it.

Lavender dress?

"I . . . I haven't seen it, ma'am. I swear." The maid's fingers trembled slightly. She fisted them and held them at her side. "Are you sure it's not at the bottom of your trunk?"

"Of course I'm sure. Don't you think I've checked?" Curls bouncing and skirt flying, an indignant Mrs. Jacobson stomped across the room to confront Lunsford. "Sheriff, this woman has stolen my dress."

"Now, ma'am," he drawled. "Let's not jump to any hasty conclusions."

Too late, Scott already had.

The maid knew the whereabouts of the dress. So did he.

Maddie had worn it to his room last night, and he'd undone most of those ivory buttons himself.

The proof he'd wished for had just been handed to him, and Scott felt like he'd been slammed in the gut with a giant tree branch.

"I insist you arrest her." Mrs. Jacobson would not be put off.

Her husband creaked to a standing position with the aid of his cane. "Now, dear."

Scott cut by him and made a beeline for the hotel room door.

"Hey, where you going?" Lunsford called after him.

The shouting inside his head drowned out whatever else the sheriff said. Scott thundered down the stairs, his boots like sledgehammers on the wooden steps. At the bottom, he stopped, suddenly aware of the multitude of curious eyes upon him.

"Is everything all right, Mr. McSween?" the clerk asked from behind the counter.

"Yes, thank you." Scott nodded brusquely before continuing to the hotel's front entrance.

But everything isn't fine, he thought as he stepped outside and was hit with a blast of hot air. Maddie Campbell had just gone from being his lover and the woman he wanted to court, to a known accomplice of the robbers.

How could he have been such a fool?

Chapter Sixteen

"Good morning."

Maddie stared at the twin brown boots in her line of vision. A spear of apprehension sliced through her.

Is it him? Has he finally come to check on me as he promised?

She gazed up—one hesitant inch at a time—from where she knelt on the floor in the center aisle of the company store. Long legs, leather belt, dark shirt open slightly at the collar, and . . . red hair?

Not him!

"Excuse me, ma'am," the customer said. "Can you tell me where to find the tobacco?"

Shaking like a leaf and trying to hide it, Maddie pointed toward the front of the store. "Over there. Next to the rack of periodicals."

"Thank you." He inclined his head and left.

Maddie sank down onto the back of her calves. Tears pricked her eyes. She didn't know how much more she could endure. Waiting and worrying had become like a heavy hand in the small of her back, forcing her ahead despite her protests.

It had been ten days since Scott left her at the gate to Eden after asking permission to court her. Ten days since the fire . . . since the Jacobsons were robbed and he'd learned about Mrs. Jacobson's missing dress. Gertrude had rushed back to Eden after the incident to tell Maddie about it, terrified of being arrested. Thank goodness the hotel agreed to pay for the dress and nothing more had come of the matter, at least as far as Gertrude was concerned.

Maddie didn't think herself so fortunate.

Scott was too clever not to suspect her. So what game was he playing and why hadn't he told the sheriff? Gertrude said he'd left the hotel room in a hurry shortly after Mrs. Jacobson accused her of stealing the dress—the dress he'd stripped off Maddie in their haste to make love. She doubted he'd been so blinded by passion that he didn't remember unfastening all those tiny buttons.

"Quit your lollygagging and get back to work," Mr. Abernathy snapped. He trudged past Maddie, leaving muddy tracks on her freshly scrubbed floor.

Maddie threw down her washrag in disgust. How she despised him.

Anger at her boss momentarily freed her from thoughts of Scott and put some stiffness in her sagging backbone. One day, when money wasn't so scarce and her future looked brighter, she'd quit her job and never, ever, work for the likes of Mr. Abernathy again. She and Josephine would leave Edenville and start over in a new town, like Tucson or Phoenix.

Ruthlessly shoving a stray lock of hair from her face, Maddie picked up the washrag shook it out. Who was she kidding? She'd never leave. The residents of Eden were living hand to mouth, on the brink of starvation. They had no food to speak of and two more days to survive until the Brubakers arrived.

Each night Maddie walked the floor of her tiny shack, rocking a wailing Josephine in her arms and wishing with all her heart for a cup of milk or a hard-boiled egg—anything to make her daughter's hunger subside just long enough for her to fall asleep.

They'd be in worse shape if not for the Ladies' Aid Society. The kindhearted members, upon hearing about the fire, had launched a campaign to help. They'd shown up the day before yesterday in a wagon loaded with loaves of bread and jars of preserves. Each family in Eden received enough food to last them the day. For a short while, at least, hope soared.

It didn't last. By the next day everyone was hungry again. Today, they were hungrier still.

Any reservations Maddie had about stealing from the Brubakers were vanquished by the cries of her hungry, listless child. She would not let Josephine die, not when she could prevent it. Like Delilah had said at the council meeting, the Brubakers had more than enough riches to go around.

True, Scott was closing in on them, but Maddie had greater problems to worry about. In two days, when the Brubakers arrived in Edenville and made their regular pilgrimage to the mineral spring, Maddie would don men's clothing and return to her life of crime. Any danger of being caught was inconsequential to saving her daughter's life and those of the other children.

"Sorry." Constance, who had come out of nowhere, inadvertently stepped on Maddie's skirt. She bent to lift the hem and shake off the dirt. As she did, she whispered, "You have a visitor waiting for you out back."

Maddie's pulse leapt. It could be only one person. "Wait." She stood on wobbly legs, but Constance had already disappeared to another part of the store.

Smoothing her apron and bolstering her courage, Maddie headed straight for the stockroom, glancing frequently over her shoulder to make sure no one followed. Her breath sounded like a bellows in her ears. Walking at a sedate pace took considerable effort.

At the rear of the stockroom was a door leading outside. She busied herself for a minute longer, erring on the side of caution. When no one appeared to question her, she pushed open the door and stepped through.

Barrels, boxes, and crates were stacked high along the wall of the building, creating a maze. The odor of rotting garbage and human urine made Maddie want to retch. She cupped a hand over her nose and mouth, swatted at flies, and continued along the narrow twisting alley. Shadow and sunlight alternately danced across her face. Her shoe slipped in something wet and sticky.

All at once, a strong male hand reached out from between two towers of crates, grabbed her by the arm, and yanked her off her feet. She landed with a start against a familiar male chest. Cool hazel eyes met hers.

"Samuel Robert Weatherspoon! You scared the life out of me."

"Shh." He put a finger to her lips. "I don't have much time and there's a lot I need to tell you."

Maddie said nothing more and just listened, the two of them huddling between the crates. As he'd done often in the past, he came to her today—at great personal risk—to impart valuable information the women of Eden would use in their robberies.

"McSween is planning to ambush you at the mineral spring," he said.

Maddie gasped in shock. "How did he find out?"

"An educated guess, most likely. You'll have to call off the robbery."

What other choice did they have? "Thank you for warning us."

"You've heard the Brubakers are arriving by train the day after tomorrow?"

She nodded.

"They aren't. The story is false. It's being circulated in an attempt to capture the robbers should they board the train. The Brubakers are actually arriving by private stage. On Friday, not Wednesday. Late afternoon. Taking the southeast route through Ghost Horse Pass. Only a few people know about it."

"I'll tell the council tonight." News of the delay would not be received well. Maddie worried that widespread panic might erupt in Eden.

"How are your food supplies holding out?" he asked.

"They aren't." Her voice hitched.

"Will you ambush the Brubakers at Ghost Horse Pass?"

"I can't say. That's up to the council. But my guess is we will. There are a lot of good places to hide in the cliffs, if we can get up there." She groaned, sick at heart. "We have to do something. We aren't going to last much longer." Her small salary, which she'd received the day before, had gone to pay the farrier. Granny Fay's horses had needed new shoes, and the women needed the horses.

"Here." He took her hand and placed a small pouch in it.

"What's this?" When she realized the pouch contained coins, she asked, "Where did you get—"

"Don't ask if you don't want to know." His eyes

twinkled with a mischief she'd seen all too often during their childhood together in West Virginia.

"Which means you didn't come by it honestly," she teased.

"You're a fine one to talk," he teased back, but then his smile faded. "It's not much. Only about twenty dollars. But you should be able to buy a little something to eat."

Yes. Maddie could already picture sacks of flour and beans lying in the back of the surrey. They'd stop at the Mexican produce vendor on their way out of town for baskets of onions, carrots, and cabbage. Twenty dollars wouldn't buy a whole lot, but tonight at least, everyone in Eden would be eating biscuits and vegetable soup.

Overwhelmed with emotion, she said, "I miss you so much."

He folded her into an affectionate embrace. "Let's leave here today. Me, you, and Josephine." He took her hand, the one clutching the pouch. "We can buy train tickets with this money."

"We can't leave. There's a price on your head. As long as you stay in Edenville, you're safe. No one will find you. And I can't leave Eden. Not yet." She thought of Scott and the future they were never going to have. "But when this is over, yes. Maybe then we can all go away. I pray it's soon."

"I have to go. My boss has me at his beck and call these days."

"I should go, too."

"Hurry, before that pig Abernathy realizes you're missing. He doesn't need another excuse to run you ragged."

After a quick glance around to ensure the alleyway was clear, he dashed off and ducked behind the side of the neighboring building, his coat tails flapping in the breeze.

Maddie crept out from the behind the crates. Before stepping through the door to the stockroom, she remembered to drop the pouch of coins into her apron pocket.

How she wished she had three hundred more such pouches. Then she, Constance, and Dora wouldn't have to rob the Brubakers. She'd take her share of the money and get as far away from Eden as possible.

Instead, come Friday late afternoon, she'd be holding her pistol to Hammond Brubaker's head, demanding he turn over all his money and his wife's jewels. She prayed it would be enough to feed the population of Eden for a few more weeks.

When was it ever going to end?

From down the street, Scott watched Maddie and Constance leave the company store and walk to the end of the main road where the old nurse, Granny Fay, waited in the surrey. There, they were joined by another woman Scott didn't recognize, and the four conversed for numerous minutes while sitting in the surrey.

Maddie withdrew an object from her apron pocket that, when passed around, elicited an excited response from her companions. Eventually, they were joined by Gertrude Michaelson, the maid from the hotel. She also displayed great enthusiasm when presented with the object.

Rather than head out of town, Granny Fay turned the surrey around and drove to the company store. Scott followed, keeping a discrete distance behind.

"What are you up to?" he muttered to himself when everyone except Granny Fay climbed out.

Gertrude went inside the store while the rest remained behind. Ten minutes later, Gertrude emerged, accompanied by a young clerk toting a large sack of flour. Scott had been watching the store all week, more closely on the days Maddie worked. Until today, he'd seen nothing out of the ordinary.

Why hadn't Maddie and Constance purchased the flour earlier while they were working? And what was the object Maddie had given Gertrude?

Suddenly, the answer came to him. *Money.*

Maddie had given Gertrude money to buy the flour. Stolen money? That would explain why Maddie hadn't been the one to purchase the flour. Had she stolen the money from the company store? Or, as he suspected, had she gotten it from the robbers as payment for helping them?

Blood racing, he inched closer.

The clerk loaded the bulging sack onto the surrey's floor, then returned to the store. He emerged twice more, each time carrying a sack and loading it into the surrey. With a friendly salute, he bid the women good-bye. Maddie, Constance, and Gertrude walked alongside the surrey, probably because the load would be too heavy for the mismatched pair of sorry nags pulling it.

Before reaching the edge of town, they turned down a side street. A minute later, Scott spotted them. They'd stopped to barter with a Mexican vendor selling produce out of a ramshackle lean-to.

Baskets laden with vegetable were piled into the surrey on top of the sacks of flour. Money changed hands, and the women were off again. Scott had to duck into a doorway to avoid being seen. The moment they passed him, he cut across the street and sprinted toward the livery stable where his horse was boarded.

Against the rules or not, Eden was about to have another male visitor.

* * *

Not fifty yards from Eden, Scott concealed himself behind some paloverde trees and watched the bustle of activity. The food delivery had generated much excitement among the members of the small community. Rage at Newlin and his greed erupted anew inside Scott. How could anyone with a shred of decency allow helpless women and children to go hungry? And what about the citizens of Edenville? Yes, a few had stepped forward, but most lived in such fear of Newlin that they didn't dare defy him.

Scott watched the cooking operation unfold for a good hour. By then, the muscles in his legs and back were protesting loudly. He wouldn't have minded the discomfort if he'd seen anything of interest, but he hadn't. The trip was a complete waste of time.

"What were you expecting?" he asked himself. "That the robbers would suddenly appear and join the women for supper?"

He stood and immediately wished he hadn't. Grunting, he hobbled to his horse, working out the kinks in his legs. And then, through the low hanging branches of a tree, he saw someone crawling between the rails of the rickety fence surrounding Eden.

Maddie!

She wasn't alone. Josephine skipped alongside her mother. As if in answer to his silent bidding, the two strolled toward him, stopping every few steps to pick flowers. His heart thundered faster and harder with each step they took.

Was she there to meet someone? The robbers perhaps?

Pain and discomfort forgotten, Scott stooped down and crawled behind a leafy bush.

Again he waited, and again he was disappointed.

No stranger materialized from out of nowhere for a clandestine meeting. Maddie and Josephine were enjoying a walk before supper and picking flowers. Nothing more.

Scott decided he'd seen enough when Josephine suddenly broke away from Maddie and ran off, straight toward his hiding place.

"Come back," Maddie called and took chase.

Josephine skidded to an abrupt halt not ten feet away from Scott and plopped down on her knees. Cooing, she plucked a cluster of tiny white blooms sprouting from the dry ground.

Scott didn't dare move. He didn't dare breathe.

Awakened from his nap, his horse snorted and shook his head. The movement must have caught Josephine's attention for she looked up . . . right at Scott.

She screamed, hopped to her feet, and bolted straight for her mother. Wrapping her arms around Maddie's leg, she clung on for dear life.

"Sweet pea, what's wrong?" Maddie touched her daughter's shoulder and squinted in the general direction of Scott. "What did you see?"

Scott did the only thing he could. Snatching the reins, he pushed the brush aside and led his horse out of the wash, pretending he'd just that moment arrived.

"Hello, Maddie."

Her nervous glance flitted from side to side as if she expected the sheriff and his deputies to spring from behind the trees. "Scott! What are you doing here?"

"I wanted to see you."

"Oh." She shifted uncomfortably at his blunt reply. "Why didn't you ride up to the gate?"

He touched the brim of his new hat and flashed a smile. "I was trying to avoid more bullet holes."

"I'm sorry about that." Her lips, normally full and lush, thinned.

Scott thought of the night they'd made love, when those same lips had tasted his naked flesh—every inch of it. With great effort, he pushed the memories aside. His body was slower to respond.

"Guards off duty?" he asked, knowing they weren't. Only temporarily distracted by the smell of supper cooking.

"They won't shoot at you if you're with me."

She pried Josephine loose from her leg. The little girl resisted, staring at Scott with large, luminous eyes set in a thin, dirt-smudged face. She probably didn't see many men, and it had been over a year since her father died in the mining accident.

"Just in case, you won't mind if I stick close to you?" Scott winked at Josephine while directing his comments to her mother. "The guards may not share your opinion, and I'm mighty fond of this hat."

Maddie smiled.

He felt a kick of desire so strong, he gulped air.

"Are you all right?" She gazed at him curiously.

"Fine," he lied and changed the subject, asking a question he already knew the answer to. "I heard about the fire. Did you lose much?"

"Yes, but we're managing."

He disagreed. She'd lost weight, and there were dark circles under her eyes. He wanted to choke Newlin with his bare hands.

"When was the last time you ate something?" he asked.

Her chin went up a notch. "This morning."

"Right." Scott unfastened the straps on his saddlebag, reached inside and withdrew a handful of soda crackers. "Here." He held them out to Maddie.

Josephine watched his every move like a cat stalking its prey. A very hungry cat.

"I told you, we're fine."

"Maddie," he said, impatient at her display of foolish pride. "Take the crackers." When she continued to refuse, he added, "If not for you, for your daughter."

He'd found her weak spot. She gave all but two of the crackers to Josephine, who stuffed one after the other in her mouth. While she chewed, she stared at Scott with shy curiosity. Maddie ate her crackers almost as quickly as her daughter, then wiped the crumbs away with an embarrassed smile.

"Thank you."

Scott removed his canteen from where it hung on the saddle horn. He handed it to Maddie after unscrewing the lid. "The water's not tainted," he said when she hesitated.

"I'm sorry." A hint of pink colored her cheeks. "I don't know what's gotten into me."

"You don't trust me."

"It's not that so much." She helped Josephine take a few thirsty swallows.

He chuckled. "Let's not be dishonest with each other on top of everything else. You don't trust me, and I don't trust you. Not where the robbers are concerned."

"You're right." She raised the canteen to her own lips and paused. They stared at each other until the air crackled with tension. Licking her lips, she tilted her head and drank deeply.

Scott watched her throat move, watched a tiny stream of water escape the side of her mouth and slide down her chin. His thumb itched to wipe away the water and stroke her soft skin in the process.

How he wanted her. Despite her deception, despite the possibility she'd made love with him solely as a means to throw him off the robbers' tracks, he wanted her. Now and always.

What the hell was wrong with him?

"Here," she said, returning the canteen.

He started to replace the lid, then changed his mind. Holding the canteen to his mouth, he captured her gaze as she had his. When he had her full attention, he indulged in a good, long drink. Imagination or not, he swore Maddie's taste lingered on the canteen's rim. Given his druthers, he'd have his lips pressed firmly against hers.

"Why are you here?" she asked when he finished.

"Isn't that obvious?"

"To spy on me?"

"Yes."

Scott's horse stood patiently while he replaced the canteen on the saddle horn. When Josephine displayed an interest, he patted the horse's nose and said, "Go on. He's very gentle. Nothing but a big ole puppy dog."

The little girl somehow understood him, for she approached the horse, and the two became instant friends. They were charming to watch and though he'd never been around children much, Scott found himself affected. Maddie, too, judging by her tender expression.

With sudden clarity, he understood something which had eluded him until this moment. "She's why you do it."

"Do what?" Maddie asked, going still.

"Help the robbers."

Her head snapped around. "I never admitted to anything."

"You don't have to." He stepped closer. "Your

daughter is hungry. She wears tattered hand-me-down clothes and sleeps in a hovel. There's not a person alive who would condemn you, who wouldn't do exactly the same thing in your shoes."

"I can think of one." Bristling, she spun sideways. "Your employer, Thaddeus Newlin."

He caught her before she got far and turned her back around. "Don't go."

She made a sound, a combination of distress and frustration. "There's so much you don't understand." Her voice caught.

"How can I when you won't tell me?"

"If you're expecting a confession, you're wasting your time."

He drew her against him. "You don't have to confess. I already know you lied to me about the dress you wore that night." He didn't have to specify which night. Her quick intake of breath told him she recalled the exact date as well as he did. "It belongs to Mrs. Jacobson. Did the robbers give it to you as payment for helping them?"

"I'm not going to answer any more of your questions."

"Yes, you are." His fingers inadvertently tightened their grip on her. He exerted a conscious effort to relax them. "One more question, Maddie. Please."

"Scott." Her tone was less firm, her stance less rigid than before.

"Did you come to my room just to keep me busy while the robbers were stealing from the Jacobsons?"

She didn't immediately answer, which was an answer in itself.

He closed his eyes, his attempts to fend off the hurt a dismal failure.

Fool, he told himself. *You should be glad your suspicions are confirmed.*

"That's not the reason I made love to you," she said softly, hesitantly.

His eyes slowly opened.

She'd adverted her head. Lifting a hand, he cradled her chin and forced her to meet his gaze.

"Then why?" Hoping was stupid. He'd learned long ago it was an exercise in futility. Yet, he did hope and was rewarded for his efforts.

"I . . . desired . . . you."

"And do you still?"

"Yes."

Her reply sealed both their fates.

"Maddie, sweetheart." His arms went around her.

She offered a token resistance. "Josephine will see us."

"You think so?" He liked the way the soft feminine curves of her body melded with the hard plains of his. What he didn't like was the lack of flesh on her bones. Her recent weight loss concerned him. When he got back to town, he'd do something about getting her and Josephine some food. "Looks to me like she's pretty busy."

The little girl was indeed preoccupied with feeding stalks of dried grass to the horse. If she were aware of what Scott and her mother were doing, she gave no indication. Taking full advantage of their semiprivacy, Scott kissed Maddie.

He'd been right. Her mild protests were strictly for show. She responded to his tongue delving into her warm, moist mouth by standing on tiptoes and parting her lips wider. Her sigh of contentment incited rather than soothed him. The fingers climbing his back urged him to take further liberties. He happily obliged, and his demands for more were met with total and complete capitulation.

One kiss melted into two, then three. Scott didn't stop until a bell rang in the distance. At first he thought it might be in his head. Eventually the bell's tinny peals penetrated the sensual mist surrounding him.

Maddie withdrew, her agitation evidenced by quick and jerky movements. Was she remembering the last time they'd kissed outside Eden and the resulting trouble?

"I want you and Josephine to come away with me when this is over and the robbers are caught. I earn good money. I can take care of you both."

He hadn't planned on asking her to marry him, but, to his surprise, he didn't regret his impulsiveness. For something he hadn't felt in a very long time filled his chest and made it swell until he thought the seams of his shirt might burst. The feeling was so unfamiliar, it took him a moment to recognize it and put a name to it.

Joy.

Chapter Seventeen

Thunderstruck, Maddie asked, "Are you proposing?"

"Yes." He chuckled, then instantly sobered, tenderly brushing a strand of loose hair from her face. "I'm sorry. I really botched that. Would it help if I got down on one knee?"

He was making jokes, which in itself was amazing. She didn't think Scott McSween capable of humor. He was, however, very capable of anger, which is how he'd react if he found out her true involvement in the robberies.

It was neither a risk she was prepared to take nor a lie she was prepared to live.

"Do you love me?" she blurted, startling herself with her question.

"I . . . I care for you. Deeply."

Care for her deeply?

His honest admission shouldn't have pained her. They'd only known each other a month. In that time she'd lied to him, intentionally misled him, manipulated him, and seduced him like one of the prostitutes at the Strike It Rich. And yet, his words did pain her. Stupid and silly and unrealistic as it might be, she wanted him to love her.

Maddie had married once before for convenience. She'd agreed to be someone's wife to evade a bad situation. And while she had developed strong feelings for William, there were days she sensed something missing in their marriage. Her parents, for all their woes, had married for love, and part of her had envied their devotion to each other. She didn't want to repeat past mistakes by accepting a proposal from a man who didn't love her.

Did she love Scott?

Yes, she did. At least, she was falling in love with him. She wouldn't have given herself to him out of wedlock if some part of her hadn't been madly head over heels. Which made his proposal tempting.

Maybe once they'd robbed the Brubakers, and if they got as much money and jewels as Delilah seemed to think they could, Maddie could quit leading the robberies. Scott truly would be a good provider and a good father to Josephine. He'd see to it they wanted for nothing, and he'd protect them with his life if necessary.

But would he protect her from Thaddeus Newlin if he learned of her double life, especially when he only cared deeply for her?

There were also the women of Eden to consider. They'd become her family—and they were her responsibility. She'd made them a promise to help get back the money Newlin stole from them. Maddie was a liar and a thief, at one time an out-and-out cheat, but she had yet to ever break a promise.

"I hate seeing you and Josephine living in squalor," Scott said. "Let me give you a better life." He pulled her to him.

It was a shame he didn't love her, for in that moment, Maddie fell a little more in love with him.

Guilt squeezed her insides. She had to refuse his proposal. He didn't deserve a wife who'd spend every day they were together lying to him and hiding her past.

"I'm . . . honored and flattered, but I can't accept."

"Why?"

She felt him tense. "It's not easy to explain."

"Is it because I didn't say I love you? Lots of couples marry for reasons besides love."

"If love, or lack of it, were the only reason holding me back, I'd marry you in a heartbeat." A sob broke loose, and she hid her face in his shirt front. "I can't leave my friends. Please try and understand."

"They'll get along without you."

"Perhaps. But there's more to it."

"Tell me. I might be able to help."

"You can't. Not unless you're able to force Newlin to hand over twenty thousand dollars."

"That much?"

"There were one hundred and sixty-seven miners killed. At six dollars a day, it adds up fast. The really sad part is with almost three hundred of us in Eden, it wouldn't last long. Not with prices what they are in Edenville."

"And you wouldn't feel right leaving your friends behind to marry a well-to-do private investigator?"

"Yes."

He lifted her away from him. For once, his expression wasn't guarded. Genuine affection and a hint of admiration shown in his gray eyes. "You aren't single-handedly responsible for saving them all, Maddie."

Not singlehandedly, but she was responsible. And committed.

"Maybe someday I can leave Eden." Maybe even with Scott, though she doubted it. "When there's enough money in the community treasury for every woman and child to buy a train ticket out of Edenville or settle into a new home."

"What about Josephine?" He glanced over at the little girl playing with the horse. "Are you willing to let her continue suffering because of a misplaced sense of duty?"

"That's not fair," she moaned. "Josephine is hardly the only child suffering."

But oh, how she wanted to give her daughter a life where she didn't wake up every morning and go to bed every night hungry. Scott could make that happen. But he could also leave her and Josephine in the same or worse circumstances if he found out Maddie had deceived him.

"You're right," Scott said. "That wasn't fair." He hugged her soundly, and she detected his body stirring. "I want you, Maddie, and I'm willing to fight dirty to have you."

"If things were different . . ." She sighed at the utter unfairness of it all.

"Do one thing for me, please," he asked.

"What's that?"

"Don't say no right away. Think about my proposal for a few days."

"I said I can't—"

He cut her off with a quick kiss. "Just think about it. And in another week or two, when the robbers are sitting in jail, I'll ask you again."

Maddie's stomach did a somersault. She wasn't sure what upset her more, the prospect of sitting in jail or Scott learning it was she who'd led the robberies.

"Your supper is ready, and I need to leave," he said.

"Thank you for the proposal. It means more to me than you'll ever know."

"I'm hoping for a yes."

He kissed her again. Though she tried to resist, he very quickly coaxed a shuddering response from her.

"Maddie." He laid his cheek against her. "Whatever your decision, swear to me you'll stay away from the robbers. They're going to be caught soon, and I don't want you to be implicated. Newlin will punish anyone who's helped them, man, woman, or child."

If what Scott said was true, the entire population of Eden could be arrested.

"Swear to me." He strengthened his hold on her.

There was nothing left for her to do but tell him what he wanted to hear. "I swear."

He relaxed his hold on her and smiled. "Go. Eat. I'll stop by the company store tomorrow. Tell Granny Fay not to wait for you. I'll bring you home after we've had dinner."

"Scott, I—"

"Dinner, Maddie. Tomorrow. In fact, have Granny Fay bring Josephine with her in the surrey. The three of us will dine together. A real family outing."

"I won't change my mind about your proposal."

"You still need to eat," he reasoned.

"All right. You win. We'll have dinner with you."

His grin was triumphant, and Maddie silently reprimanded herself for agreeing too readily.

She went to Josephine and stroked the little girl's hair, then tugged on her arm. "It's time to leave, sweet pea. Say good-bye to Mr. McSween."

Josephine hugged the horse's front leg and spoke garbled parting endearments. He tolerated her affection with good-natured calmness and a swish of his tail.

As they turned to go, Scott waved. To Maddie's utter astonishment, Josephine smiled brightly and waved back.

Her resolve, weak to begin with, crumbled to pieces.

Lulu cracked opened the door to Delilah's suite at the Strike It Rich and slipped inside. She shut the door behind her, wincing as the latch clicked loudly into place. The parlor and adjoining rooms were empty, save for an orange-striped cat asleep atop a footstool. Lulu remembered when Delilah's son, Henry, begged his mother to keep the stray. Henry no longer lived with Delilah, but the cat did.

The town madam had recently gone downstairs, making her customary grand entrance into the saloon where she would oversee the girls and check out the customers. If any of the males clamoring for her attention appeared to be free with a dollar or otherwise struck her fancy, she'd claim them for herself. The rest were left for the girls to pick over and divvy up.

Walking in a straight line to the side table where Delilah kept the liquor decanters, Lulu poured herself a glass of whiskey. The dark gold liquid seared her throat. A second large swallow helped dispel the burning. The remainder of the whiskey went down like water.

Lulu poured herself a second glass. With the exception of Delilah, Fat Mike didn't allow the girls to drink while on duty. If a client chose to bring a bottle along with him to her room, she could partake, but only in moderation. Fat Mike didn't tolerate drunks.

Unfortunately, he had a dandy of a drunk in Lulu.

God, she despised her job—despised her job, her life, and everything in it, especially the miners. Most of them were dirty and stank, and she loathed their grubby hands mauling her. Her dear sweet Virgil had never come to their bed without first washing up and shaving.

She'd loved him for that and all the other simple and endearing things about him. He was just nineteen when they'd wed, barely a man. They were both young, and Lulu appeared even younger because of her petite stature. The miners' wives would look at Lulu with her apple-round belly, cluck their tongues, and exclaim how she was still a child herself, not old enough to be starting a family. She'd been called Mary Louise in those days. Delilah had made her change her name to something shorter when she began working at the Strike it Rich.

Lulu wiped a tear away and contemplated having a third drink. Why did Virgil have to die in that terrible accident? Why had she lost the baby?

She'd probably never learn the answers to those questions. Sometimes, when she drank enough, she stopped caring, but only until morning when she woke up, hungover and miserable.

Her fingers had just closed around the neck of the whiskey decanter when she heard the knob on the door rattle. Setting her empty glass onto the silver tray, she had just enough time to rush to the settee before Delilah swept into the room.

Frowning, Delilah demanded, "What are you doing here? You're supposed to be downstairs."

Lulu's heart thudded erratically as she searched the room for a plausible excuse. Spotting a pair of gloves next to the oil lamp, she snatched them up. "I came for these. I've had this awful rash on my hands the last few days." She feigned a pout in a bid for sympathy. "It's getting worse, and I didn't want to put off any of the customers."

"Why didn't you say something?" Delilah went into her bedroom and returned a minute later carrying a small jar. "Here, try this salve. It works like a charm for me."

"Thank you."

Lulu didn't meet Delilah's eyes. The kind, almost maternal, affection shining there made her feel reprehensible for lying. The town madam was good to all the girls, but especially Lulu, perhaps because she'd lost her baby and Delilah had so recently given up her son.

"I'll be sure and return it soon."

"No rush." Delilah rummaged through an open trunk in the corner. "I'm glad you're here, actually. I wanted to talk to you." She produced a black and red fan from the depths of the trunk and snapped it open. Examining the fan for holes, she said, "I just heard Hector Boone is expected later. You remember him?" Delilah had a keen memory where customers were concerned.

"No."

"He's the stage depot manager." She folded shut the fan and heaved a sigh when Lulu continued to shake her head in confusion. "Tall, wiry, wears spectacles. He took a real shine to you his last two visits."

Lulu suddenly recalled the man. "He doesn't drink. Won't touch the stuff," she said with a twinge of disappointment.

"That's him. I want you to keep yourself available until he comes in, which according to his friends should be in another half hour. Make sure it's you he picks."

"Why?"

Another sigh from Delilah. "Don't you remember? I told you the Brubakers are arriving by private stage the day after tomorrow. I want you to pump Hector Boone for any information you can."

Ah, yes.

Delilah had visited Eden the other day, taking some money and attending a meeting. Because of her son, or maybe because she was a busybody by nature, she liked keeping abreast of the goings-on there. Lulu hadn't paid all that much attention when Delilah told her about the women's plan to rob the Brubakers. She'd heard about the fire, as had everyone in Edenville, and she certainly pitied the women their latest tragedy. But she had no wish to become embroiled in their dangerous and illegal escapades.

"It might be kind of hard to pump Mr. Boone for information, since he don't drink." And neither would she, not with him for a customer.

Delilah tapped the tip of the fan against her cheek and wiggled her eyebrows. "Honey, there are plenty of ways to inspire a man to talk besides liquor. Haven't you learned that yet?"

Lulu couldn't stop the sudden onslaught of tears.

"Hey there." Delilah came over and put an arm around her. "What's wrong?"

"Nothing." Lulu hiccupped softly.

"I know you don't like being a . . . doing what we do," Delilah said. "And to be brutally blunt, you aren't very good at it. They'd welcome you back at Eden if that's what you want."

"It's not what I want." Slowly, Lulu brought her tears under control.

"What, then?"

"I want Virgil and my baby," she blurted with more anger than she'd intended.

"That's not possible, love."

"No, it isn't." Lulu straightened, fitting a glove onto the fingers of her left hand. The smile she wore surely looked as phoney as it felt. "So where I live, what I'm doing, really doesn't matter now, does it?"

At eight-thirty, Lulu sat at a corner table, listening to a shaggy-haired miner with stained teeth drone on and on about his job, trying his best to impress her when she couldn't care less.

Where was Hector Boone, the stage depot manager?

The man had yet to appear, and Lulu was sick to death of entertaining miners. This particular one couldn't keep his hands to himself. Every few minutes his fingers snuck under the frilly hem of her dress and toyed with her garter. And every few minutes she gently shoved his fingers away.

"Lulu, get over here," Fat Mike hollered from behind the bar. For a heavy man, he moved with considerable speed, filling drink orders quickly as they came.

He's mad, she thought and braced herself. She should have taken at least one customer up to her room by now. A glance around the saloon confirmed Delilah hadn't yet returned and probably wouldn't for the remainder of the night. A fancy-dressed, high-stakes gambler had sauntered into the saloon earlier. His first shot of bourbon was personally delivered by Delilah. Not much later, the two of them disappeared.

Lulu was on her own.

"S'cuse me a minute, handsome," she purred and left the miner, vowing not to return to his table. Sashaying over to the bar, she asked Fat Mike, "You want something?"

He leaned forward, his congenial smile in contrast with the warning he delivered. "I'd better see someone following your sweet ass up those stairs in the next fifteen minutes or you're fired. You got it?"

Lulu got it. And without Delilah in the vicinity to bail her out, she didn't have much choice except to do what Fat Mike told her.

She pivoted on the heels of her shoes, leaned against the bar, and took mental stock of the men, weeding out those who'd come strictly to play cards and socialize from those who'd come for a bit of hanky-panky. Why, for pity's sake, did most of them have to be miners?

"Can I buy you a beer, miss?" A vaguely familiar man in a black suit and bowler hat eased along the bar toward her, his gaze at first apprising and then appreciative. "You look like you could use one."

He had no idea how right he was.

She smiled beguilingly, caring not one whit about Fat Mike and his silly no-drinking rule. "Why, thank you. That'd be right generous of you. And I'll have a whiskey if you don't mind."

"The name's Otis." He signaled Fat Mike for a bottle and two glasses. "Otis Tarrington. I'm a notions salesman originally from Ohio."

She refrained from gulping the entire glass and took only small sips. "I've seen you in here before."

"I make the trip to Edenville about once a month."

"Tell me, sir." She sidled closer. At least this one didn't smell. "What's it like being a notions salesman?"

Lulu didn't require the full fifteen minutes Fat Mike had allotted her to entice Mr. Otis Tarrington up to her bedroom. What's more, it bothered him none that she polished off most of the bottle he brought with them. He was a talker, which suited her just fine. While he conversed, she drank. Eventually, he ran out of things to say and groped her breasts. Lulu set her glass down on the bedside table and resigned herself to the inevitable.

Twenty minutes later, he climbed off her naked body, panting and sweating. By then, Lulu was pleasantly and thoroughly inebriated.

"That was nice," he said, gathering his pants from the floor.

"Yes, it was," she answered on cue. She'd been in another world during the entire ordeal. The sound of liquid being sloshed into a glass reached her ears, and she roused herself.

"You want the last of this?"

When had he gotten out of bed?

"Why, yes." Sitting up, she waited for her head to stop spinning before taking the half-full glass he offered. "Thank you, Mr. Boone."

He sat down next to her. "My name's Otis Tarrington."

She squinted at him and almost burst out laughing. The lug was actually hurt she'd forgotten his name. If he only knew how many men's names she'd forgotten over the past year.

"Otis, of course. I'm sorry. I was supposed to meet another gentleman tonight. Mr. Hector Boone." She batted her lashes at him, which felt heavy and thick. "I'm glad he didn't show."

"Hector Boone, the stage depot manager?"

"You know him?"

"Sure. I travel by stage as often as I do by train."

Guzzling the last drops of whiskey, Lulu fell back onto her pillow. "I was supposed to pump him for information."

"What kind of information?"

Because Otis Tarrington seemed genuinely interested and it had been ages since anyone had wanted more from her than a quick roll in the sack, Lulu told him.

"About the Brubakers. They're arriving by private stage Friday afternoon."

"Really? I heard they were coming by train tomorrow."

"Shh." Lulu giggled and put a finger to her lips. "It's a secret. Don't tell anyone."

"How'd you find out?"

The interest in his eyes changed, becoming sharper, which put Lulu on guard. She abruptly changed her story.

"Someone in the saloon was saying something the other day."

"Who?"

"Some feller who works in the mining office." She flung off the bedsheets and teetered to her feet. "Never seen him in here before." Her sluggish heart accelerated, and the tide of blood pumping through her veins cleared her head somewhat.

"Are you all right?" Otis asked, swiveling around to watch her dress. The bedsprings creaked in protest.

"Peachy." She pushed his hands away when he reached out to help her with her dressing gown. "Sorry, but your hour's up. You need to get outta here and settle your tab with Fat Mike."

Not needing to be told twice, he nodded and proceeded to dress.

"Thanks," he said before departing. "It really was nice."

"Yeah, sure." She shut the door in a hurry, resting her pounding head on the unyielding surface.

What all had she said to Otis Tarrington? Something about the Brubakers arriving by private stage.

It doesn't matter, she told herself. *He's just a traveling salesman and will probably be gone by morning.*

But she couldn't shake the feeling she'd revealed too much, or the giant stab of guilt pricking her middle.

Delilah was going to be mighty angry with her when she found out—if she did find out. Then what would Lulu do?

She'd figure it out tomorrow. Right now she needed something to take the edge off her headache.

Shielding his eyes from the glare, Scott stepped off the train and onto the depot platform, his boot heels making hard contact with the wooden planks. The late morning summer sun beat down on the large and disappointed crowd gathered to meet the Brubakers, unmercifully bright and hot. Its intensity would only worsen as the day progressed.

But then, as far as Scott was concerned, the day had already gone to hell in a handbasket. What was one more irritation?

"Well that was a complete and utter waste," Sheriff Lunsford grumbled when Scott joined him at the far end of the depot. "What'd'ya think happened?"

Beside them the train's engine hissed and spit, punctuated by the occasional groan.

"I'm not sure. The robbers may have decided to ambush the Brubakers at the mineral spring. The train was always a long shot."

Scott, along with a half dozen of Newlin's guards in the guise of passengers, had ridden the train from the Vista Linda Mine to Edenville. Hoping to set a trap for the robbers, Scott had circulated a story around town that the Brubakers would be on the train and that Hammond Brubaker's health was in a state of decline, giving the impression he'd be an easy target.

The trap had failed. The train arrived in Edenville

without incident. No one was more irritated than Scott. He wasn't accustomed to failures.

"Maybe you scared them off," Sheriff Lunsford said. "They were a hair's breath away from being caught, according to Mrs. Jacobson. If you had busted into that hotel room, we wouldn't be standing here now."

How often had Scott berated himself for exactly the same thing during the last two weeks?

He'd made a mistake. More than one. He hadn't followed his instincts and forcibly entered the Jacobsons' room when his gut told him something was amiss. And he'd allowed his desire for Maddie to distract him at a critical moment when he should have been paying attention to his job. He didn't, however, regret making love with her. Never in a million years would he regret that.

But, damn it, he'd been weeks on this case. The robbers should be in jail and awaiting trial by now, a fact Thaddeus Newlin reminded him of daily.

If Maddie would just accept his marriage proposal, Scott could go back to concentrating on work. She needed protecting, even if she didn't agree with him. The gang of robbers exercised far too much influence over her, and Scott didn't like it. He wanted her and Josephine the hell out of Edenville and tucked safely away in a nice, cozy home. Denver, maybe. Maddie would love the mountains.

Anger erupted inside him as it frequently had of late, ever since the other day when he, Maddie, and Josephine, dined together in the Edenville Hotel. Watching them relish their simple fare of chicken and dumplings had both amused and disturbed him. No one should be that hungry. It was easy to see why the women of Eden hated Thaddeus Newlin. He'd taken everything from them, right down to the food in their mouths.

When supper ended, Scott escorted them to the local

millinery where he'd made prior arrangement with the shop owner. Ignoring Maddie's vehement protests, he'd purchased her and Josephine matching bonnets. His intentions were purely selfish. He wanted to prove to Maddie his ability to provide for her and her daughter.

Afterward, they visited the livery stable so Josephine could show off her new bonnet to his horse. He again attempted to convince Maddie to consider his proposal. She refused, stating the same reasons as before. He countered, giving the same arguments, and the outing ended on a sour note.

What was this force driving him to save a woman who clearly didn't want to be rescued?

As each day passed and he made no further progress on the case, his frustration mounted. Who were the robbers? Where were they hiding, and what were they planning? It was as if they'd disappeared into thin air.

Scott had become increasingly convinced they were miners, perhaps survivors of the accident, friends and fellow workers of those who died. It made sense and would explain their connection to the women of Eden. He'd stopped by the company store several times to chat with Maddie since their supper together. She was his only real link to the robbers, besides their intended victims, the Brubakers. When questioned, she'd claimed to know nothing. She was either an accomplished actress or telling the truth. Scott didn't know which to believe.

It took a second or two for him to realize Sheriff Lunsford was speaking to him. "Sorry. What did you say?"

"I asked what your next move is."

"Ambush the robbers at the mineral spring." In light of the train fiasco, however, he would be wise to reconsider his strategy.

"That won't be for several more days. Mr. Newlin won't like the delay." Sheriff Lunsford's enjoyment of Scott's predicament showed in his gleaming smile.

"No, he won't." Scott wasn't looking forward to his regular meeting with the majority partner. His one consolation was that the Brubakers would be arriving the day after tomorrow, safe and sound. Only a few people knew about the private stage and they, according to Newlin, were impeccably trustworthy.

Scott had his doubts about Lunsford. He'd changed his opinion of the sheriff since arriving in Edenville. Lunsford wasn't nearly as competent as Scott first thought, and he was definitely hiding something, though Scott hadn't figured out what, or even if his secret was related to the robberies. But it was clear Lunsford harbored a grudge against Scott and would prefer he fail. Why, Scott had no idea. He didn't want the sheriff's job. When Scott turned in his badge five years ago, it was for good.

"I'm heading over to the mining complex to meet with Newlin," he said, and put action to words.

"Wait. I'll tag along if you don't mind."

Scott did mind, but he refrained from stating as much out loud. Better to keep the sheriff close until he found out exactly what the man was hiding and if it affected his case.

"Hey, McSween," called a friendly voice. "Good to see you."

Scott recognized the man in the black suit and bowler hat climbing the steps to the depot platform.

"Tarrington," he said when they met up. "You know Sheriff Lunsford."

"Sure do. Howdy, Sheriff." They all shook hands.

"You leaving town?" Scott asked.

"On my way to Prescott." Tarrington smiled broadly.

"Business has been hopping there lately, and I intend to cash in."

Scott wasn't much inclined for idle conversation with the talkative salesman. He opened his mouth to give an excuse when Tarrington interrupted him.

"All these folks here to greet the Brubakers?" He perused the gathering and shook his head. "Guess they didn't hear the Brubakers aren't coming till Friday."

"What did you say?" Scott couldn't believe his ears.

Tarrington repeated himself. "I heard tell the Brubakers are arriving Friday afternoon by private stage." He looked from Scott to the sheriff for confirmation. "It's not true?"

"Tell me where you heard it first."

"At the Strike It Rich last night. From one of the girls."

"Impossible," Lunsford croaked. "No one knows about the stage."

Scott didn't correct him. Instead, his mind raced as he mentally reviewed the list of people who'd been informed of the Brubakers' true schedule.

"I admit the little lady was three sheets to the wind and probably confused." Tarrington shifted his valise of samples from one hand to the other, the contents rattling slightly. "Though she mentioned Hector Boone and seemed rather convinced."

The stage manager, thought Scott with increasing alarm. Three sheets to the wind or not, Tarrington's "little lady" was privy to some highly confidential information. There was a leak in Newlin's office the size of a barn door. From his contemplative expression, Lunsford had drawn the same conclusion.

Or was it guilt that paled cheeks beneath his tan? Had Scott just stumbled onto the sheriff's secret?

"Do you remember the girl's name?" Scott asked.

"Lulu, I think," said Tarrington. "Pretty young thing with the saddest eyes. She can sure put away the liquor."

Scott turned to Lunsford. "You know this Lulu?"

"Yes." He nodded. "She was one of the Eden widows. Lost her unborn baby if I remember correctly. She took up with Milton Shanks, the bank manager, soon after that. He tired of her before long and tossed her out on the streets one night with nothing but the clothes on her back. She went to work for Delilah and Fat Mike over at the Strike It Rich."

Excitement ricocheted through Scott as his mind made the connections. Lulu was in possession of confidential information. She was a former Eden widow. The Eden widows, Maddie in particular, were in partnership with the robbers. It stood to reason the robbers also knew about the Brubakers arriving by private stage.

Forget the mineral spring! The robbers were going to attack the Brubakers' stage on Friday. His gut practically screamed at him, and this time he listened.

"We need to talk with Newlin right away," he told Lunsford.

"Agreed." The sheriff's eyes narrowed to slits. "You trust me?"

"For now."

So he was clearly more intelligent than Scott gave him credit for. But intelligence didn't absolve him of guilt. Lunsford could easily be the leak. His sister was head of the Ladies' Aid Society, vocal advocates of the Eden widows. Granted, the link was small, but there.

"Tarrington." Scott clapped the notions salesman on the shoulder. "It's vitally important you don't say anything to anybody about this. You understand?"

"Not a problem, especially since I'm leaving. And after Prescott I'm going to Tucson—"

Scott heard nothing more of what Tarrington said. The sound of his own footsteps as he and Sheriff Lunsford raced down the steps leading to the street below drowned the man out.

It was a stroke of luck Scott had run into Tarrington. He would have just enough time to devise a plan before the Brubakers arrived.

"Where's the most likely place the robbers would attack the Brubakers?" he asked Lunsford, his breath short as they hurried to the sheriff's office where Scott's horse was tied out front.

"Ghost Horse Pass is my guess. It's the place I'd pick if I were them."

And where I'll be waiting, thought Scott.

He was close to catching the robbers—could taste victory on his tongue. It would be twice as sweet when they were arrested, which, if all went well, would be in a little over forty-eight hours.

Chapter Eighteen

The stage was coming!

Maddie heard the horses in the far-off distance, and her heart rate soared, exceeding the staccato beat of their thrashing hooves. She closed her eyes and pictured dirt and pebbles flying as iron-rimmed wheels sped over deep ruts left in the road by countless other vehicles traveling the same route.

Five minutes at most until the stage rounded the bend, a blind corner she'd chosen specifically for the advantage it provided.

Constance and Dora scurried down the steep hillside to take their places in the middle of the road. Constance lost her balance and rode the last few yards on her bottom. Landing feet first, she brushed off the back of her men's pants and tucked in her shirt before taking her place beside Dora. Maddie squatted behind a boulder, its strategic location giving her a view of the road below and the approaching stage, visible now a mile or so away. A thick cloud of brown dust trailed in its wake.

The three women had left Eden late the previous night, walking the fourteen miles to Ghost Horse Pass under a moonless sky. Heat and the difficult terrain nearly did them in. Dora had fallen, spraining her ankle. She'd hobbled the rest of the way and complained not once about the acute pain she must have been suffering.

By the time dawn broke, they'd reached their destination and set up a modest campsite. After eating a meager breakfast, they napped for a few hours until the blazing sun drove them to find shade beneath the scrub brush.

After that, it was only a matter of waiting.

No one had been much in the mood for conversation. Dora rubbed the ache from her injured ankle and hummed a ditty. Constance scribbled a letter to her sister back in New York. Maddie knew Constance and Archie had been invited to return to New York and live with her sister, but neither sibling had the money for fares.

Maybe after today, if the Brubakers were carrying as much cash and jewelry as folks said they did, there would be a little extra for Constance. She had certainly earned special consideration.

So had they all.

More and more lately, Maddie had been thinking about passing the leadership of the robberies to someone else. Lavinia had once commented there were individuals in Eden capable of taking Maddie's place. Maybe she was right.

Then you could accept Scott's proposal and leave Eden, a voice inside her head urged. *Isn't that what you want?*

The stage, with its team of six galloping horses, exploded from behind a sloping hill a half mile up the road. Startled from her momentary lapse in concentration, Maddie reached for her Colt pistol with fingers uncustomarily shaky. Resting the barrel of the gun on the boulder, she willed her lungs to cease their rapid expanding and contracting.

She signaled to Dora and Constance, who signaled back and moved into position. Dora lay down in the middle of the road, arranging her body at an awkward angle as if she'd passed out. Constance stood in front of Dora, arms raised. The denim jeans and chambray shirts they wore were particularly scruffy in the hopes of passing themselves off as a pair of prospectors.

Suddenly, the stage rounded the blind corner, the horses charging at Constance and Dora like the devil's army freed from hell. The noise was deafening, and Maddie had to resist covering her ears.

"Help us," Constance hollered and waved wildly. Her and Dora's staunch bravery in the face of being trampled to death was admirable.

"Whoa, there!" the stage driver hollered. He leaned back and yanked hard on the reins, forcing the horses' heads to the right. The man riding shotgun reached for the brake. A grinding screech echoed through the gully, sending a flock of sparrows into frightened flight.

The stage and horses came to a stop mere feet from Constance and Dora, who, to their credit, hadn't moved. Both right wheels had gone off the road and into a ditch, leaving the stage tilted at a precarious angle.

"What in blue thunder are you doing?" the driver hollered, visibly vexed. "Trying to get yourselves killed?" He removed his hat and dried his sweaty forehead with the sleeve of his shirt. The horses stood on trembling legs, their heaving sides lathered with sweat and their nostril flaring. One of the lead horses pawed the ground impatiently.

"Kin you hep us?" Constance answered, imitating a male voice. She wrung her hands and fidgeted like a nervous old man. "My pardner here done collapsed fer no reason. I think he might be dying on me. We been together fer prit near ten years."

"Charlie," the driver ordered the man riding beside him. "Climb on down and see what's what. And make it snappy. We got a schedule to keep."

Maddie followed the man with the point of her gun. She didn't want to shoot him, but she would if he tried anything. Their plan was to draw whoever came to lend assistance close enough so Constance could pull her gun on him and hold him hostage. Dora would then spring to her feet and pull her gun while Maddie kept watch on the stage with its driver and passengers.

The man wore his hat pulled down in the front and the raised collar of his shirt hid his chin and throat. As Maddie watched him walk cooly and confidently toward Constance and Dora, the hairs on the back of her neck stood unnervingly on end. A tingling—not the good kind—irritated her middle.

She glanced quickly at the stagecoach, and the uneasy tingling intensified. Why weren't the passengers sticking their heads out to investigate or complain to the driver? Most people would want to know what was going on.

Something was wrong! Dreadfully wrong. Maddie felt impending danger clear to her toes.

She hesitated only a second before pulling the trigger.

The stage driver took the bullet in his right elbow, exactly where she aimed it. Blood spurted, showering his shirt front. He dropped the reins with a loud cry. Her next bullet careened off the toe of his boot.

"Son of a bitch!" The driver jerked and threw himself onto the seat. "Help me, would you? I'm a sitting duck up here."

The doors of the stage flew open and the passengers poured out, weapons drawn. There were three of them. All men. Not Mr. and Mrs. Brubaker.

Maddie had barely registered that one of the men was Sheriff Lunsford before aiming her pistol at the man with Constance. She figured to incapacitate him as she had the driver, but in the few seconds it had taken her to render the driver useless, the man had disarmed Constance and maneuvered her into a choke hold, his gun pressed directly into the back of her skull.

Dora started to rise. Without letting go of Constance, the man kicked Dora viciously in the side, and she fell face first on the ground with an "Oomph."

"Goddamn you!" Constance howled, fighting to get away. "Leave her alone."

Her flailing arm knocked the man's hat, and it toppled off, leaving him bareheaded.

He stared up to where Maddie hid behind the boulder, zeroing in on her exact position. His steel gray eyes flashed in the sunlight. "It's over," he shouted. "Come down now."

Maddie's heart missed several beats as she stared into Scott's face. She shouldn't have been so surprised to see him with the sheriff. Early in their acquaintance, he had bragged of always getting his man.

When she didn't immediately move, he said, "If

you're thinking of picking me off like you did Hank over there, think again. One shot from you and your pal here gets it in the head."

No longer disguising her voice, Constance yelled, "Shoot him."

Maddie didn't think she could, not without risking her friend's life. Once before Scott's gun had gone off when he was struck with a bullet, and two men had died as a result. She would not allow the same fate to befall Constance and Dora.

Holding her pistol by the barrel, Maddie lifted it in the air and tossed it down the side of the hill.

"That's fine," Scott said. "Now come on down. Nice and easylike."

Maddie tugged the kerchief tied around her neck up and over her mouth. With calm resignation, she climbed down from her perch to where her lover and the man who wanted to marry her would have her arrested and put in jail.

"Please God," she quietly prayed. "Take care of my Josephine."

Scott didn't once take his eyes off the man slowly trudging his way down the hill. The ragged clothes he wore were ill-fitting and hung from his gangly frame. His boots flopped as if five sizes too big. Even with a kerchief over his mouth, Scott could see the man's features were fine and immature.

He's nothing but a kid.

And, Scott reminded himself, a hell of a shot for someone so young. Gun or no gun, he wasn't taking any unnecessary chances. "Hold it right there," he said when the man reached the bottom.

His prisoner, a short fellow and not particularly

sturdy, began to struggle anew, clawing at the arm Scott had wrapped around his neck. At a sharp, stinging pain, Scott let out a short grunt and tightened his hold. Risking a quick glance at his knuckles, he was surprised to see three long, bloody scratches.

The old geezer had some pretty long fingernails. Long fingernails and spongy muscles. He wasn't particularly fit for a hardened criminal.

At his feet, the third robber rolled onto his side. That one, thought Scott, didn't have much fight in him either. One swift kick and he'd folded faster than a house of cards. It was amazing the robbers had been as successful as they were and eluded capture for as long as they had. They were either cleverer than they appeared or they had help.

The women of Eden. He could well imagine Maddie aiding this bunch of misfits.

"Hands in the air," Sheriff Lunsford barked from behind Scott.

"Somebody help get me down from here," the driver hollered.

Nobody paid him any attention, least of all, Scott.

The sheriff and his two deputies had their weapons trained on the shooter, evidently considering him the greatest threat of the three. Scott agreed. The kid could have another pistol hidden beneath all those baggy clothes.

"Please let us go," Scott's prisoner whined. "We didn't mean any harm. We were just hungry." Then he started to cry.

Hungry?

"Hungry don't make stealing legal," Lunsford growled. He tipped his head at the fallen robber who was making an effort to sit up, a task complicated by the hand he pressed to his undoubtedly aching side.

"Calhoone. Get that one up and on his feet." The sheriff smiled broadly. "You fellows are going for a nice ride in the Brubakers private stage. All the way to the Edenville jail.

"No!" Scott's prisoner went from crying to blubbering like a damn female.

Something registered in Scott's head. Something too inconceivable for him to take seriously. And yet . . . He looked at the scratches on his hand again.

Could it be?

With the tip of his gun barrel, he flipped his prisoner's hat off. A long black braid uncoiled to drape over his arm—a braid he'd seen plenty often enough in the company store during his many visits.

Constance Starkweather.

Scott's stomach clenched from the impact of an invisible fist driving straight into it. For several seconds, the people around him appeared to move in slow motion.

This couldn't be happening. There had to be another explanation. But it *was* happening, and the invisible fist buried in his stomach dug in and twisted.

"Keep your grubby hands off of me!" came a decidedly angry female voice. "That big lug over there busted my rib."

"Christ Almighty!" Calhoone exclaimed, leaping backward. "He's a . . . I mean, she's a woman. With . . . breasts! And I touched one of 'em."

The deputy wasn't referring to Scott's prisoner, but the one he'd helped to stand. Scott remembered having seen her in Granny Fay's surrey once or twice, though he couldn't recall her name.

"My wife's gonna have my hide if she finds out I touched another woman's breast." The deputy rubbed his palm vigorously on his pant leg, his face a mask of shock and disbelief.

Scott turned a limp and distraught Constance over to the sheriff. He was far more interested in the shooter.

"Take off your mask," he ordered, thinking he sounded more in command of his faculties than he felt. He pointed his gun directly at the shooter's head. It was a hollow threat, and he'd bet they both knew it. Still, he forced his hand to remain steady and stepped closer. "Do it!"

The face beneath the kerchief was revealed one feature at a time. Finally, the mouth was exposed—a mouth Scott would recognize anywhere. How could he not? He'd kissed it again and again until the taste of those lips were branded in his memory forever.

"Shit," he grumbled and said no more, for there was nothing more to say.

"Maddie Campbell." The sheriff chuckled and shook his head. "Shoulda known it was you. You're the only one around these parts who can shoot off a fellow's big toe without taking half his leg with it."

Scott had a sudden image of Maddie as a little girl, a pistol clutched in her tiny fingers, shooting tin cans off a fence rail for a hat full of coins. Not much had changed over the years, except for the targets and the amount of money.

"Let's get down to business, boys." The sheriff snatched a length of rope from his deputy and tied Constance's hands behind her back with practiced efficiency. The other deputy did the same to the woman whom Scott had kicked, a deed he now regretted.

"Reckon we saved the best for last." With a spring to his step, Lunsford started toward Maddie.

"No." Scott moved in front of him. "Let me."

The sheriff shrugged good-naturedly and relinquished the rope he carried. "Only fitting I suppose since you're the one who trapped them."

For an instant, Maddie's eyes clashed with Scott's. Emotions danced in their jade green depths, then vanished before he could fully identify them. What was she feeling? Anger at being caught? Shame? Fear? Betrayal?

She offered no resistance as he slipped the rope around her wrists and bound them securely behind her back. He paused for a moment as the magnitude of what he was doing sank in. Of all the things he'd imagined doing with Maddie, escorting her to jail hadn't been one of them.

"A favor, please," she asked softly.

Pride waged a battle with compassion, and he debated refusing. "What?" he asked dully.

"Send news of our arrest to Eden so that our children can be told we aren't coming home tonight."

The children, of course. They were the reason the women stole.

We didn't mean any harm. We were just hungry. Constance's cry rang in his ears.

Though the law probably would convict the three robbers despite their gender, no person in his right mind would blame them for what they did.

Blame, however, wasn't the issue where Scott was concerned. Trust was, or lack of it.

They'd made love. He'd asked her to marry him. Repeatedly. She should have known he would never allow harm to come to her. If Maddie felt betrayed, she had nothing on him.

"Right this way, ladies." Lunsford bowed and gestured expansively. "Your carriage awaits."

One deputy laughed at the sheriff's jest. The rest of

them filed to the stagecoach and climbed inside without so much as cracking a smile. Because their hands were tied, the women required help mounting the step. Scott watched and pretended he didn't care when the sheriff wrapped his large hands around Maddie's waist and gave her a boost.

Because of his injuries, the driver rode shotgun to Edenville, and Calhoone took over the reins. Inside the stage, the sheriff and the second deputy sat on one side, Scott on the other. Maddie, Constance, and the one who'd given her name as Dorothy Margaret Seidman, huddled together on the bench seat in the middle facing the sheriff. With each bump and dip, Dora, who occupied the middle seat, hugged her side and turned so as not to knock into either of her neighbors.

"I'm thirsty," Constance said in a scratchy voice. With six of them crammed in there, the stage's interior temperature had quickly escalated from warm to scalding.

"Plenty of water at the jail," Sheriff Lunsford answered, absently picking his teeth with a matchstick.

There were canteens up top, but Scott didn't argue with the sheriff. The women were his prisoners, his responsibility.

"Will you be making special accommodations for us?" Maddie inquired.

"And what would you like?" Lunsford's tone was biting. "Your own private outhouse, I suppose?"

"Clothes," Maddie said simply.

"And a place to wash up in privacy," Dora added.

"Sorry, ladies. Not possible."

All three female spines stiffened.

"Afraid you'll have to make due with what's available, just like any other prisoner." He appeared oblivious to their dismay.

The stage rocked unexpectedly when they hit a hole in the road. Dora whimpered in pain.

"Stop at the company doctor's office first," Scott told the sheriff.

"What for?"

"Mrs. Seidman needs to have her side examined and treated."

"He won't see her." Lunsford flicked the matchstick he'd been chewing on out the window. "Newlin's orders."

"The doctor will see her," Scott said evenly. "I'll handle Newlin."

"It's your funeral." Lunsford cranked the upper half of his body around, banged on the ceiling, and shouted, "Calhoone. Stop at Doc Hardy's place first before heading to the jail."

"Yes, sir!"

Maddie pivoted in her seat to face Scott. "Thank you."

For several seconds, they stared at each other. Her narrow face and thin body were lost inside the oversized hat and men's clothes she wore. Tears she'd been unable to wipe away had left tracks in the dirt smudging her cheeks.

Scott broke eye contact first, diverting his gaze out the window at the rolling landscape. Through sheer force of will, he shut himself off from Maddie and the pain ripping him apart inside. It wasn't easy, but it should have been. Between his family and fiancée, he'd had plenty of practice. Only when he sensed Maddie turn away did he start breathing again.

A few minutes later the first buildings appeared in the distance. They were approaching Edenville.

Reaction at seeing their sheriff riding in the Brubakers' private stage spread quickly among the townsfolk, who rushed to clear the streets and make way. Eyes popped, heads bobbed, and hands raised in greeting. Two young boys darted into the street and trotted alongside the stage.

"Who you got in there, Uncle Tom?" the braver one asked. He gripped the ledge of the open window and hopped up and down as he ran, trying his hardest to peek inside.

"None of your business." The sheriff gently cuffed the boy on the ear. "You and your brother get on home. Tell your ma I'm going to be late and to hold supper for me."

"Aw, shucks," the boys complained in unison, but did as their uncle instructed.

"Whoa!" Calhoone hollered from above. The stage slowed in order to take a sharp corner without dumping its passengers.

"I'll get out here," Scott said, and opened the door.

"You ain't coming to the jail?" Lunsford lunged out of his seat as if to haul Scott back inside.

"No." His hard-won control was too weak to test by watching the cell door close on Maddie.

"Mortimer Goldwater from the *Edenville Gazette* will want to interview you. This is gonna be the biggest story to hit town since the accident."

"You talk to him." Scott jumped from the moving stage, avoiding any last glimpse of Maddie. "I'm going to Newlin's," he hollered over his shoulder.

The sheriff swung the door shut and hung his head out the window, smiling broadly. "Eager to tell the old man the good news, huh? Can't say as I blame you."

Eager to tell him I'm through and leaving town, thought Scott.

Once he finished with Newlin, he'd head straight to the telegraph office and wire his agent to see if any new jobs had come in. With luck, there'd be one far, far away from Edenville and Maddie Campbell.

Scott started to wipe his boots on the rug outside mining headquarters, then decided the hell with it. He didn't care about impressing Newlin or whether he left dusty footprints on the highly polished wood floors. He wanted only to make his final report and return to his hotel room so he could pack his bag.

Newlin's secretary sat at his desk, the perpetual watchdog guarding his master's domain. He evaluated Scott with cool hazel eyes that missed little and gave Scott reason to ponder how much of the Edenville mining operations lay in this man's hands and not Newlin's.

"Good day, Mr. McSween."

"Is Newlin in?"

"Yes, but he's tied up in a meeting at the moment. Is there something I can help you with?"

"I need to talk to him right away. We've caught the robbers."

"You . . . have?" The papers Forrester held fluttered to the floor. He quickly recovered his composure and, after bending over to retrieve the papers, rose from his seat. "I'll inform Mr. Newlin right away. He'll want to hear all about it, naturally."

Scott leaned an arm on the bannister dividing the waiting area from Forrester's desk and watched the secretary cross the short distance to Newlin's closed door, noting the slight but unmistakable wobble in the other man's stride. Interesting that news of the robbers' capture should affect the otherwise unflappable Zachariah Forrester.

Newlin bellowed something from inside his office in response to Forrester's quiet rap. Cracking open the door, the secretary delivered Scott's news in a hushed voice.

"Well I'll be dipped in shallow water." Newlin's belly laugh carried into the waiting area. "Give us a minute and then send him in."

"Yes, sir." Forrester returned to his desk. "Mr. Newlin will see you presently. If you'd like to have a seat . . ." He motioned to the four empty chairs behind Scott.

"No, thanks." Scott crossed one boot over the other and leaned heavily on the railing. "I prefer standing."

Some minutes later Newlin's door opened and a young, modestly dressed woman emerged. Cheeks flaming and eyes downcast, she scurried past Scott, who had to work at hiding his surprise. He'd assumed Newlin was meeting with the mine superintendent or a buyer.

"Good day, miss." He tipped his hat.

Except for a small gasp, she ignored him. Wenching the door open, she fled the office. The woman didn't look like a prostitute, but Scott would wager the meeting had nothing to do with mining business and everything to do with private business. He'd heard the stories about Newlin's penchant for young, wholesome women. The man had a lot of nerve carrying on in his own office.

It gave Scott yet another reason to hate the majority partner and another reason to want to leave town on the first available train.

"Mr. McSween," Forester said. "Mr. Newlin will see you now."

Scott pushed off the railing. "You sure he doesn't need another minute to button up his pants?"

Forrester's answer was an indignant sniff.

Perhaps the young woman and the indelicate circumstances of her visit were the reason for Scott's unaccustomed rudeness. He reminded himself that just because Forrester worked for Newlin didn't mean he approved of his boss's habits.

"I apologize," Scott said as he passed Forrester's desk. "My remark was uncalled for."

The secretary stared up at him, and Scott was momentarily taken aback by the intensity and depth of character in the man's expression. He'd underestimated Zachariah Forrester, and that was something Scott didn't often do.

"Were the robbers taken alive?" Forrester asked in a level voice, but Scott heard the emotional undercurrents.

"Yes."

"Very good." Forrester returned to his work. "Unnecessary loss of life is always a shame."

It seemed to Scott the secretary breathed a little easier.

"Come in, come in." Newlin waved to Scott from behind his massive oak desk.

The majority partner had neither a hair out of place nor a wrinkle in his starched white shirt. Scott briefly wondered if he'd been wrong about the young woman and the purpose of her closed-door meeting with Newlin.

"Have a seat and tell me everything." Brimming with good cheer, Newlin removed a bottle of brandy from the bottom drawer of his desk along with two glasses. He poured them each a drink and when he was done, lifted his glass in a toast. "Here's to a job well done. Sure as hell took you long enough."

Scott didn't return the toast but he did drink the

brandy—in one gulp. Liquid fire burned a hole in his middle, giving him a much-needed distraction from unwanted thoughts of Maddie's formal arrest and what must be going on at the jail. He set down his glass, which Newlin instantly refilled, and began his account.

"We captured the robbers this morning at Ghost Horse Pass."

Like a starving man sitting before a steak dinner, Newlin rubbed his palms together in greedy anticipation of the details. "That's the route the Brubakers were taking."

"Yes. I learned two days ago our plan to trap the robbers on the train failed because of a leak. They were on to us, which explains why they didn't show. The Brubakers' arrival by private stage was also leaked. We anticipated the robbers might be planning an ambush, so Sheriff Lunsford and I put together a counter ambush of our own."

"And you didn't see fit to tell me?" Newlin roared.

"The leaks most likely came from someone on your staff, here or at home. The fewer people who knew, the better chance of success."

"Impossible! My staff is completely trustworthy. Each of them has undergone an extensive background check."

"A prostitute over at the Strike It Rich knew about the Brubakers arriving by stage and told one of my acquaintances."

Scott's remark gave Newlin pause.

"Did any of the men on your staff who knew about the Brubakers arriving by stage visit the Strike It Rich this week?"

"No." Newlin shook his head, but not with conviction.

"Are you sure?" Scott remembered the look in Forrester's eyes. "What about your secretary?"

"Forrester? Absolutely not." This time, Newlin's head shake was decisive.

"Most men have needs."

Newlin laughed. "I'm positive. I don't know where Forrester finds his pleasure, and I don't care. But it's not with prostitutes." He picked up a half-smoked cigar from the dish where it sat and relit it. The stream of smoke shooting from his mouth resembled the back end of a steam locomotive engine. "Forget the leak and where it came from. All that really counts is you caught the robbers." He rubbed his palms again. "Tell me about them."

"There are three of them. Young. Pretty desperate from the looks of them." Scott watched Newlin closely, gauging the other man's reaction. "And female."

"What?" Newlin coughed on cigar smoke. He pounded his chest until the fit passed.

"They're from Eden. Widows of the men who died in the accident."

"You're full of shit, McSween," Newlin wheezed.

"Not this time. You can visit them in jail as soon as we're done here."

"Women!" He sat back in his chair and stubbed out his cigar. "Who'd have guessed it?"

I should have, thought Scott. The clues were there. Had he just chosen to ignore them or been blinded by emotion?

Damn, Maddie. Why hadn't she told him? He could have prevented her arrest, stopped her from spending the next decade or two in prison.

"I suppose them being female is why they got away with it for so long." Newlin leaned back in his chair and shot Scott a penetrating look. "Are you certain they're the one who committed the robberies? Did they confess?"

"They didn't confess, but I'm fairly certain. It'll be up to Lunsford to conduct the investigation and a court of law to decide if they're guilty."

"Court," Newlin bit out. "Just what I need is a bunch of bleeding-heart women up on the witness stand, crying their eyes out."

"They have cause to cry. You refused to pay their dead husbands' back wages and death benefits."

"And that gave them the right to steal?"

"They're hungry and homeless."

"They tortured me," Newlin shouted, outraged.

"Can you blame them? Especially after the fire."

"What fire?"

Did he really have no idea what went on in his own town, or was he lying to cover up yet another sin? Scott had dealt with some unconscionable individuals as a U.S. Marshal and private investigator, but none more so than Newlin. Scott couldn't stand to be in the same room with the man. His actions affected so many people's lives, yet he could care less.

"The fire that destroyed the women's entire food supply." Scott's voice rose by increments. "The one started by *your* employee, Jonesy."

Anger which he could no longer contain broke free, directing itself at Newlin. That man was the entire reason Maddie and the others had taken to stealing in the first place. The reason she'd refused to leave Eden and marry Scott. The reason she now sat in jail, her life and her daughter's in ruin.

Newlin's face flushed dark red. "You think I'm supposed to feel sorry for these women, don't you? Well, think again. The mining accident wasn't my fault!"

"But everything that's happened since then is your fault."

"Who the hell are you to talk to me like that?" Newlin stormed to his feet.

"I'm the man who caught the robbers. A bunch of ragtag, starving women who are just trying to put food in their children's mouths."

"Don't talk to me like that." Newlin jabbed the air with his index finger. "I don't abide insubordination in my employees."

"As of today, I no longer work for you." Scott stood and turned his back on Newlin. "Sheriff Lunsford can fill you in the on the rest of what happened."

"I'll see you never get another job in Arizona again, McSween," Newlin hollered after him.

That, thought Scott, *would be a blessing.*

"Wait, Mr. McSween." Forrester caught up with him on the porch steps outside. "You forgot your weekly wages."

Scott studied the thick envelope Forrester held out to him. It was on the tip of Scott's tongue to tell Forrester what his boss could do with the money. He didn't want it or anything else that reminded him of his part in arresting Maddie and the others. If the women and children of Eden were in dire straights before, they were worse now that their main source of income had been incarcerated.

Abruptly changing his mind, Scott took the envelope from Forrester's outstretched hand.

Leaving mining headquarters, he went directly to the livery stable. There, he rented a wagon and horses, which he proceeded to drive to the company store. Parking in front, he climbed down and tossed a gold dollar to a young boy sitting on a nearby stoop.

"Watch the horses for me, will you?"

"You bet, mister!" The boy bit down on the dollar and a wide grin split his freckled face.

Inside the company store, Scott headed straight for the manager, who stood behind the counter ringing up a sale.

"Good day, Mr. McSween." Mr. Abernathy cowered slightly, his eyes cutting to the gun at Scott's side. "How can I help you?"

Scott slapped the envelope of money down on the counter. "How much food and supplies will this buy?"

Abernathy picked up the envelope and peeked inside. His jaw dropped. "Quite a bit."

"Enough to fill that wagon out there?"

"Two or three times."

"Then do it." Scott read off a list of the items he wanted.

An hour later he drove the heavily loaded wagon through the gate to Eden, a white flag nailed to the side and flapping in the breeze.

Chapter Nineteen

Maddie replaced the lid on the chipped porcelain chamber pot and shoved it underneath her cot. Bracing a hand on the pitifully thin mattress, she stood, her muscles stiff from two weeks of captivity.

She hated being restricted to her cell, though she doubted being escorted to the outhouse with an armed guard in attendance would be any better. Their once-a-day excursions to the alley behind the jail to scrub out their chamber pots—and anything needing scrubbing, including themselves—were enough of an embarrassment to bear.

With a weary sigh, she flopped down onto her cot and rested her back against the bars separating her cell from the one Constance and Dora shared. The two other cells in the Edenville jailhouse were currently unoccupied. Since their arrival, a disconcerting and sometimes frightening assortment of prisoners had come and gone.

At least on those days Newlin allowed them to drape

a blanket from the bars, affording them a small measure of privacy. Sheriff Lunsford might be issuing the orders or granting their few privileges, but Maddie knew it was actually Newlin calling all the shots where she, Constance, and Dora were concerned.

He'd come to visit them on the day of their arrest. Though he said little, Maddie would never forget, if she lived to be a hundred the look of cold hatred in his eyes. He hadn't come to see them since, but they felt his presence in other ways.

Humiliation was his primary method of manipulating them. Requiring them to use chamber pots and wash in public were just two examples. Newlin's hired goon, Jonesy, the one who had accosted Constance in the store and set fire to their supply tent, dropped by daily. The messages he delivered from Newlin and the insults he directed at Maddie for shooting him in the shoulder were simply an excuse. Intimidation was the real purpose to his visits, which he did quite well.

Newlin had made sure they were given decent, if ugly, dresses to wear and sufficient food to eat. He wouldn't have it said the prisoners were mistreated. They might have robbed and tortured him, but he laid claim to returning their dastardly acts with kindness and compassion.

Unbeknownst to the town, he forbade the children to visit their mothers, not that Maddie wanted Josephine to see her in jail. He hired a photographer to take tintypes of the children and had them presented to the prisoners as keepsakes by the Ladies' Aid Society. To the rest of Edenville, he appeared a magnanimous, forgiving individual.

Maddie knew differently.

The tintypes were yet another torture device. Gazing at Josephine's cherub face ripped Maddie's heart to shreds, but she refused to give Newlin the contentment of knowing his ploy worked.

A hand reached through the bar to rest on her shoulder. "Don't let him get to you," Constance said, seeming to read Maddie's mind. "It's what he wants, you know."

"You're right." Maddie patted the hand, grateful once again for Constance's and Dora's loyal companionship.

"The jury ain't gonna convict us," Dora said, sitting down next to Constance so that the three of them were huddled together with only the bars separating them. "Once the jury hears what Newlin did to us, they'll lock him away. Not us."

"That's right," Constance agreed.

Maddie didn't waste her breath arguing. Newlin had as much a chance of going to prison for what he'd done to them as she had of sprouting wings and flying to freedom during her next trip to the alley.

"Yeah," Dora said. "And it's not like they're gonna hang us. We didn't kill anyone."

Granted, they wouldn't be executed. But if Newlin wielded enough influence, and Maddie feared he did, she, Constance, and Dora would spend years, if not the rest of their lives, in a federal penitentiary.

Poor, sweet little Josephine. Would she grow up without ever knowing her mother? Not so very different from Maddie and her own mother, who had been there in body but not in spirit and then not at all when she unexpectedly died.

Grief tore at Maddie with razor-sharp talons. How could everything have gone so wrong? Had the choices she'd made, beginning as a child, led her to this moment?

All she'd ever wanted was to provide a decent home for her daughter, and to right a terrible injustice. Instead, she'd destroyed her own life, her daughter's, those of her friends, and thrown away the opportunity to marry a wonderful man.

Given a second chance, she'd accept Scott's proposal. And not because he could have provided for her and Josephine. Maddie loved Scott. She'd come to that realization when he was tying her hands behind her back after capturing them at Ghost Horse Pass. For once, his face hadn't been expressionless, and the agony she saw reflected there had brought tears to her eyes and an ache to her soul so fierce she had yet to recover.

Stop it, she chided herself. Scott was long gone from Edenville, and she couldn't change the past. Indulging in useless daydreams about what might have been only added to her misery. And she had a long road of misery ahead of her to travel.

With a sudden sense of purpose, Maddie sat up straight. Dora was right. The truth would come out during the trial. She, Constance, and Dora would see to it by testifying until they were blue in the face. People in Edenville were going to learn about the atrocities Newlin had committed and, God willing, start standing up to him.

She *had* to believe decency would prevail. If not, everything she'd done in the last year, everything she'd sacrificed, would be for naught.

The door leading to the sheriff's office opened, its squeaky hinges announcing the arrival of Lunsford's two deputies, both wearing big grins, one silly, one sheepish.

"Afternoon, ladies," the first one said.

Dora rolled her eyes theatrically. "Well, iffin it ain't Stupid and Stupider. Let me guess. You're here to tell us there's been a big mistake, and we're free to go."

"You shut up," Calhoone growled. "Another smart

remark and you'll be washing your chamber pot with your bare hands."

Dora snorted. "As if I ain't already." She hopped off her cot. "That tiny scrap of cloth you call a washrag ain't fit for blowing a nose, much less scrubbing a chamber pot.

"I can get you a better washrag." Leering at her, he lifted the ring of keys from his belt and unlocked their cell door. "And anything else you want. My offer still stands."

This wasn't the first time he'd propositioned Dora, and it wasn't the first time she'd rebuked him.

"If it's just the same to you, I'd rather kiss a skunk on the lips." She tilted her head and scrunched up her mouth. "Come to think of it, I don't reckon there'd be much difference."

"I've had enough of your sass." He flung open the door and advanced.

Constance rose and placed herself next to Dora. The two linked arms. "Come any closer and I'll scream. Orders are you're not to lay a hand on us."

"Leave 'em be, Calhoone," the second deputy barked. "We ain't got time. We gotta meet the sheriff at the courthouse."

Maddie's stomach turned over. The trial was scheduled to start tomorrow. Newlin had arranged for the judge to arrive in Edenville ahead of schedule. Or so their defense attorney had informed them yesterday. Young and inexperienced, he lacked the necessary savvy to go up against the prosecutor, an influential man who sat squarely in Newlin's back pocket.

"Get the lead out," Calhoone growled at Constance and Dora. "Or you'll be washing my laundry along with yours."

Constance and Dora obeyed, but their idea of "getting the lead out" clearly wasn't the same as the deputy's. It was a minimal effort at best, but fighting back even on a small scale bolstered their flagging moral.

Maddie didn't accompany them. She was taken outside separately, with both deputies guarding her every move. Like separating her from her friends, it was another of Newlin's attempts to strike fear in her. Today she vowed his ploy wasn't going to work.

As the second deputy was leaving, his pistol trained on Dora and Constance, he said to Maddie, "You have a visitor waiting outside. He'll be along shortly."

Anticipation shot through her. Visitors were rare to the jail, per Newlin's instructions. Both Lavinia and Granny Fay had been allowed, but no one else and only with a deputy present. Through them, Maddie, Constance, and Dora had learned how their loved ones were faring. The visits had been both a blessing and a curse.

Maddie pushed off her cot and balanced on legs not altogether steady. There could be only one individual permitted to visit her without the presence of an armed guard.

Newlin himself.

He would not find her looking as disheveled on the outside as she felt on the inside. Maddie hurriedly smoothed the front of her dress and patted her hair. Because she had no towel or washcloth, she wiped her face with the collar of her dress. She had just finished when she heard the door to the sheriff's office open.

Bracing herself, she spun around to face the lily-livered coward and give him his due. At the sight of her visitor, the fight drained instantly out of her.

Scott!

Either she teetered slightly or the floor beneath her feet rippled. She wasn't sure which.

He stood inside the doorway, his height and breadth filling the opening completely. They stared at each other for indeterminable seconds. Finally, when she could withstand no more, he moved into the room and approached her cell. The door closed behind him, shutting out the rest of the world and leaving them entirely alone.

"Hello, Maddie."

His astute gaze absorbed every detail of her appearance. Suffering a moment of shyness, she glanced away. How must she appear to him with her stringy hair and wrinkled clothes? He, on the other hand, looked marvelously handsome in his leather vest and freshly laundered shirt.

Taking a moment to ready herself, she relaxed her clenched fists and breathed deeply. Scott's visit might be just another of Newlin's attempts to rattle her.

She swallowed before speaking. "Hello, Scott."

"How are you?"

Contrary to his neutral expression, emotion seeped into his curtly delivered words. Maddie silently berated herself. She'd been wrong, Scott wasn't one of Newlin's pawns. He was here of his own accord. And seeing her locked in jail must be as difficult for him as it was for her, though for different reasons.

"I'm fine." She came toward him, not stopping until she stood directly in front of him. "I want to thank you," she said, her own emotions at war. If he didn't cease his intense perusal of her, her resolve to remain in control would waver.

"For what?"

"Delivering the food and supplies to Eden."

"You heard about that?"

"Lavinia told me." Maddie paused, her throat constricting. She'd been overwhelmed and profoundly grateful when the head councilwoman informed her of Scott's generosity. Having worked in the company store, she knew how much the food and supplies had cost him. "They would have starved without you."

"It's not just me. A lot of people have been helping out."

"Only because you led by example. Once they saw that you weren't intimidated by Newlin, they began to contribute, too."

"You underestimate the citizens of Edenville."

"I think not. Most would die rather than go up against Newlin. Even to help a bunch of starving widows and orphans. Until now."

Though none of the other donations had equaled Scott's in size, every little bit helped. Maddie no longer worried herself sick that Josephine wasn't getting enough to eat.

"I wish there were some way I could repay you," she said with heartfelt sincerity.

"I wouldn't let anything happen to Josephine. You know that, don't you?"

"Yes, but—"

He didn't let her finish. "Do you remember the day we met in the company store, and I offered you a licorice rope?"

She nodded. How could she forget?

"You told me you couldn't take something back to Eden for your daughter without taking something for all the children. I wanted Josephine to have food to eat."

"So you purchased enough for everyone." Tears gathered behind Maddie's eyelashes. Scott was without question a man of his word. If he promised to protect her daughter, he would for as long as he remained in Edenville. Another small burden lifted from her. "You're a good man, Scott McSween."

"No, I'm not. If you think that, you don't know me very well."

"I do know you. It was your former fiancée who didn't, and she's more the fool for it."

His eyes flashed hot and angry. "Damn it, Maddie. Why didn't you tell me about the robberies? I would have helped you."

"I couldn't tell you. Surely you see that."

"You think I would have had you arrested?"

"I . . ."

"What kind of bastard do you take me for? I wanted to marry you, for God's sake."

"It's not that cut and dry."

"It is. You either trust someone or you don't."

"That's right," she answered, her anger flaring to match his. "And if I'd told you about the robberies, I'd have betrayed the trust everyone in Eden placed in me."

"I wouldn't have turned you in," he reiterated with no less conviction.

"Can you say that with absolute certainty? You're a lawman, and I'm a lawbreaker."

"I haven't been a lawman for five years."

"Really?" Impulsively, she reached between the bars and laid her palm on his chest, over the place where he'd once worn his badge. "Then you know yourself even less than I do."

He didn't argue. How could he when she was so clearly right?

"Why are you here, Scott? I thought you left town."

"I planned to. Haven't quite gotten around to it."

He smelled of shaving cream. She closed her eyes and was immediately thrown back in time to the night they'd made love. He'd smelled of shaving cream then, too. And like that night, the spicy, very masculine scent intoxicated her.

"Is it because of the trial?" she asked. It suddenly occurred to her he might be staying behind to testify.

"No. I'm not needed. Lunsford can give an account of the arrest."

"So why then?"

"Guilt, maybe. It's not every day I arrange for the arrest of three women."

"You have no reason to feel guilty."

"Don't I?" His brows arched quizzically.

"You were only doing your job."

"I was only doing my job once before, and I killed two innocent men."

Maddie couldn't help herself. She stood on tiptoes and brought her face close to his level. "This isn't the same thing. Constance, Dora, and I aren't innocent, and no one died."

He squeezed his eyes shut. "But you could have. What if I'd shot you?" He covered her hand with his, pressing her fingers deep into his chest. His free arm snaked out to wrap around her waist and pull her flush up against the bars. "I couldn't have lived with myself if anything had happened to you." His voice was low and harsh and reached inside her to coil around her heart like a tightly wound lasso.

"Scott, I—"

He kissed her, effectively putting an end to her protest and bringing a small piece of heaven to her dingy jail cell.

She barely registered the bars pressing into the sides of her face. Scott was all she felt, heard, smelled, and tasted as his lips and tongue worked their incredible magic.

Maddie forgot momentarily about her bleak surroundings and entered a world where only the delicious pressure of Scott's mouth on hers existed.

Hope, unexpected and delightful, erupted within her—like a tiny seedling sprouting from the barren desert floor. Was it truly possible that she and Scott had a future? With him kissing her like he was, she dared to believe.

Slowly, reluctantly, he ended the kiss, brushing his lips over her cheeks before releasing her and stepping back.

"Good-bye, Maddie."

"What?" The implication of what he'd said penetrated her foggy brain. "You're leaving?"

"I have to."

Of course he did. She stared into his eyes and saw the despair there. The truth hit her with crippling finality.

Scott's kiss was one of farewell, not an assurance that they would be together one day soon.

"Will you come to the trial?" she asked in a flat voice. She didn't want this wretched meeting to be the last time she saw him.

"No." He gripped the bar, squeezing until his knuckles turned white. "I'll stay in town through the trial, but I won't watch the proceedings."

"I understand."

"Who's caring for Josephine while you're . . . here?"

"Granny Fay."

"I've set up a bank account in Josephine's name. Not much. Just enough to buy two train tickets out of here and take care of her for a year or so."

"I can't let you do that. Not on top of everything else." Sadness mingled with appreciation to form a large ball of pain that lodged in Maddie's chest. She didn't want Josephine living in Edenville where she'd grow up the daughter of a convicted criminal. Yet she hated the idea of Josephine moving away.

"I would have done more if you let me," he said.

Married you. Given you a home. Loved you.

His unspoken words chimed inside Maddie's head.

"I'm sorry," she whispered.

"Me, too." He let go of the bar. "I have to go."

Of course he did. Maddie held her jaw rigid. She gave herself credit for not giving into impulses and grabbing on to his shirtsleeve.

"Good-bye then," he said.

When she didn't respond, he left, closing the door behind him.

She waited several seconds. When he didn't return, she went to her cot and collapsed upon it.

The tears she assumed would flow somehow didn't. It took a while for her to realize it was because her insides were completely and utterly empty.

Newlin chewed the end of his lit cigar, his attention focused on the proceedings. Tobacco juice seeped into his tongue and gums, the bitter taste a reflection of his current mood. What was taking so long? And why in hell didn't the little twerp get to the damn point? Newlin sucked hard on the cigar and exhaled a thick stream of smoke. A trio of ladies sitting in front of him coughed and fanned their hands in subtle reprimand. He ignored them.

At another overruled objection, he groaned and smacked his forehead in disgust. He and the judge would be having a talk after court adjourned today. A long talk. The man needed to do a better job of shepherding the defense attorney. The trial was already in its fourth day, two days longer than Newlin deemed reasonable, and the end wasn't in sight. In his opinion, the women should have been tried, found guilty, and sentenced by now.

The current target of his frustration paced in front of the jurors, arms waving in the air and making a far better impression on the twelve handpicked men than he should have. Newlin's advisors had assured him the young and inexperienced defense attorney, a Mr. Samuel Phelps from Phoenix, would flounder when faced with the older, more experienced, and enormously charismatic prosecutor. But Mr. Phelps surprised everyone and rose to the occasion, earning the jury's sympathy by playing up the women's long-suffering plight against poverty and despair. If the rumors were to be taken seriously, the entire town of Edenville was following in the jury's footsteps.

"Tell me, Mrs. Campbell," Mr. Phelps prompted, "how many ladies from Eden have been attacked in the last year and a half?"

"Four," she answered.

"Were they badly injured?"

"Bruised and beaten. One suffered a dislocated finger and two others were molested before help arrived."

The packed courtroom came alive with murmured disapprovals and lowly spoken outrage. Since the beginning of the trial, it had been standing room only, everyone from the merely curious to the morbidly fascinated attending.

Hands folded primly in her lap, hair pulled back in a neat bun, and a plain dress that didn't quite hide the lush figure beneath it, Maddie Campbell, the robber leader, was making an impression. The wrong impression as far as Newlin was concerned. Rather than coming off as victims—which he and the other mining partners rightfully were—Maddie Campbell had painted them as an unscrupulous and greedy lot who evicted three hundred widows and orphans from their homes without a dime to their names.

The bitch.

His loathing for her burned nearly as powerful as his lust.

Since her arrest a few weeks ago, Newlin had spent his nights fantasizing about her and how, given the opportunity, he'd first slake his desire and then throttle her until he'd wrung the last breath from her body.

She deserved to be punished for the humiliation she'd forced on him in his railroad car and in the mine tunnels. She deserved to die for lying on the witness stand and turning the town—*his* town—against him.

"Tell us about the fire, if you please, Mrs. Campbell," Mr. Phelps coaxed in a gentle voice.

Maddie delicately wiped her nose with a lacy handkerchief and compressed her lips as if to prevent a sob from escaping.

"Take your time." Mr. Phelps's soulful expression encompassed the entire jury. "We know this is hard for you."

The crowd gasped in shock and horror as Maddie recounted the details of the fire and the subsequent starvation of the community.

Newlin, his loathing reaching fever pitch, pictured her naked and tied spread-eagle on his bed, pictured himself carving designs in her smooth, bare flesh with the tip of a razor-sharp knife.

Heads swivelled in his direction when she finished her story, the eyes boring into him accusatory. He wanted to shout that he hadn't set the fire and wasn't responsible for the crime his employee committed. Instead, he ignored the stares and chomped down on his cigar, the end of which had become a soggy, pulpy mess.

She's going to pay, he vowed. *So help me God.*

"Order, order," the judge demanded. His gavel hit the table with a sharp rap. Once calm was restored, he spoke again. "Bailiff, what time is it?"

"Seven minutes past five o'clock, Your Honor."

"Considering the lateness of the hour, I suggest we reconvene tomorrow and continue questioning the witness then. Does either counsel have any objection?" They did not, and the gavel banged again. "Court is adjourned until eight o'clock tomorrow morning."

"All rise," crowed the bailiff.

The crowd stood in unison and converged on the front door, creating an impossible bottleneck.

Newlin scanned each face until he found the one he was looking for. When Sheriff Lunsford's eyes connected with his, Newlin tipped his head imperceptibly to the right. Lunsford gave a single brisk nod in return, acknowledging the silent message.

Meet me in my office.

At the stroke of five forty-five, Newlin stood looking out his office window, a fresh cigar wedged between his index and middle fingers. As he watched a crew of second-shift miners leave the complex, he chased each puff with a sip of brandy. His thoughts were centered on the problem of Maddie Campbell and what to do about her.

"I want the Campbell woman dealt with," he said.

"As in eliminated?" Behind him, Sheriff Lunsford sat up straighter in the chair where he'd been slouching.

"You have to ask?"

"Mr. Newlin. I mean no disrespect, but I believe

what you're proposing is a dangerous plan. The townsfolk have taken the women of Eden, Maddie Campbell in particular, into their hearts."

"Which is exactly why I want her eliminated. She will *not* be found innocent. Do you hear me?"

"If anything happens to her, you'll be the first person they come looking for."

"Believe me. I'll have an airtight alibi." He spun around, smiling for the first time in four days. "My wife and I will be entertaining the Jacobsons and the Brubakers at my house tonight. Dinner will undoubtedly run late."

Lunsford shook his head. "People will talk. I'm not sure even you have enough clout to fend off their accusations."

"I want her dead! Tonight." The fury of his raised voice echoed off the walls as did the crash of shattering glass when he threw his brandy goblet into the far wall. "You get the job done, you hear me?" His head pounded with such intensity, his vision blurred. "Have Jonesy do it. Everyone in court today heard Maddie Campbell accuse him of setting their supply tent on fire. They'll think he took revenge on her."

"Possibly." Lundford pushed his hat back and scratched behind his ear. "But I doubt it. He works for you. It won't require a genius to put two and two together."

"Then we'll just have to take extra precautions."

"How?"

Newlin fought the urge to kick the nearest object. What had gotten into Lunsford lately? He wasn't usually this obtuse. "How the hell am I supposed to know? That's what I pay you for."

"I don't like it."

"You don't have to like it. You just have to do it."

"Where's Jonesy staying?" The sheriff hauled himself out of his chair.

"Ask Forrester." Newlin returned to the window, effectively dismissing the sheriff. He was tired of having to think for everybody on his payroll.

He heard his office door open, then shut. Silence descended on the room. Seconds later, however, the door opened again and Lunsford stuck his head inside.

"Forrester's gone."

"He can't be. I didn't give him leave to go."

"Well, he ain't here."

Newlin charged across his office and out the door, nearly knocking Lunsford down.

An empty outer office greeted him, fueling his rage to new proportions. If the spilt inkwell on Forrester's desk was any indication, the secretary had left in a hurry.

"When I find him," Newlin bellowed, "I'm going to fire him so fast his head will spin."

Maddie pressed the cherished photograph of Josephine to her breast and closed her eyes.

"I love you, sweet pea," she whispered. "God protect you and keep you safe."

"You did real good today in court," Dora said. Her disembodied voice floated through the darkness from the next cell. "Did you notice the way them jurors looked at Newlin? I swear, I never thought I'd live to see the day folks in Edenville would finally see that man for the monster he is."

"I'm afraid the jury is still going to find us guilty. They almost have to. We were caught red-handed." Maddie placed the tintype of Josephine under the folded quilt she used as a pillow and lay down on her cot. The clock in Sheriff Lunsford's office had recently rung ten o'clock but Maddie was still too agitated to sleep. Dora, too, evidently.

Not so Constance, who slept peacefully. Maddie envied her friend. The trial had taken a heavy emotional toll on each of them. Where Constance was concerned, exhaustion had prevailed. Maddie's mind, however, refused to shut down enough to let her body slumber. She fretted, wanting to be alert for her continued testimony tomorrow. But her fretting only made her inability to sleep that much greater.

It was a vicious circle from which she couldn't escape.

"You don't know for sure," Dora said. Judging from the sounds of movement, she'd sat up. "What was it our attorney said? We could be found innocent if the jury believes we weren't in our right minds because of being constantly hungry and mistreated like we were."

"They might." Maddie didn't think so. Maybe if they'd stopped at robbing Newlin. He wasn't about to let them get away with torturing him. "I'm hoping the judge will take pity on us during sentencing."

"He will," Dora insisted. "How can he not after today?"

Maddie wished she had half of Dora's confidence, but life had knocked her flat on her behind too hard and too often during her life.

"We'd better get some sleep." She turned onto her side, tucking her hands under the quilt so that her fingertips touched the tintype of Josephine. "We have a big day tomorrow."

"Yeah. Good night." Dora yawned and within a few minutes, she, too, fell asleep.

Maddie was less fortunate. The minutes crawled by as sleep continued to elude her. She lay in the dark, singing lullabies in her head, the same ones she sang to Josephine. When she first heard noises coming from the other side of the door, she thought it might be her overtired mind playing tricks on her.

But the dark figures bursting through the door with a thunderous crash were no trick of the mind.

"Who is it!" She sat bolt upright in bed, simultaneously digging in her heels and scooting backward.

"What's going on?" Constance yelped. She and Dora scrambled from their cots. "Maddie, are you all right?"

"Yes." Maddie rolled over and automatically reached for her rifle. She grabbed only air. Hissing a curse, she hit the floor with both feet and faced the intruders, standing with her back to the wall.

The commotion died as fast as it had came. Suddenly, a funnel of light filled the jail, swaying to and fro. It originated from a lantern attached to the arm of a man, his face distorted by shadows. As soon as he spoke, Maddie recognized him, and a fear like none other she'd known turned the blood in her veins to ice.

"Hello, ladies," said Jonesy. "And how are we doing this fine night?" His voice reverberated with false cheer.

"Get out now or we'll scream for the sheriff," Dora cried.

"Don't need to scream." Jonesy sneered as he moved toward Maddie's cell. Two large men loomed behind him "Who do you think let us in?"

"Oh, dear God." Maddie realized her earlier prediction was about to come true. Newlin wasn't going to let them get off the hook. But what were his plans for them? She didn't have to wait long for an answer.

"I suppose you're wondering why we came." Jonesy fit the key into the lock on her cell door and turned it. "Well, we're gonna have ourselves a little party." He laughed loud and menacingly. "A lynching party."

Chapter Twenty

"What's that!"

"Just some ruckus." Delilah patted her customer's knee. He was the nervous type, and the commotion on the street below had him ready to leap out of his skin. "It's Saturday night, and you can always count on the miners raising one kind of hell or another."

If she didn't get the silly little twit calmed down, they'd be stuck in her suite all night. The saloon downstairs was packed, and Delilah had her eye on one or two more prospects.

"You just sit tight," she cooed, "while I shut the window."

She had barely risen from the settee when someone banged on her door.

"Who's here?" The man fidgeted in his seat, his spectacles riding down the bridge of his nose. He pushed them back in place with his index finger.

"Relax, love. I'll send whomever it is away." The wide smile she showered on him vanished the instant she turned to answer the door. "Why now?" she grumbled to herself.

The banging resumed, louder and more urgent. "Delilah, you in there? It's me, Lulu. Open up."

Delilah yanked the door open, her patience at an end. Lulu had been driving her crazy lately, and the younger woman's drinking, which she hid very poorly, had gotten out of hand.

"What's all the fuss about?"

"It's Maddie," Lulu wailed, hands pressed to her cheeks. "They've got her."

"Got her . . . what?"

"Outside." Lulu's red-rimmed eyes blazed. Her hair hadn't been combed and her clothes were the same ones she'd worn the day before. "Oh, Gawd, Delilah. They're gonna hang her."

"What are you talking about?" Delilah stared at Lulu. "How much have you had to drink?"

"They're hanging Maddie. From the water tower." Lulu grabbed Delilah by the shoulders. "You've got to stop them," she ended on a sob.

Delilah knew then it wasn't the whiskey talking. "Those sorry-ass, good-for-nothing scalawags!"

Forgetting about her customer, she flew out the door and down the hall. Lulu hurried to keep up. Delilah took the stairs at a run, her petticoats swishing. She ignored the dozens of inquisitive stares directed at them as they darted through the crowded room.

On the boardwalk outside the front entrance they stopped long enough for Delilah to get her bearings. A mob had formed at the end of the street, loud, raucous, and increasing in size by the second.

Could Maddie truly be in danger of being lynched? From what Delilah had heard, the citizens of Edenville sympathized with the prisoners.

All at once, Delilah knew.

Newlin! The bastard was behind the lynching. Who else had the nerve or stupidity not to mention the money and influence, to attempt something so brash and reckless?

"This is all my fault," Lulu babbled, still weeping. "A few weeks ago I told that salesman about the Brubakers arriving by private stage. At least, I'm pretty sure I did. I don't remember much. He must've said something to that private investigator."

"You imbecile!" Delilah wheeled on Lulu, the pieces of what happened coming together. She immediately reined in her temper. Losing it would accomplish nothing except waste valuable time. "Stop your bawling and listen to me. We have to hurry."

Delilah's sharp tone reduced Lulu's crying jag to sniffles. "Gawd, I'm sorry," she said.

"Forget it. What's done is done. Saving Maddie is all that's important."

"How we gonna do that?"

"To start with, you get yourself over there fast." She shoved Lulu down the step ahead of her and pointed her in the direction of the mob. "Do whatever you have to do to stall the lynching."

"But I can't—"

"Throw yourself in front of Maddie if you have to. Pretend to faint or vomit. I don't care, just stall the lynching."

"What about you?"

Delilah didn't answer. She raced across the street and barged into the sheriff's office. Upon seeing him seated behind his desk—reading the newspaper like it was just another night on the job—she promptly lost the temper she'd held in check with Lulu.

"You slimy dog. I knew I'd find you here. What's the

matter? Don't have the stomach to watch the fruits of your labor?"

"Get out, Delilah."

"The hell I will."

"This doesn't concern you."

"No? I say it does. My son lives in Eden. *Our* son. Henry. You remember him, don't you?"

Lunsford wouldn't meet her gaze. "I care about Henry."

"Not enough to acknowledge him. And you're letting Newlin's men murder the one person who's kept him fed this past year."

"She stole."

Delilah gave a short, sarcastic laugh. "Were you born dense or has being under Newlin's thumb for so long squashed the smarts right out of your brain?? They didn't steal, they simply took back the money *he* owed *them*."

"Regardless, my hands are tied." He busied himself with some papers on his desk. "I can't stop what's been started."

She wouldn't let him ignore her. Walking over to the desk, she braced her hands on the edge and lowered her head until her face was inches from his.

"You were once a fine man, Tom. Fair and honorable. Folks admired you. Boys wanted to grow up and be just like you. I loved you so much I gave birth to our child. What happened?" When he didn't answer she shook her head in disgust and backed away, nearly choking on her disappointment. "Shame on you for allowing Newlin to turn you from a respectable lawman into a pathetic bootlicker. I pray our son doesn't take after his father."

With that, she twirled on her heels, not bothering to

view the effects of her cutting remarks. Sailing out the door, she ran smack into Scott McSween. He caught her with both hands.

"Newlin's men are trying to hang Maddie!" She grabbed large folds of his shirt in her hands. "At the water tower on the edge of town."

He thrust her aside. "Is the sheriff in there?"

She understood his gruffness wasn't directed at her but at the situation. "Don't bother." She clung to his arm, pulling him back. "He won't help. I've already tried. Newlin has him on too short a rope."

McSween didn't hesitate and took off down the street.

Delilah started after him. "Thank heaven there's at least one man in this town who isn't afraid of Newlin."

As he ran toward the mob, memories crashed over Scott like raining debris in the wake of a detonation.

Another lynching, another guilty prisoner.

But he wasn't a U.S. Marshal any longer, and it wasn't his job to protect Maddie.

Or was it?

Hell yes!

He would lay down his life for her if necessary—and from the looks of things, it might be. Regardless of what crimes she'd committed, she didn't deserve to die. She didn't even really deserve to go to prison. Scott had failed her before, but he wouldn't fail her tonight.

Damn his stupid pride. He should have stayed closer to her, especially after he'd figured out Lunsford was on the take.

Panting so hard his chest hurt, Scott reached the edge of the mob and pushed through without regard for anyone who had the misfortune of standing between him and the three men who had Maddie. Hands clawed at him, lanterns blinded him, and voices yelled into his ears. He fended off everyone and everything, revolted by the fanaticism that overtook normally decent folks during a lynching.

A scream rent the night. Maddie's scream! Jonesy had flung her over his shoulder and was carrying her to the noose hanging from the water tower beam. It swung back and forth like a grisly pendulum, counting the seconds until death took its passenger.

Jonesy's accomplices formed a tight circle around him and Maddie. They raised their rifles in the air, attempting to incite the crowd. With a maniacal laugh, Jonesy set Maddie down on two stacked crates that raised her to the height of the noose.

One of his accomplices, the taller one with a full beard, grabbed her by the hair and yanked her head sideways. With his other hand, he reached for the swinging noose. Maddie screamed again and fought the ropes that bound her wrists behind her back. The crowd pressed closer. One spectator lunged forward, shouting something Scott didn't understand. The second, shorter accomplice shoved him back.

In the next instant, Scott broke free of the mob, his Colt drawn.

"Shoot the dirty varmint before he kills her," a wizened old-timer beside Scott squawked. "Hurry!"

"Don't let them hang her," another shouted. "She ain't done nothing wrong."

It took several seconds for Scott to fully comprehend that the mob was attempting to stop the lynching, not encourage it.

He was only too happy to oblige the old-timer's request. Those nearest to Scott ducked their heads when the shot rang out.

The man with the beard never quite got the noose around Maddie's neck. His hand wouldn't function properly with two of its fingers missing.

"Jesus Christ!" he hollered. Dropping to his knees and folding into a ball, he buried his mangled appendage in his stomach. Blood had splattered in all directions, spraying him and Maddie both.

Scott broke free of the crowd, frantic to get to her. Jonesy, however, had other plans. He and his remaining accomplice stepped directly in front of Scott.

"Don't move one inch closer," Jonesy snarled, his rifle leveled at the center of Scott's chest. "We got our orders."

He bet they did. Newlin's orders.

Scott moved considerably more than an inch.

"He said to hold it right there." The remaining accomplice also had his rifle aimed at the middle button of Scott's shirt.

Scott was confident he could take Jonesy out before taking a bullet himself. He was less sure about Jonesy's partner, but willing to try. After all, he'd shot two men once before at another lynching—that time by mistake.

In the background, Maddie sobbed. "Scott. Please. Don't shoot. They'll kill you."

Newlin's flunkies were going to hang her and yet she pleaded with him to put down his gun. Unbelievable.

No warning shot in the ceiling this time. Scott pointed his pistol at Jonesy's head. "Lower your weapon or I'll shoot." He sensed the crowd surrounding him part.

Jonesy grinned. "How about you tell Mr. Lucifer

hello when you see him." His finger tightened in the trigger. "Because you're going straight to hell."

"You tell him first," said Tom Lunsford from behind Scott.

"What the—"

Jonesy never finished his sentence.

The bullet from the sheriff's gun whizzed past Scott's head, so close his ear rang. Jonesy's feet flew out from under him, and he landed sprawled on his back at his accomplice's feet with a nauseating thud. He didn't get up.

His accomplice yelled an obscenity and tossed down his rifle. Hands in the air, he said, "Don't shoot. I'm unarmed."

Scott kicked the rifle out of reach as he covered the few feet separating him and Maddie. While the assembly cheered her rescue, he lifted her off the crates and into his arms.

Burying his face in her hair, he said in a choppy voice, "Don't ever do that again."

"I won't." She both laughed and cried, her limbs quaking from the aftershock of fright.

"I love you, Maddie. I've been such an idiot." With one hand, he unbound her wrists, his own fingers trembling.

"I'm so sorry." She threw her arms around his neck as soon as she was able. "I love you, too."

As he hugged her to him, his gaze found Tom Lunsford and a silent understanding passed between them. The sheriff broke contact first when the town madam appeared out of nowhere and hauled off and slapped him.

"That's for the way you treated me in your office," she huffed, then hopped into his arms and kissed him full on the mouth. "That's for saving McSween's and Maddie's lives."

"When this is all over," Scott whispered in Maddie's ear, "I want you and Josephine—"

Another gunshot shattered the night. Startled gasps and angry shouts followed.

Maddie cried out as Scott threw her to the ground and fell on top of her, shielding her with his body. "Are you hurt?" he asked in a gruff voice.

"No." The green eyes staring up at him were huge. "What was that?"

Every one of Scott's muscles tightened to the point of snapping. "My guess is Newlin's not through with you yet."

Thaddeus Newlin slipped the small revolver inside his shirt and swallowed a curse. His bullet had missed the Campbell bitch by mere inches. Well, he wouldn't make the same mistake twice. When next he pulled the trigger, she'd be dead.

"Where in tarnation did that come from?" demanded a crouching spectator, arms curled protectively around his head.

"Did anyone see who did it?" someone else asked in a high-pitched voice.

"What do you bet it's one of Newlin's men?"

"This time he's gone too far." The incensed speaker rose to her full height. "Trying to first hang and then gun down a poor, innocent widow guilty of nothing more than trying to feed starving younguns."

The indignant rants didn't affect Newlin in the least. Pushing the old hat he wore further down on his head, he maneuvered to the edge of the crowd. Luckily, no one had seen him fire at Maddie Campbell, and no one recognized the shabbily dressed vagrant as Thaddeus Newlin, majority partner of the Edenville Consolidated Mining Company.

He reached the opposite side of the water tower just as McSween was helping the Campbell woman to her feet. Surveying the area, he positioned himself in front of her, his tall, broad body forming a barrier between her and danger. Newlin opted to wait until McSween lowered his guard before making another attempt.

An elbow in his side disrupted his concentration. "Watch it," he snapped.

"Excuse me." The man who inadvertently bumped into him paused a moment longer than necessary to study Newlin's face. Apparently deciding any resemblance between the majority partner and this grimy drifter was just a coincidence, he moved on.

Newlin did the same.

Moseying over to a wagon parked in the shadow of the water tower, he leaned against the side. As he predicted, once the excitement died down, people began to drift away, though not soon enough for him. Jonesy's body was carried off and the other two fellows, whose names Newlin couldn't remember, were escorted to jail.

He didn't give the loss of his three men a passing thought. If they had done their job right in the first place, Maddie Campbell would be swinging from the water tower and Newlin would be watching with a big smile on his face. In truth, Lunsford had done Newlin a favor by killing Jonesy.

Newlin gnashed his teeth, bemoaning the absence of a cigar. The sheriff presented a whole different problem. He should have stayed in his office where he belonged instead of preventing the lynching. But Newlin would resolve that situation in due course.

There were more important matters needing his attention tonight.

At long last, the moment he'd been waiting for arrived. Cheers rose from the remaining spectators as McSween lead Maddie away. Every pair of eyes were riveted on the couple, not him.

"Easy now." Newlin reached inside his shirt, the nerves in his body on fire. "Slow and steady." His fingers encountered smooth, cool metal and closed around it.

A heavy hand came crashing down on his shoulder at the same instant a sharp pain pierced his side.

"Drop the gun," said a familiar voice in his ear, low and lethal, "or I'll stick this knife so far into you, it'll poke out the other side."

Newlin cranked his head around to see his assailant. His laugh sounded more like a wheeze. "Forrester! Christ, man, quit horsing around and cover for me."

"Not this time. Not ever again." The scar along the side of Forrester's face stood out like a white brand in the lantern light. His dark eyes glittered with an abhorrence so strong, Newlin recoiled slightly.

"May I remind you, you work for me." Along with insubordination, insolence was an unforgivable sin in Newlin's book.

"I'm afraid you're sadly mistaken about that."

The knife in Newlin's side dug a fraction deeper.

"Who then?" He snorted, more bothered by his employee's threatening demeanor than he let on. "Oh, wait. Don't tell me. It's Hammond Brubaker, right?" Wouldn't it be just like Brubaker to plant a spy in his camp?

"Wrong again." Forrester inclined his head at the approaching surrey. "I work for them."

A half dozen women from Eden piled out of the surrey before it came to a complete stop and scrambled toward Maddie Campbell, arms outstretched.

"The Eden widows?" *Impossible! Not to mention ludicrous.* "You're joking."

"Think, Mr. Newlin. When have I ever joked with you?"

"You goddamn traitor. You won't get away with this."

Red streaks of rage nearly blinded him. He'd been betrayed again. First by Lunsford and now by his most trusted employee. Hell, the entire town was turning against him, calling him names and maligning his reputation. And it was all Maddie Campbell's fault.

Killing her would be tantamount to bliss.

Ignoring the knife in his side, he withdrew his pistol.

"Don't do it," Forrester warned.

Newlin paid him no heed.

Moonlight and lantern light glinted off the gun's shiny surface, forming silver and gold rings on the barrel. Time slowed to a crawl, then stood still. Noises faded into the background.

"Die, whore," Newlin muttered.

"He's got a gun," Forrester yelled. "He's going to kill her."

Newlin waited a fraction of a second too long before pulling the trigger. Forrester's knife pricking his ribs affected his aim, and his bullet missed its mark again.

The mob turned as one, their eyes going first to his gun and then his face. Their confusion lasted only briefly. With shouts of outrage, they descended upon him.

"Get the dirty scoundrel!"

"He tried to kill Maddie."

Newlin stared at the approaching mob—most of them female—too stunned and too horrified to react. What had gotten into them? Didn't they understand?

These were his people. They needed him. Without him, without the mine, they'd have nothing. Maddie Campbell would have ruined everything. She had to die.

"Help me, Forrester," he choked.

"Gladly, sir."

Forrester removed his hand from Newlin's shoulder only to place it in the middle of his back.

With one hard thrust, he pushed Newlin forward.

Stumbling, Newlin landed directly in the midst of the melee. He fought like a lunatic but to no avail. Dozens of hands grabbed him and tossed him around like a beanbag in a child's game.

"He's trying to escape!"

"Don't let him get away."

"Stop. It's me," he cried weakly as he fell beneath the onslaught of stampeding feet. "Thaddeus Newlin."

"Murderer!" a woman's voice, heavy with whiskey, screamed in his ear. "You killed my husband and unborn baby."

And then he heard nothing at all.

"Maddie," shouted a deep male voice, "over here."

After almost losing her, Scott would have preferred to hold Maddie straight through next week. Releasing her was bad enough. Releasing her so that she could run to Zachariah Forrester was worse. Watching him scoop her up in an exuberant hug and kiss her soundly on the cheek was reason for Scott to smash his fist into the nearest available solid object.

"Sam!" She threw her arms around Forrester's neck. "Thank God you're all right. I've been beside myself with worry."

Sam?

Unable to stand idly by while the woman he loved—

the same woman who'd just professed to love him, too—kissed and hugged another man, Scott walked over to them. "Am I correct in assuming you two have met before?"

Forrester set Maddie down. His arm, however, remained around her waist. Protective and friendly. Especially friendly. And . . .

Not for the first time Scott noticed the scar on Forrester's face. Maddie bore a scar as well, on her stomach. What was it she'd told him about her scar? She'd gotten it as a baby when the Confederate shoulders attacked her mother.

"Scott." Maddie beamed. "I'd like you to meet Samuel Robert Weatherspoon, my—"

"Your brother," he interjected. Everything suddenly made sense, or partial sense.

"I couldn't tell you." She went to him, taking his hand and holding it to her breast. "Not without endangering Sam's safety. You understand, don't you?"

"I understand that you and Forrester, make that Sam, are brother and sister." *Not lovers,* he thought but didn't say. "Everything else is a little fuzzy." He turned to Sam, but not before gathering Maddie to his side. "How did you wind up as Newlin's secretary?"

"It's a rather long tale."

Sam's grin, so full of life, wasn't anything like Zachariah's. Dimples slashed his cheeks and a lock of hair fell forward over his face, giving him a boyish appearance. Here, thought Scott, was the young bookmaker and swindler Maddie had talked about.

"I'm all ears," Scott said.

Maddie shook her head at her brother. "Maybe you shouldn't."

He shrugged off her concerns. "I didn't exactly come by the position in the usual manner."

Somehow, Scott wasn't surprised by the revelation. "Tell me, is the real Zachariah Forrester alive and well?"

Sam laughed. "Fine and dandy when last I saw him, if not a touch irate over the loss of a few personal possessions."

"And what was he doing when last you saw him?"

"Heading home. Back to Philadelphia, I think."

"At your suggestion?"

"I might have mentioned Philadelphia." Sam clapped Scott on the back. "I came to Edenville after Maddie wrote me about the accident. I wanted to help her. Mr. Forrester and I met on the train. We talked. He told me about his job. As I listened, it occurred to me there might be a way for me to help not just Maddie, but all the women of Eden."

And what better way to feed them information than posing as Thaddeus Newlin's secretary? Sam had been the reason the robbers were always one step ahead of the law.

A loud disturbance erupted beside them. Mr. Abernathy crashed through the throng of people who had congregated around the fallen shooter. Pale and shaken, his hair sticking out in all directions, he stumbled in midstep.

"What the . . ." Scott didn't wait. He pushed Maddie behind him.

"It's Mr. Newlin," Abernathy shouted. He stared at Scott, who might as well have been invisible. Whatever the company store manager saw, it wasn't him.

Scott automatically looked around for the majority partner.

"He's dead." Abernathy's voice trailed off. The hands clutching his disheveled hair shook. "The whole left side of his head's caved in."

"Dead!" Maddie gaped at Scott and her brother.

"I'll see what I can find out," Scott said. Before he traveled two steps, Sheriff Lunsford emerged from the crowd and came toward him. "Is it true?" Scott asked. Is Newlin dead?"

"Yes."

"When did it happen? And how?"

Behind the sheriff, people began to scatter like hungry bees leaving the hive in search of nectar. Shouts rang through the street announcing Newlin's untimely death.

Lunsford tipped his hat at Maddie. "Glad to see you're fit and in one piece, ma'am."

"Thank you. But what about Mr. Newlin? Was he killed at home?"

"That's him right over there." Lunsford indicated the body lying in the street. "He's the one who shot at you, Mrs. Campbell. He was behind the lynching attempt as well. Jonesy's partners confessed."

Scott didn't reveal Lunsford's participation in the lynching. Ultimately, the sheriff had saved Maddie's life and for that, Scott owed him.

Beside him, Maddie's knees buckled. He deftly caught her and hauled her upright. "Sweetheart?"

"I'm fine."

She didn't look fine. Her cheeks and lips had lost every drop of color. "Was he murdered?" she asked.

"Someone killed him. Can't say for sure who or why." Lunsford rubbed his chin with the knuckle of his index finger. "There were at least thirty people within spitting distance but none of them saw anything. Could've been an accident. Witnesses say he lost his balance and went down. A well-placed boot, intentional or not, can do a lot of damage. Beats me what he was doing out here, dressed like he was."

"He wanted to watch Maddie hang and not be recognized." Scott couldn't say how he knew, he just did.

"I reckon you're right, McSween." The look on the sheriff's face said more than his words. "Would you mind bringing Mrs. Campbell by my office tomorrow morning? I need to ask her a few more questions for my report. You, too, Mr. Forrester."

"Certainly," Sam replied. "Happy to."

Neither Scott nor Sam offered to set the sheriff straight on Sam's real identity.

A buggy, fancy as any Scott had ever seen, pulled up beside the wagon. The driver climbed down and after handing off the reins, went to assist his lone passenger. From the rear of the buggy, he removed a large, awkward object and placed it on the ground. Only when the driver stepped backward did Scott see what it was.

A wheelchair.

With considerable effort, the driver assisted his passenger down from the buggy and sat him in the wheelchair. Adjusting the man's legs and handing him a cane, the driver then pushed his passenger over to Newlin's prone and lifeless body.

After saying good night, Sheriff Lunsford excused himself in order to join the man. They remained by Newlin's side for several long minutes, chatting with the company doctor and the undertaker, both of whom had just arrived. When the man finished, his driver pushed him back toward the buggy.

Scott would have liked to converse with the man but felt he'd be intruding. He got his wish, however, when halfway back to the buggy the man glanced in their direction. Signaling his driver to halt, he beckoned Scott, Maddie, and Sam over.

"Mr. Forrester," he said, when they were close enough to talk. "I'm glad you're here. Please report to mining headquarters tomorrow morning at eight o'clock sharp."

It wasn't necessary for the man to introduce himself. They all knew Hammond Brubaker, either personally or by reputation.

Being confined to a wheelchair didn't detract from the power and authority he exuded, an impression enhanced by prominently muscled arms and shoulders. Yet there was kindness in his face, the plains of which were ravaged by chronic pain.

"I'll be there." Guilt flashed across Sam's features. "Is something the matter?"

Scott wondered whether the former secretary feared being found out as an imposter.

"Not at all," Brubaker said, brushing aside Sam's concern. "We need to discuss your promotion."

"I don't understand."

"With Newlin gone, I require a capable and experienced manager to assist me in running the company. I can't think of anyone more suitable for the position than you. Interested?"

"Yes, sir!" Sam's reservation gave way to full-fledged enthusiasm. "Very interested."

It looked to Scott as if Sheriff Lunsford wasn't the only one turning a new leaf. If what Maddie had told him were true, Samuel Robert Weatherspoon had just landed his first legitimate job, albeit under an assumed identity.

"Mrs. Campbell. It's good to finally meet you." He reached out and captured Maddie's hand in both his. She didn't shy away from his wheelchair as Scott imagined some people did. "I can't express how sorry I am. This whole horrid affair should never have happened. None of it should have. Please accept my apology. Rest assured, Thaddeus Newlin acted alone. I speak for all the rest of partners when I say none of us wished you ill."

"Thank you," Maddie said, returning his handshake before letting go. "Please accept my apology for attempting to rob you and your family. We wouldn't have done it if we weren't starving."

Scott gave her arm an encouraging squeeze when she returned to his side. A lesser person might have thrown Brubaker's apology back in his face. But then, Maddie wasn't just anybody. Scott's heart filled with love and pride.

"Nonsense." Brubaker jabbed the tip of his cane in the dirt. "What happened to you poor ladies is unforgivable. Once I'm in place as majority partner, I'll see to it your husbands' back wages and death benefits are paid in full."

"Sir?"

Scott sensed Maddie's excitement. It mirrored the emotions soaring inside him.

"Newlin was an unscrupulous scoundrel, but I don't have to tell you that." Brubaker signaled his driver, who resumed pushing the wheelchair toward the buggy. The three strolled alongside him as he talked. "While it's true the operation suffered after the accident, our financial losses were never as bleak as Newlin implied. We'll pay you back, Maddie. May I call you Maddie?"

She smiled and nodded.

"It may take some time. Newlin's shares will have to be transferred over to me before I can authorize payment. Banks and attorneys will slow the process. But it will happen. You have my solemn promise."

Tears glistened in her eyes.

"Oh, and one more thing." They stopped, having reached the buggy. Brubaker maneuvered the wheelchair so that he faced Maddie. "I'm going to do my best to see to it that all charges against you and your friends are dropped. Though from what I heard, the jury would have found you not guilty."

No one, least of all Hammond Brubaker if his reaction were genuine, expected Maddie to bend down and plant a kiss on his forehead.

"I'll never forget your generosity, sir," she told him before straightening. "None of us will."

"Well, well." He harrumphed. "My pleasure."

Sam whooped and reached for Maddie, then caught himself. "Congratulations, Mrs. Campbell," he said with reserve appropriate for the solemn Zachariah Forrester.

Scott picked up where Sam left off. "Does this mean we can finally get married?" he murmured into her hair as he held her tight against him.

Her head snapped back, and her green eyes shimmered up at him with joy and anticipation. "Are you proposing again?"

"As often as it takes to get you to accept."

"Yes!" She clasped his head in her hands and planted little kisses all over his face. "Yes, yes, yes."

He howled at her unabashed joy and realized it had been a long time since he'd enjoyed a good laugh. Maddie was the one responsible for rescuing him from the dark place he'd lived in the past five years. He thought he might spend the rest of his life repaying her for that minor miracle.

Her wandering mouth happened to brush his. Desire ignited inside him, hot and sizzling like a struck match. Mindless of their audience, he gave her the kind of kiss a man gives a woman who's just agreed to marry him. Maddie, never one for shyness, reciprocated with like fervor.

Somebody shuffled his feet. Somebody else cleared

his throat. Scott finally took the hint. Maddie's seductive smile greeted him when they broke apart.

"You won't mind leaving Eden?" he asked, not sure how she'd feel about parting from her brother after so recently being reunited. Or her friends, who had become like sisters to her.

"Not with Mr. Brubaker repaying the money."

Sam extended his hand to Scott. "Welcome to the fam—" He caught himself and started over. "Well done, Mr. McSween. Best of luck to you and the future Mrs. McSween."

"This is indeed cause for a celebration," Hammond Brubaker said after offering Scott his congratulations. "I have no wish to stick my nose in where it doesn't belong, but I heard you mention leaving Eden. It was my intention to speak with you tomorrow but perhaps now is a better time. I'd like to offer you a job, McSween. As head of security for the company."

"A permanent job?"

"Yes. I've been impressed with you from the beginning. Of course, the position would require you live in Edenville. There would also be some traveling between the three mines. I'm afraid you'd have to leave your new bride for one week of every month."

"That's not a problem," Maddie gushed. "I won't mind. Oh, wait." She winced. "I didn't mean to speak for you, Scott. You haven't even said you'd take the job. But if you want to take the job . . ." She covered her mouth with her hand. "I should just be quiet, shouldn't I?"

"I can really use you, Mr. McSween." Amusement lit Brubaker's craggy features. "If you need a few days to think about it, I understand and will gladly wait."

"I don't need a few days." Scott gazed down at Maddie, wondering what he'd ever done to deserve her. "I'll take the job. As it so happens, I've been thinking of settling down for a while now."

"Oh, Scott!" Maddie squealed. "We don't have to stay on my account. Josephine and I will go anywhere you want us to go. I know how much you like to—"

He shut her up with another kiss, this one quick and hard.

"Fine and dandy," Brubaker said. With the aid of his driver and his cane, he stood on wobbly legs that didn't entirely support him. All three men helped lift him into the buggy. "Edenville Consolidated Mining Company has a new manager and a new head of security along with a new majority partner," he said when he was comfortably situated. "I think, gentlemen and lady, we have a promising future ahead of us filled with some exciting changes."

Scott heartily agreed.

"I'll take you home," he said to Maddie as they waved good-bye to Hammond Brubaker.

"Home. That sounds nice." She snuggled more securely into the crook of his arm only to squirm out a second later. "Sam! Where are you going?"

"To celebrate my promotion," he yelled back at them.

Both she and Scott had been too preoccupied with their enjoyment of each other and the moment to notice her brother's departure. Scott caught sight of Sam up the street, heading for the Strike It Rich. As Zachariah Forrester and Newlin's secretary, he'd maintained a quiet existence. The new Zachariah Forrester, company manager, evidently intended to kick up his heels.

Sam would be an interesting addition to his life, thought Scott. As would his soon-to-be stepdaughter.

Upon saying "I do" to Maddie, he'd go from being alone—and lonely—to having an instant family.

And he couldn't be happier. It was long overdue, but fortune had finally smiled down on him.

Have you ever been to San Francisco?" he asked as they ambled toward the livery.

"No." She laughed as if she found his question preposterous. "Why?"

"I was thinking it might be a nice place to go for a honeymoon."

"Oh, Scott!" Her eyes lit with excitement.

"We can take Josephine."

"On our honeymoon? You wouldn't mind?"

"I did some checking around these last few weeks. There's a prominent hearing specialist who practices in San Francisco." He stopped and swung her around to face him. "I'll wire him tomorrow to let him know we're coming."

The next thing Scott knew, he was holding a jubilant Maddie in his arms, and she was squeezing him as if she'd die rather than be parted from him.

"Thank you," she whispered into his neck.

"Thank *you.*" He tipped her chin so that their gazes met. "If I haven't told you before, you saved me from a terrible, wretched life."

"And you saved me, my darling." She reached up and sifted her fingers through his hair before pulling his head down to receive her hungry mouth. "Heart, body, and soul."

Their kiss likely drew the attention of those folks out for a late night stroll but neither of them cared.

"Shall we tell Josephine about our engagement tonight?" Maddie asked when they at last separated. "She's going to be absolutely delighted."

"Delighted to have a new father or delighted about seeing my horse again?"

"Don't be silly. She adores you." Maddie poked him lightly in the arm, then soothed the spot with slow, sensuous strokes. "And so do I."

Scott's mind drifted off track, only to be brought sharply back by Maddie's next comment.

"Can we stop by the jail for Constance and Dora? I don't want them spending another night there if they don't have to."

"Sure." There went his plans for a romantic moonlight ride back to Eden.

He didn't mind. Not really. There would be plenty more opportunities for romantic rides. Many more nights sleeping with Maddie curled by his side. In fact, every night for the rest of their lives.